M.G. HERRON

THE ARES INITIATIVE

TRANSLOCATOR TRILOGY BOOK 3

THE ARES INITIATIVE

Copyright © 2018 by M.G. Herron

Cover designed by MiblArt

MG Publishing LLC

Translocator Trilogy

The Auriga Project

The Alien Element

The Ares Initiative

The Translocator (Books 1-3)

The Gunn Files

Culture Shock

Overdose

Quantum Flare

The Gunn Files (Books 1-3)

Other Books

The Republic

Boys & Their Monsters

Get science fiction and fantasy reading recommendations from MG Herron delivered straight to your inbox. Join here: mgherron.com/bookclub

1

———

SHIFT

Remethiakara nearly ripped the mothership to pieces as he shifted into hyperspace.

The massive living spacecraft heaved, quaked, and hurled him to the floor of the bridge. His head cracked against a hard edge—the armrest of the pilot's chair, most likely. The impact would have been enough to break his skull, but he was spared a life-threatening injury by the thin but durable fabric of his armorsuit. It was still enough to split the outer shell of the helmet and send him tumbling back-ward, end over end, until he struck against a circular doorframe.

Air was driven from all four of Remethiakara's lungs as his body impacted the shapeshifting carapace that made up the walls of the mothership. He focused on trying to regain his breath even as blood filled his mouth from a cut on his tongue. The ship continued to rattle around. He couldn't make out anything but blurry shapes, streaks of brownish-purple, an azure luminescence flecked with black. Red spots crowded his vision as the multiplied gravity of the ship's acceleration flattened him against the wall with such force that his organs lurched inside him.

He managed to choke down one ragged breath. Then another. It felt like breathing with weights on his chest, but it kept him conscious. A ghoulish sound like flesh being rent from bone suddenly crowded out the other sensations. His whole body tensed.

At first, he thought it was one of his own limbs breaking. Then he realized it was happening not to him, but to the mothership that carried him. Due to their truethought connection, her autonomous neural system screamed in his mind—a sharp sound that he felt as much as heard, a small needle being gouged straight into his eardrum. He closed his eyes and held on as an aft compartment was torn away from the tail of the ship, shredded as it passed through the hyperspace continuum, and scattered through a billion miles of space.

He felt the ship's pain as his own pain, but muted, distant. The purpose of the pain was to allow the pilot—in this case, him—to identify the breach and respond quickly. A nanosecond after the aft compartment was torn away, Remethiakara hurled a sharp mental command at the mothership's receptors. The living vessel's vascular system clotted to seal the breach, preventing the rest of the atmosphere from bleeding out.

He did not need to see it to know it happened. He felt it as a flash of physical knowledge—similar to the way it felt when one of his servitor bots stitched up a deep cut in the soft flesh at the small of his back.

The pain faded to a dull throbbing as the breach was finally sealed. The sense of panic and urgency that had been transmitted to him with the sensation subsided. And the mothership finally achieved equilibrium with the hyperspace continuum into which he'd thrust her.

When the quaking rumbled down to a low vibration, and the artificial gravity returned to normal levels, Remethiakara sagged to the floor. There had been a high probability that forcing the ancient mothership into hyperspace would tear him and the spacecraft to pieces. Getting away with a lost limb was perfectly acceptable—even to be expected. But he also knew that were he to try the maneuver a second time, he would certainly not make it through alive.

Not that there was enough juice left in the star shard to make another shift.

He only had one chance to get this right.

Remethiakara pushed himself to his feet and surveyed the rest of the damage the shift had caused.

One of the fragile eggs containing his precious offspring had jostled free of the stasis pods where he'd put them for safekeeping. He hadn't been sure how much of the ship would hold up in flight, and decided to keep them close. But they were too large and awkward at this point in their gestation for the stasis pod lids to close, and the straps he'd used to secure them had come loose in the turbulence.

The eggs shouldn't be anywhere near the low gravity of space travel this late in their development. But what choice did he have? After the savages had swarmed through the Wall and overwhelmed his defenses with the help of more advanced Earthlings and their quantum teleportation device, he'd been forced to discard the old plan to ensure the preservation of his race.

Remethiakara bent down and gingerly ran his hand along the broken shell of the cracked egg—then jerked his hand up to his helmet, now gashed in a similar way. He swallowed his panic, jerked the busted helmet off over his head, and took deep draughts of air through his slitted nostrils and thin, lipless mouth.

Another of his children had been killed, this time by his own actions. That knowledge caused an inescapable feeling of guilt to clawed its way up from deep in his lower stomach. Globs of half-formed flesh were visible through the crack in the egg, floating in a thick amniotic fluid. He could see the curve of what might have been a neck. What a terrible waste. What a tragic loss.

He closed his eyes and looked away.

The young leader of the savages had destroyed four eggs. His own carelessness had ended the life of another. There were only four left.

With shaking hands, Remethiakara checked the remaining straps. Coming out of hyperspace might be rockier than going into it, and he couldn't take any chances. These four eggs were his last chance to uphold his duty, his last chance to ensure the survival of his race, a nomadic species who had wandered the stars since the destruction of their native world.

Remethiakara rose to his feet abruptly and strode back to the center of the bridge, where a column of blue light in front of the pilot's chair held a large chunk of meteorite suspended in its beam. The sable geode was so black that, from a certain angle, it looked like a hole in the light rather than an object suspended within it.

In reality, it was an ancient source of power called a star shard. Wrought by the intense heat of exploding stars, his race had been using their concentrated energy to power their motherships as they made way from planet to planet for aeons.

This particular star shard Remethiakara had

recovered by tracking a human woman who had shown up on the planet where he'd been living. He used the star shard she brought with her to create a singularity that took him back to Earth.

There he learned that a group of intelligent Earthlings had managed to harness the shard's energy with their own transport technology...but that they didn't seem to grasp the true extent of the shard's power. Their tech was inefficient, their defenses thin. Eventually, Remethiakara's long patience had been rewarded. He cut through them easily and reclaimed the star shard as his own.

But then they had killed his children and destroyed the place he had called home for the last thousand years.

They would pay for that.

Remethiakara tossed the busted helmet aside and reached out with his gauntleted hands. The blue light bent and crackled, shooting sparks into his fingertips. He manipulated the beam. The display inside the helmet would normally show energy readouts. Without it, he cast the readouts directly into his cornea. An array of numbers and symbols no Earthling would be capable of comprehending superimposed themselves on his vision. After spending a moment tweaking the complex mathematical formula in his mind, he clenched his jaw.

It was as he suspected. The ship was just too large to expect anything else. Raising the mothership from what was meant to be the living vessel's final resting place on Kakul, traveling through the planet's atmosphere, and shifting into hyperspace had taxed the star shard to such an extent that its power was already nearly depleted.

If he was lucky, there would be enough energy left to complete his journey and little, if any, leftover. Was it enough to construct an incubator for the eggs until he could establish a more permanent settlement? He hoped so.

Remethiakara thrust his hands back into the blue-white beam of light and checked on the course of the jump. Noting that the two planets had moved away from each other more than the ship's systems had predicted since the last time this ancient mothership had journeyed between the stars, he made some adjustments which took the unexpected orbital drift into account.

All Remethiakara could do after that was wait. He passed the time by monitoring the energy drain on the shard, and carefully feeding the eggs through a complicated manual link with the living mothership, using what little power the shard could spare to sustain them.

The end of the jump felt like it would never come.

Then it seemed to come abruptly.

He prepared better this time, strapping himself in beside his eggs.

The mothership quaked and lurched, throwing the metallic sphere of his last servitor bot across the bridge and smashing it to uselessness against the doorway.

The floor rumbled and there was a change of speed, like stepping off a fast-moving vehicle onto solid ground.

Remethiakara braced, then slowly relaxed as nothing happened for a moment. *Was that it?*

He unbuckled himself and thrust his gauntlets into the beam of light. The walls of the mothership turned transparent—or rather, they simply transmitted through the vascular systems what the outer membrane was experiencing visually, so that it seemed as if he could see directly into the black emptiness of space from deep within the heart of the mothership.

The velocity shifted abruptly again. This time he was expecting it, and it merely hurled his body back into the pilot's chair, piling seven or eight gravities of force upon his chest. He fought to remain conscious as a cold blue planet blurred past on the starboard wall, followed by a massive orange one with an enormous ring system.

Then the spacecraft went completely still as the vessel exited hyperspace.

He slumped down, his chest heaving.

And felt his slitted nostrils and lipless mouth expand into a helpless grin.

Despite the hiccup in the landing, the ship had ended up not only in the right system, but almost exactly on target. Off by only a few hundred thousand miles. Not bad for a derelict mothership that was six thousand or so years past its prime.

Now the starboard wall was filled with the great red curve of a desert planet receding behind him.

Meanwhile, directly ahead, a tiny green and blue speck was just becoming visible in the distance.

He stood there for a long time, smiling, as the planet known as Earth slowly grew larger in his viewframe.

After another day it was the size of his fist.

It wouldn't be much longer now.

If his brief encounters with modern Earthlings were any indication, they had already made note of his ship and were now making their own preparations.

He suspected that his arrival would not be taken lightly.

THE ARES INITIATIVE

Five days after Amon Fisk first spotted the alien spacecraft entering the solar system, three unmarked Black Hawk helicopters landed on his campus. The choppers thundered out of the north through a fading blue sky and came down inside the high barbed-wire fences. He'd forgotten to eat dinner again and the sight of their matte black hulls, strangely unmarked, made his empty stomach turn.

He glanced at Dr. Enzo Badeux, who stood next to him wearing creased khakis with brown loafers. His expression was unreadable.

Five days. It had been five days since he watched the spacecraft skip past Pluto and appear inside the orbit of Mars in the blink of an eye. Amon had been subconsciously bracing for impact ever since. That level of sustained stress diminished one's appetite significantly. A dull ache had also appeared between his shoulder blades.

Due to what they had seen, everyone assumed the vessel was of alien origin. Astronomers at the SOLARPulse-1 detection array on the lunar base clocked the unidentified spacecraft traveling at nearly two hundred and fifty thousand miles per hour, over four times the maximum speed any human spacecraft had ever achieved.

The secret had moved quickly through the organization, but thanks to protocols put in place by Dr. Badeux after they first discovered the Translocator could transport people and objects not only to the moon, but with a little modification, to distant planets, they had managed to keep the information out of the media's hands.

Keeping knowledge of the spacecraft away from his wife was a simpler matter. Seven days ago—two days before they spotted the spacecraft—she had taken her team back to Kakul via the Translocator to do more archaeological research on the stone temple. The Lunar Terraform Alliance had green-lighted a two-week exploratory mission, and apart from sending an encoded signal daily to let the LTA know they were safe, Eliana and her team were effectively cut off from communications.

Doubt gnawed at his empty stomach.

"Do you think it was a good idea to leave the exploratory team on Kakul?"

"I assure you," Enzo said. "Eliana is perfectly safe. Signals indicate they are even ahead of schedule." Enzo's perfectly relaxed manner gave him an aloof charm that rarely cracked, even under the kind of stress he'd endured since two days ago, when they took a preliminary analysis of the spacecraft to NASA, who then ran it up the chain to the proper governmental authority.

Now, that authority was here, landing on *his* campus. The campus's official name had been changed to the "Austin Lunar Research Center," but since Amon had purchased the land and buildings over fifteen years ago for Fisk Industries, it was difficult to give up the habit of thinking that the sprawling grounds, Gothic buildings, and research labs belonged to *him*.

Old habits died hard.

"Who do you think is in charge?" Amon yelled over the roar of the rotor blades as a pilot centered the first helicopter over a bright yellow H surrounded by a circle.

Dr. Enzo Badeux shrugged. "I am merely the director of the Lunar Terraform Alliance, an international research organization. They, are the U.S. military," he shouted back, as if that explained things to his American friend.

When Enzo noticed the serious expression on Amon's face, he added, "They called thirty minutes ago to tell us they were coming, but failed to specify who was on board. I assume it was for security reasons. It is not my place to ask such questions."

Amon grunted. "You Europeans are too concerned with protocol. Anyway, we'll know soon enough. I hope they're here to help."

"I refuse to let anyone shut down the project, Amon. Do not worry. We have already received your president's blessing."

Amon gritted his teeth. That was a factual statement. They *had* received President Roscoe's blessing to keep the Translocator operational, if under the watchful eyes of a battalion of U.S. Army soldiers with high security clearances. That was why the campus was no longer his. It was at the president's suggestion (read: orders) that the LTA had transformed the former campus of Fisk Industries—*his* campus—into the military installation it was today, complete with a gate that could be defended easily, and guard towers spaced every hundred yards along the barbed wire-topped walls.

Unfortunately, that knowledge did nothing to assuage Amon's fear that the arrival of this alien spacecraft was no mere coincidence. This problem was too big for a little barbed wire.

And it was probably his fault, too.

For that reason, the presence of the Black Hawks brought him a faint sense of hope—news had traveled up the chain to someone important. Someone who was in a position to take action.

But who? Was it the president? Was it someone he could trust?

Ten Marines rushed from the first Black Hawk and fanned out, their postures relaxed but alert. They wore black body armor and cradled carbine rifles in their arms. This was a secure area, yet they were still on their guard. Smart and cautious. The huge squad leader, a man with a white scar along the jutting edge of his chin, made a circular motion with one hand. The other two choppers came down, one on the left and one on the right.

A second squad of Marines indistinguishable from the first hopped out of the chopper on the left. Instead of rifles, they carried crates and heavy black duffel bags. The last two men to jump out of the chopper balanced between them a thin, transparent rectangle that Amon instantly recognized as a slab of tempered hologlass. That explained what some of the extra luggage was for. A holo that big still wasn't an easy machine to port around.

The last man to get out wore fatigues and a matching camouflage patrol cap, but carried no weapon. His face was deeply tanned, lined with age, and perfectly inscrutable. He spotted Amon and Enzo and made a B-line for where they stood. A small retinue of assistants, also wearing military uniforms but carrying clipboards and phones and laptops instead of firearms, followed in his wake.

"This looks promising," Amon said to Enzo out of the corner of his mouth.

Enzo lifted one shoulder in a nearly imperceptible shrug. "We'll know soon enough," he said, parroting Amon's words back to him.

"Gentlemen," the distinguished man said when he finally reached them. He spoke with a lazy drawl, dragging out the word and betraying his southern heritage. "Good evening. I'm General Joseph Wade."

"Hello, sir," Amon replied. "Nice to meet you."

"*Bonjour, Général,*" Enzo said. "Welcome to the Austin Lunar Research Center."

Amon had to admit the new name had a nice ring to it. Everything always sounded so elegant coming from Enzo.

General Wade inclined his head. He was tall man, six foot three with salt-and-pepper hair in a high and tight, and a clean-shaven face showing a five-o-clock shadow. He wore no jewelry of any kind, not even a wedding band.

"Thank you, Enzo. Amon, it's good to meet you in person finally. You're...not as tall as I thought you would be."

Amon barked out a laugh. It felt good to laugh. "I'll take that as a compliment. We have much to discuss. Director Badeux was wise to suggest we prepare a room."

The Marines insisted on sweeping the building

ahead of the general's entry. Amon hid his frustration while they accomplished the task. Was it not enough that the building was in the middle of a military base?

When they determined it was clear, Amon strode into the vast lobby of the headquarters building, then up the stairs across from the indoor waterfall, which burbled calmly, unfazed by the unusual activity. "This way, please."

Amon led the group to a large conference room that could seat about fifty. Several tables, dozens of chairs, and a folding stage were all pushed against the left wall. The Marines swept the room and then took up posts outside the door and at all three of the building's exits. The leader of the first squad of Marines returned to the conference room a minute later to join Amon and Enzo, the general, and his retinue.

"I'd like you to meet Major Bautista," General Wade said. "He's the platoon leader of the Ares Initiative strike forces, and will be coordinating efforts on the ground."

Amon really looked at the major for the first time. He was a few inches taller than the general even, which meant he towered over Amon. He had light brown skin and a brooding All-American look about him—thick jaw, low brow, handsome in an I-can-pull-you-apart-like-a-rotisserie-chicken kind of way. A pale scar across the bottom of his jawline stood out from his skin. His left ear had the faintest trace of cauliflower ear, the result of too much time spent with your ear pressed to the wrestling mats. Major Bautista inclined his head to Amon and Enzo.

"The Ares Initiative?" Amon asked. "What's that?" He managed to sneak a glance at the director. His unflappable expression of studied indifference was marred only by a slight crease between his eyebrows.

So he's never heard of the organization either. That's odd.

"In due time," General Wade said calmly, brushing off the question. "Sorry to drop in on you like this, but it was a necessary precaution. Only a few people know I'm here right now, and I'd like it to stay that way. The public will know what you found soon enough, and then where I am and what I'm doing won't be such a big story." The general met Amon's eyes. "I know you have questions. Just hold onto them for a moment longer. The mobile command center is almost ready. Tammy?"

One of the assistants had already begun to assemble the holodisplay and other equipment the Marines dropped off. The sheet of hologlass went horizontal over the conference table.

"Almost ready, sir," responded an Asian woman in her late thirties. "Just need to seal the room and authorize the encryption."

She set a device the size of a hockey puck on the table and clicked a small button on its side. Amon felt his ears pop as the room was sealed, like a bubble, from prying ears.

"Interesting," Amon said, reaching for the device.

Tammy rapped the back of Amon's hand with her knuckles.

"Hey!"

"Hands off."

Enzo and the general both smirked. Major Bautista just quirked one eyebrow slightly before settling back into stone impassivity.

Gadgets were almost irresistible to Amon. He itched to dissect tools and electronics, and as a wealthy inventor was not used to being denied. But he had learned better than to mess with territorial women—learned slowly, as the distant and fraught relationship with his wife continued to remind him of late. She still hadn't forgiven him for trying to keep her from returning to Kakul.

He contented himself by studying the pocket-sized jamming device with his eyes. When the woman gave him a severe look, Amon showed her his palms. "I'm not going to touch it. Just looking."

While they waited for the final preparations to be made, the general unbuttoned his jacket, laid it over the back of a chair, and seated himself at the head of the table.

"Ready, sir," Tammy said.

"Excellent. Gentlemen, if you'll join me, please. Tammy, go ahead and connect the call."

Major Bautista sat on the general's right, Enzo on his left. Amon took the chair next to Enzo. No one had mentioned a call, but he supposed he should have expected it. The lights in the conference room dimmed slightly, and the holo screen came to life with a soft internal glow, like someone turned a light bulb on and held it under water.

Precise figures of a dozen more people flickered into existence around the table. There was suddenly a stern-looking white woman across from Amon. A genial African man sat to her right, and a dapper gent with eyeglasses next to him. They kept appearing until the whole table was populated.

Amon recognized none of them. Each sat in their own chairs that were transferred with the hologram, as if they had been sitting at the table with them but invisible all along. The colors of their images were slightly paler than they would have been in real life, and their forms flickered just slightly when they moved. Even Amon, who had been working with sophisticated and expensive holos for over a decade, was impressed by the image clarity.

"Thank you all for your patience," General Wade said. "As we discussed previously, I am now located at the Austin Lunar Research Center with Amon Fisk and Director Badeux, of the Lunar Terraform Alliance."

A dozen heads inclined politely.

Amon put one hand in the air and waved at them.

"Uh, hello. Didn't know this was going to be a group chat."

A few faces smiled or grimaced. Most of them glared. Amon put his hand down, swallowing hard.

Awkward.

"As you both know," General Wade continued, addressing Amon and Enzo directly this time, "the Lunar Terraform Alliance was formed as a collective initiative with cooperation from over a hundred countries. However, the initial discussions that led to the alliance were not as smooth as they might have been. There were, shall we say, disagreements among certain parties about what the funding should be used for. For example, it was the opinion of the American leadership, as well as Mexico, the UK, Russia, and China"—the general nodded around the table to several different representatives—"that some of the funding be directed toward planetary defense."

Amon's ears perked up at the last bit. He'd asked Enzo once about using the LTA's resources for planetary defense, and learned that it was a sensitive subject best left untouched due to strained international relations. He took a second to be grateful it had not been an original thought.

"But when agreement could not be reached on that subject, defense was left out of the alliance we ended up with." This time the general held an open hand in Enzo's direction.

"The smaller countries banded together to oppose the idea," Enzo said, picking up the thread of the story with ease. "They worried that if things were to go wrong in some way—say, if tensions ramped up between the United States and Russia—they would get caught in the crossfire of any weapon systems developed by the LTA for the purposes of planetary defense."

"Which I can understand," General Wade said. "But once the can of worms was opened, we couldn't very well ignore it. When our military strategists war-gamed the problem of planetary defenses with the capabilities we had at the time, it became clear that too many possible edge cases resulted in unacceptable outcomes. As a result, President Roscoe was able to convince a select few of those who were interested in authorizing LTA funds for planetary defense to form a separate, more covert alliance."

Amon finally understood. "The Ares Initiative."

"That's right, Mr. Fisk. The Ares Initiative. Welcome aboard, gentlemen. This is the first time a Class 1 emergency meeting has ever needed to be called. I think it goes without saying that what we say here does not leave the room. Understand?"

Amon nodded.

"Good. And now, Amon, I believe you were the first to make the discovery. Would you please inform the rest of the group?"

All eyes turned to Amon.

Oh, Amon thought. *Oh, God. He didn't tell them.* No wonder they hadn't found his sense of humor very amusing. They had a good idea of the stakes, but it seemed to be up to him to relay the specifics.

The old fear of public speaking came back in a flash of cold sweat. He gripped the arms of his chair under the table, and wished Eliana were here at his side. Though things had been tense between them lately, she was the only one who truly knew his fear and could help him overcome it. He took a shaking breath and paused for a second, thinking of her warm presence, imagining her reassuring hand on his arm. Slowly, he grew calmer, and got the old fear under control.

Enzo seemed to notice Amon's hesitation. He opened his mouth to stall for him, or maybe tell the story in his place, but Amon reached a hand out to grip his friend's arm. "It's my fault. I'll tell them. They deserve to know. And if they can help then it doesn't matter who's to blame."

Enzo gave him a look they had shared many times since the discovery of the spacecraft. The "I know it's not your fault" look. Amon ignored his friend and continued.

"As I'm sure all of you know, the SOLARPulse-1 detection array went online at the Lunar Base last week. Dr. Badeux and I went up there to see it for ourselves. It's got predictive modeling capabilities we've only dreamed of. It can map the dance of objects in our solar system and beyond, practically in real time. Part of the reason the array was built is to identify what we call Near Earth Objects, or NEOs. Usually this means asteroids and large comets. This time we discovered something else—an alien spacecraft."

A few pairs of eyebrows around the table shot up. Most took deep, steadying breaths and leaned back in their chairs.

"What is the danger?" a dark-skinned man asked. Amon couldn't place his accent specifically, but guessed by that and his brightly-patterned shirt that he was from somewhere in Africa.

"Well, we don't know," Amon said. "What we do know is that it seems to be on a course to intercept Earth in about eighteen hours." One or two people cursed under their breath. More than a few crossed themselves as their lips worked in prayer. "It's got a strange design, more like an insect than a spaceship like we think of them, and we can't tell if it's carrying weapons systems of any kind. It's massive, easily ten times the size of our largest ships, and moving at a remarkable speed.

"It gets weirder. We don't actually know how it got here. According to Stanis Rachmaninoff, the lead astronomer in charge of SOLARPulse-1, it 'skipped' into our solar system. The first time our systems detected the spacecraft was inside the orbit of Pluto. The next time, inside the orbit of Mars. It hasn't skipped since then. Maybe it can't, now that it's so close to the gravity well of the planets."

"How is this possible?" asked a severe blond woman in a suit tailored in a classic London style. Apparently the fashion had come back around.

"That doesn't matter," Amon said. "What matters now is that we take steps to mitigate the problem."

The dapper-looking gent on the left across from Amon leaned forward, setting his forearms down on a table in his own office that was higher than the level of the conference table, giving him the impression of leaning on air. "But where did it come from? Who's piloting it?"

Amon took a deep breath and sighed. "All good questions."

The man licked his lips and glanced around the room before speaking softly. "We heard of the incidents at Fisk Industries, including what happened to your wife. Her publications have been noticeably absent of certain details. Is this related?"

"That's not been confirmed," Amon said, filing away their detailed attention to his wife's career for deeper examination later.

"Amon, you have every right to be protective, but please make an effort to cooperate," General Wade said. "I already told you, nothing leaves this room. I promise. Now, tell us what you know. It could be important."

Amon clenched his jaw. Eliana was still on Kakul.

He didn't want to say anything that could jeopardize her safe return. But they had him backed into a corner, and truthfully, he wanted to help. He built the Translocator, which led to all of this in the first place. He couldn't escape his responsibility now.

"When my wife went to that other planet, she encountered an alien known as Xucha. The natives think he's some kind of god. Whatever he is, he's dangerous. He proved as much to us when he commandeered the Translocator and came to Earth through a wormhole for a brief period of time. He stole the star shard from the lab here."

Someone let out a low whistle from between their teeth. All eyes were watching Amon intently now.

"During that...encounter, Eliana went back through the wormhole to Kakul. This alien took her. We were able to rescue her with the help of the native warriors, some of whom she befriended. The alien's lair was located and destroyed in that mission. Of that much I am certain. I thought he was killed, but we never found a body. So it stands to reason that this spacecraft could belong to him."

"The other thing we know for certain is the timetable," General Wade said. "As Amon relayed, the spacecraft will reach Earth in eighteen hours. But we can't afford to wait until that happens. Our deadline for a decision is thirteen hours from now. That's 0800 tomorrow morning.

"Thirteen hours!"

"No…"

"How is that possible?"

Over a dozen pairs of eyes bore holes into Amon. He squirmed in his chair. Then they each turned away from the table and spoke to invisible people apparently standing behind them.

"What if the spacecraft is bringing an army?" the African man asked.

"What if it's carrying a plague?" said the dapper gent.

"It could be carrying any number of things," General Wade said in his cool drawl. "Let's not create complications that don't exist yet."

"Do we have the capability to destroy it?" asked the blond woman in the London-style suit.

General Wade glanced at Major Bautista, who leaned forward and spoke for the first time. "Cruise missiles are in place and standing by. One of them is a nuclear device."

General Wade looked back at Amon and Enzo. "Does the spacecraft have any weapons? Shields?"

"We don't know," Enzo said. "But I will try to find out."

"Please do. I want to know everything we can," General Wade said. "Speaking of which, Amon, I need you to do something else for us."

"What's that?"

"If your wife has any more information on this

alien or his technology, we must know about it. You said she spent time with him, when she was being held captive."

All eyes snapped to him. Amon bit the inside of his lower lip hard. With Eliana on the mission, he had been hoping to keep her out of this. Hadn't he already put her life in enough danger? "She's back on Kakul, sir. Doing more archaeological research. Her team isn't scheduled to return for another week."

"Amon," General Wade said, rocking back in his chair slightly. "The fate of the world is at stake. Surely you can convince her to return early."

Or let Earth get blown to smithereens and leave her safely on Kakul, he thought bitterly. *Wouldn't be the worst thing.*

Amon glanced at Enzo as his stomach tied itself up in a complicated knot.

"Yes, sir," Amon said, though he didn't feel the certainty his words conveyed. "I'll see what I can do."

3

HIDDEN BELOW

Eliana gazed over a heap of tumbledown limestone that had once been the great stepped pyramid of *Uchben Na*.

The observatory that had crowned the pyramid now lay on its side like an overturned sarcophagus. The broad front stairway had split, chunks of the steps and the symbolic snake that adorned its edges thrown in every direction. Moss-covered walls had been shaken into their constituent bricks. And all around the sunken foundation, the weed-grown courtyard of the ancient stone city was littered with limestone chunks, from pieces as big as her fist to blocks the size of her torso.

More than just crumbling where it stood, the pyramid seemed to have been demolished as if from an explosion within, and then collapsed into an enormous underground cavity.

She hadn't been here when it happened. None of the locals lived in the stone city, either. Not even Rakulo had seen it.

She turned to look at the young chief. "Tell me again what happened."

Rakulo sighed, crossing his arms over his broad bare chest just beneath the welts of fresh tattoos, an intertwining, sinuous pattern that started on his upper chest and extended over his shoulders like a warrior's protective pauldrons. They indicated his status as their people's chief, like his father before him. The people had apparently been in a hurry to make it official, now that the internal strife among them had been settled once and for all, and the false god Xucha driven from their midst.

"I was in the village when it happened. The ground shook violently, and we heard thunder, except the night sky was clear. And we found the temple destroyed like this the next day. Honestly, Eliana, I don't see why it matters. It's better this way. Good riddance. My people are saying it must mean that there *are* gods out there, listening to our prayers, after all. That they saw our pain and struck down the temple of the pretender for us—the symbol of our suffering. That this is perhaps our reward for driving him away."

It took her a while to piece together what Rakulo was saying. It was uttered in short, terse phrases in his native language, and she had never heard the phrase 'temple of the pretender' before. They had always called the temple by the same name as the stone city, *Uchben Na*, which meant "ancient mother" in their native tongue. A new name for the pyramid indicated more than anything how things had changed since her last visit. She almost didn't catch the meaning.

Almost.

By "pretender," Rakulo was referring, she realized, to Xucha, the alien being whom his people had worshipped as a god. Rakulo's ancestors had sacrificed their children to Xucha for countless generations, coerced through a system of social and physical retribution to do so. Some of the alien's methods of control had been overt, like the hundred-foot sheer metal barrier surrounding this peninsula, effectively trapping Rakulo and his people within its confines. Other methods had been more subtle, like how children tended to fall ill when their parents went against Xucha's will.

Eliana had witnessed one child die of this mysterious god-given sickness the first time she came to Kakul. She had been there when the child's mother howled her grief to the amethyst sky, the lifeless young boy still clutched in her lap. That child had been Rakulo's younger brother, Tilak. So Eliana could guess how he felt about the ruined temple, though he did well to contain his anger, never once raising his voice. Xucha had only been out of the picture for a month, yet that control alone showed how the young chief had matured in the year since his brother's death.

It was only through persistent opposition that his people had managed to throw off the yolk of their oppressor. Tilak's death had merely been one loss of hundreds in their long drawn-out rebellion. She put her hand on Rakulo's shoulder. "Okay."

Eliana had only arrived to see the final wave of that rebellion come crashing down. Then she had been drawn into the conclusion, when Xucha kidnapped her and revealed his true identity as an ancient alien from a faraway planet.

She learned that his real name was Remethiakara. He had shown her a confused smattering of his own race's history before Rakulo had snuck into the lair and caught them both by surprise, giving Eliana the opening she needed to escape, and being stabbed in the gut for his trouble. Eliana could see the jagged line below Rakulo's ribcage where Xucha had sunk the blade in.

"What are they doing?" Rakulo asked, gesturing to Eliana's team of anthropologists on the opposite side of the ruin.

Lakshmi, Ross, and the twins—Talia and Turner —paced around the edge of the pyramid, taking readouts from metal probes that had been stuck into the ground every fifty feet or so. They were asking their own questions—of the site itself.

Eliana pursed her lips. She didn't have words in Rakulo's language to explain that they were using a technique called an electrical resistance survey. Instead she just cut to the point of it. "They're using the sticks in the ground to find out what's beneath—rock, water, or empty air."

He bobbed his head, obviously distrusting of their strange methods. "Water," he said. "The underground rivers must lead here."

"Probably," Eliana said. "But what else might have happened down there that could have caused the sudden collapse?"

He glanced at her out of the corner of his eye. "Does it matter?"

"If it does, I'll certainly let you know when we find out."

"No, thank you. I should get back." Rakulo turned to walk away.

"Rakulo," she called after him. "Have you thought any more about what I said?"

He paused, but didn't look back.

"At least come visit my world. I think you'd like it there if you gave it a chance."

His knuckles cracked as his hands made fists at his sides. "I can't leave my people."

She hesitated only a moment before responding. "They can all come, too."

He said nothing.

"I know it's hard to believe, but are we so different? You're from my world, originally, I think. You should at least get the choice to return if you want to."

He finally turned back to face her. "Kakul is my home. My people need me. We are still exploring beyond the Wall."

"I know."

"I would like to visit your world," he said after a moment, his voice very low. "Maybe one day."

"Have you found anything on the other side of the Wall?"

His eyes darkened. "Barren land, mostly. Dry, dusty, no plants except a few scrawny cactus. Not good for much of anything. It's…" He hesitated a moment. "It's very strange. I expected something else."

"Well, if you change your mind, my invitation still stands."

"Thank you. I must go now."

She let him walk away.

This was the first time the Lunar Terraform Alliance had agreed to send her back as part of an official mission. They had two whole weeks here.

The first week had gone smooth enough. She introduced her team to Rakulo and his people, and spent a day or two showing them the lay of the land.

Rakulo's people seemed indifferent to their presence, although the gifts they brought were not turned away—candy and toys for the kids at first, and then basic necessities like matches, flashlights, reusable water bottles, pots and pans, needle and thread, and other practical things.

Eliana had figured that the only thing Rakulo and his warriors would be interested in were weapons, like the steel knife Amon had given to Rakulo, and the laser cutter they had used to make openings in the vast Wall. Knowing this, she gave Rakulo a large illustrated hardback book of military history that showcased all kinds of weapons and warfare. His eyes had grown wide with wonder when he first saw the illustrations inside.

A high-pitch buzzing cut through the air. On the opposite side of the ruins, Ross stood astride a broad slab of limestone wielding a stone saw, sweat glistening on his ebony arms. Lakshmi and the twins stood to one side, masks pressed over their mouths, as he touched the spinning blade to the rock. Stone dust billowed into the windless air.

The pitch of the noise shifted into a sickly croak as the blade hit a snag. It cut out a moment later and was slowly filled in with sounds of the jungle—birds singing, cicadas buzzing, and overhead the watchful silence of the pale violet sky.

Eliana cupped her hands over her mouth. "Everything all right?"

"No worries!" Ross called back. "Just a tree root or something. I think I managed to cut through it."

Turner held out a hand and Ross passed him the saw. Then Ross tied a rope around the slab of stone, and with Turner and Lakshmi's help, hauled it up to ground level and pulled it to the side.

Ross clicked on a flashlight and peered down into the hole he'd cut in the large slab.

"Boss," he called out in his low voice. "Might wanna see this."

Eliana hopped down onto the rubble pile and climbed across the uneven heap that had once been the proud and beautiful pyramid, watching her footing as she maneuvered around the fallen obser-vatory. Somewhere under there, the blood-encrusted sacrifice stone was still buried.

This pyramid seemed to be built after the model of *El Castillo*, the famous Mayan pyramid located in Mexico back on Earth. Rakulo had shown her that, like the tropical rainforest in the Yucatan Peninsula, this area of jungle on the planet of Kakul was dotted with cenotes, great rainwater-filled sinkholes. A little research had confirmed her memory that there was a cenote below *El Castillo*, too.

However, *El Castillo* still stood on a solid bed of limestone. No one had had actually *set foot* in the cenote beneath it, and its significance was up to anthropological interpretation.

Lakshmi spoke when Eliana came near. "Took us

three days to move enough limestone to cut here, but our measurements were correct, boss. There's a small pocket of air right under here that didn't cave in all the way."

Eliana accepted a small flashlight from Ross and knelt down on the stone. The square he had cut was three feet wide. It opened into twenty to fifty feet of empty air below. Maybe more.

At the bottom sat a flat layer of water, dark like ink and covered in debris. Leaves and small sticks slowly drifted through the beam of the high-powered flashlight in a uniform direction, meandering around piles of limestone bricks where the foundation of the pyramid had broken through. She tilted her head and followed the drifting leaves to where they disappeared under a pile of rubble. Limestone bricks stacked up haphazardly against that wall, covering the opening through which the water still moved.

"Looks like Rakulo was right. Water. It's flowing toward the pile of rubble on that side, so this is part of the underground aquifer that runs through this area. It's blocked up now, although the water doesn't seem to be gathering here, so it must be getting through."

The water was shallow, maybe only a few feet deep. If the pyramid hadn't collapsed, this would have been an ample space, maybe even a nice swimming hole if one knew how to access it.

"Anything else?" Lakshmi asked, her voice strained. Eliana could tell without looking that she was biting her nails.

Eliana leaned farther into the opening. "Not that I can see. I was really hoping…" Her breath caught in her throat when the ray of light skipped over a thick root system hanging down from the ceiling like a bundle of cables. She had almost missed it!

She traced the system up to the ceiling. It was thick, the roots wrapped up into bundles, and then the bundles tangled into thicker cords. They came out of the wall and threaded along the ceiling before going directly into the rock foundation of the pyramid itself.

She had seen root systems like these before—she suspected that they weren't entirely natural even if they did seem to be alive. She had watched as Rakulo severed a set of them in the cenote they called the Well of Sacrifices, to disable the energy-consuming biotechnology that Remethiakara had planted there —that was how the alien had stolen nutrients from living things thrown into the water, and used it to nourish his offspring in their eggs and power strange machines in the tower outside the Wall where he lived.

"I don't think that root you hit belonged to just any old tree, Ross."

She traced the roots down with her flashlight— the bottoms dangled free. As she looked she saw that there were four such … plugs. She had no other word for them. None of the plugs connected to anything. They dangled far above the water's surface, so they couldn't get sustenance that way. If they were alive, Eliana knew she would have seen the same greenish glow that she saw in the systems Rakulo had destroyed. These ones were already dead, but not rotted out or deteriorated. As if they'd been severed only recently.

"I think something else was down here. Something big, and very much alive."

"What could it have been?"

"Not a clue."

4

PART OF THE PROBLEM

Rakulo wished for nothing more than to visit Eliana's world again. His hands rose unconsciously to the welts on his shoulders where his new tattoos were still healing, a constant reminder that being chief came with certain responsibilities that made his wishes immaterial.

He walked back along the river in what his mother might have called a "mood." He didn't care a speck about what Eliana and her friends might find beneath the temple of the pretender. Where was the sense in trying to dig up old ghosts?

She had always been fascinated with the stone city; Rakulo would be happy if it *all* sank into the ground, never to be seen again. It would be good riddance to painful reminders of all that had been lost.

Despite a life living within the confines of

Xucha's Wall, he'd never felt as trapped as he did right now. Even though he'd driven Xucha off and cut holes in the Wall, effectively removing the barriers that kept his people penned up like turkeys for the slaughter over countless generations, his ties to Kakul and to the people in his care were stronger than ever. He loved them truly. He felt responsible for their well-being and safety.

But that didn't change his desire to explore the unknown world, to go where no man had gone before —at least, where none of *his* people had ever been.

Rakulo had always been driven to know the truth of things. His sole ambition had once been to go beyond the Wall. Now that he'd done that, why wouldn't he want to go beyond the *world*, too? What else was out there for him—for his people—if someone with courage took the first step?

As he approached the edge of the village, Rakulo spotted his friend Quen. The warrior's massive frame and broad brown back were recognizable from a distance. He was on his knees beside the last row of maize plants in the large field at the north end of the village. As Rakulo approached, he saw that Yeli, Gehro, and a few others were there with him, pulling weeds and tending to the plants with care. Several of the tall stalks of maize had begun to wilt, their roots torn up and turned dark and sickly brown. A handful of dead plants had been removed and set aside entirely, their spots in the rows ominously empty.

"How's it going?" Rakulo said as he approached them.

Quen sighed, and brushed the dirt from his hands as he stood. "More of the same. Some damn critter keeps uprooting the maize. They're stealthy. You can hardly tell it happened until the plant starts to die."

Gehro, standing at the back of the group, caught Rakulo's eye and shrugged.

Gehro had forgotten more about living off the land than the young chief had ever known. Once they had realized something was wrong with the crops, Rakulo asked the old forest dweller to come down to the village and give his opinion.

"This is like nothing I've ever seen," Gehro said. "But let's give it time, eh? It's normal to have a few bad seeds in a bunch. Take care of the ones you've got left."

Quen wiped his head, nodded, and turned to Yeli. He regarded her seriously—she was with child and just beginning to show a telltale baby bump.

Yeli shook her head and laughed when Quen whispered something that the others couldn't hear. "I'm not *that* pregnant, Quen. I can keep working a while longer."

He gave her a crooked smile, nodded, and they

walked off down the row to continue checking the rest of the plants.

Ever since he found out Yeli was pregnant, Quen had become very concerned with daily life in the village—crops, and clean water, and the entertainment of the other children, for which Quen himself often became a centerpiece. The boys would climb over him like a tree while he lumbered around the dirt field where they played ball. Yeli would look on from the shade and smile. The sight of those two happy together helped to ease Rakulo's burden, or at least to give his anxiety a purpose.

Gehro put an arm around Rakulo's shoulder. "Let's walk."

They began to move toward the village. Once they were out of earshot of Quen and Yeli, Gehro said in a normal speaking voice, "Quen is right, Raku. Something is destroying the plants, maybe even eating the roots. I didn't want to say so in front of the others, but it worries me."

"Why?"

"If it was a bird or a lizard, I would recognize the markings. I don't know what's doing this."

Rakulo pursed his lips. "It's nothing to worry about. Harvest isn't too far away. We'll plant an extra field next year to give ourselves some leeway."

"Still, it begs the question. What is it? And why?"

"You can keep an eye on it for me. I have other things to worry about."

The old man frowned.

"I'm sorry, I didn't mean it like that."

Gehro dropped his hand and let out a dry chuckle. "Does being chief make you unhappy?"

Rakulo sighed. "No, it's just that I never truly wanted this responsibility."

"That's what makes you good at it. Those with the desire to rule often do so with only their intent in mind, not the well-being of others."

As he gathered his thoughts, Rakulo walked for a moment in silence beside the wizened old man.

"I'm afraid that if I tell people something has set out to destroy the maize, they will distort my words and say that it is a supernatural punishment for my transgression against Xucha. Either way, it's my fault."

"It's not your fault."

"But it is."

Gehro gave him the side-eye. "Is there something else you wanted to share?"

"Once we're inside."

They were meandering between houses in the village now, the mud daub walls and thatch-roofed huts where Rakulo's people made their homes. They rounded a corner and approached the hut where Rakulo grew up. It was unusual for a chief to live with his mother, but then these were unusual times. Rakulo knew that she still felt the absence of his father and younger brother keenly, so he had decided to continue sharing a shelter with her so she wouldn't feel isolated with her sorrow.

They found Ixchel inside, pinching one of the "metal" needles between two fingers. Ixchel was patching a child-sized tunic that had once belonged to Rakulo, and which she intended to give to Yeli as a gift when her baby was born.

"Hello, mother," Rakulo said. "Can I talk to you for a minute?"

"Talk," she said, not looking up from her sewing. "Rakulo, these needles are incredible. Can you ask Eliana if she can bring more of them next time she comes?"

"I can, but mother, this is important. I need to tell you both about what Citlali and I found beyond the Wall."

Ixchel lifted her face. Noticing Gehro for the first time, she set her work aside and regarded the men while intertwining the fingers of both hands. "Out with it, then."

"The land beyond the Wall is barren. Sand and dirt and not much more. No jungle. No river. The only living thing out there is Xucha's tower and a few cacti. That is, it until we found the tracks and the mounds."

"Tracks and mounds? What do you mean?" she asked.

"I thought at first it was just the way the wind blew the sand into dunes, but then I realized they were tracks of some kind of animal. Not like any tracks I've ever seen."

He squatted down so he was close to the packed dirt floor and drew two sets of horizontal lines that ran parallel to each other.

"Looks kind of like something ants would make. Or maybe spiders."

"I thought that, too, but this drawing doesn't do the scale justice, Gehro. The tracks are as wide as my arms." Rakulo held his arms apart to demonstrate. "We have cut thirty holes in the Wall. If these are spiders that big…" He shuddered.

Gehro cocked his head to one side and pursed his lips.

"You didn't explain the part about the mounds," Ixchel said. "What do you mean? Like, mounds?"

She nudged her bare breasts with her hands, which won a belly laugh from Gehro.

She gave him a look. "I'm a widow, you know."

Gehro cocked an eyebrow. "Is that so?"

Rakulo rolled his eyes, felt his cheeks heat up a little, and barreled on before the situation spiraled any further out of his control. He did not wish to deny his mother another chance at happiness, but there was no reason he had to be *present* for those discussions.

"Not those kind of mounds, mother. Please try to focus. The tracks lead to large mounds. I thought they were sand dunes until Citlali located an entrance. They may be burrows of some kind for whatever creature makes those tracks."

His mother put a warm hand on his arm and squeezed reassuringly. She traded a look with Gehro that he couldn't read. "Do you think they're dangerous, Rakulo?"

Rakulo felt very young all of a sudden. He was no longer the naive youth that thought he could climb over the Wall with a rope. But he wasn't the strong leader his father had been, either. For all Chief Dambu's faults, Rakulo had never once seen him look as uncertain or scared as he felt right now.

Rakulo cleared his throat. "Could be. I don't know what makes tracks like that. They could be harmless as caterpillars. But that's the only sign of life we've seen. Surely that's not a coincidence. My whole life, I thought that there was something for us beyond the Wall. Something that we were being denied."

"And now?" Ixchel said.

"It's not what I thought I would find. I don't know what to think," Rakulo said, lowering himself onto a stool that leaned against a wall. He set his head back and looked up at the thatched roof, where the magical bracelet Eliana had given him—the one that would send a "signal" to her friends—was hidden. It was his backup plan if everything went to shit.

Are you already resorting to backup plans? Come on, Raku. Think.

He closed his eyes and focused on the problem at hand. "What if the Wall wasn't built to keep us in, but to keep everything else *out*? The desert and whatever those creatures are. Does that mean I made a mistake by cutting holes in the Wall?"

"Maybe. You could try to patch them up again," Gehro suggested. "Or build gates in front of them."

Rakulo groaned. He hated that idea. "Only if there's no other choice."

Ixchel took a deep breath and sighed. "I don't have all the answers, Rakulo. You're the chief now. You must do what you think is right."

An idea forced its way into his mind as if it had a will of its own. *Go to Eliana's world and find what you're searching for. But what* are *you hoping to find?*

"I can't help but think that we were destined for something greater. I thought I would find it beyond the Wall, but what if..." Rakulo licked his lips and lifted his head. He looked into his mother's big brown eyes. "What if we went to Eliana's world. She invited us. Everyone."

His mother let out a disgusted noise, half exhalation, half growl. "And leave Kakul? This is our home, Rakulo."

"I know, but—"

"My son is buried here."

Gehro gazed at his feet and remained silent. Rakulo shifted his glance to Gehro.

"This forest is big enough for me. So what if there is nothing beyond the Wall? I'm an old man. I am content with my situation."

"Rakulo, listen to me," Ixchel said, lowering herself to her knees beside the wooden stool. "For the first time in ages, we have a *good* man as chief—someone who has a chance to become a truly great leader. Your fears and worries are valid. It is the chief's job to worry about these things. But leave our home? Rakulo, it is too much to ask."

"Those mounds outside the Wall are not invented. Neither is whatever is killing the maize."

"So deal with those problems. We've had a bad harvest before; the sea will sustain us. We've eliminated predators—one of them called himself a god, and *you* killed him."

"I can't be sure of that. I never found his body."

She waved her hands at the air, then raised her eyebrows, as if daring him to challenge her. "You drove him away. No one else has fallen sick, or been taken in the night. Hm?"

"What if we could have a better life on that other world? Eliana says that our people came from there originally. And the things they brought with them. Have you ever seen people like them before?" He gestured to the object on his bed that Eliana brought — a large, illustrated codex showing the warrior people of Earth on full display. "Their clothes are so different…these tools they bring us are remarkable, you said so yourself. Look at these magnificent beasts they ride." He gestured to the colorful paintings of proud men holding weapons in their arms, and riding bark-colored beasts of war.

"Those are drawings."

"These things exist on their world."

"So what?" Ixchel stood again, and picked up the baby's tunic and the metal needle and thread. "Since they were gifts, we shall use these things and treasure them. But we do not *need* them, Rakulo. There is a difference."

Rakulo bowed his head. It took an enormous effort of will to beat back the competing desires that vied for dominance within his conflicted soul.

His mother's voice came softly, almost a whisper. "Kakul is my home, Rakulo, and so it shall ever be."

"I know," he finally said, and sighed. "It's mine, too."

That's part of the problem.

5

OFF VECTOR

Amon descended to the basement level of the Austin Lunar Research Center, where the Translocator was kept, his whole body thrumming with nervous energy as he imagined Eliana's annoyed reaction to him showing up, unannounced, to end her expedition early.

But what choice do you have, man? General Wade is right.

As the elevator dropped, he shook his hands out, adjusted the collar of his shirt in the reflective silver walls, yanked at his slacks, and cursed himself for not putting sneakers or hiking boots on his feet that morning rather than the expensive, brown leather dress shoes he wore. Though they were comfortable, they weren't suited to stomping around in a rainforest on another planet.

Amon checked his watch. It was approaching

midnight, and he had promised to meet FBI Agent Moreno for breakfast tomorrow morning to get an update on the manhunt for Lucas Lamotte. The detective had made a breakthrough identifying some of the early victims of Lucas' Translocator mutilations, and Amon was itching to hear what they'd found.

Given his current timetable, that wasn't likely to happen. He pulled out his phone and dialed the FBI agent's number. But he didn't want to reveal too much, given the secrecy of this situation. Not even to the FBI.

"Agent Moreno, this is Amon. I know I was the one who requested a meeting tomorrow, but something came up at work and I don't think I'll be able to get away. Can you meet me at my cam—I mean, at the Austin Lunar Research Center, first thing in the morning? I won't have phone service for the next several hours, so if you return my call and I don't answer, I'm not ignoring you."

He ended the call and pocketed his phone again. His problems were starting to stack up, and not in a good way. At least he had confidence that a good man was on the case.

The elevator door slid open on the lowest level and Amon hurried out, taking long purposeful strides down the corridor.

The keening noise of the Translocator, like an amplified camera bulb charging up, echoed through the hall and then vaulted into the sub-audible range. He felt a subtle shift in the air as the machine activated and—he knew without having to see it—translocated an object. A billion tiny particles instantly dismantled, sent through space using high-frequency quantum teleportation, and reassembled at the destination point.

Amon slowed his walk, took a deep breath, and crossed the threshold of the open blast door right as the concentric rings of the stabilization sphere wound down and came to a stop. Branches of excess electricity shot off the silicon nodes in the hundred-foot arch that brushed the high ceiling.

"Aptitude?" Reuben called out.

"Transfer modeling at ninety-nine point seven percent accuracy," responded Audrey, who was waving a quantum wand over an object on the floor —a pair of sneakers that looked very familiar to Amon.

"Location?" Reuben said.

"Tenth of a degree off vector. What's the power ratio?"

"Cumulative readings…" Reuben frowned. "Up by about fifteen volts from the last run."

Holograms surrounded the engineer, a half dozen blue and green graphs and live readouts cast in the air like a cockpit around his head. A baggy button-up shirt hung off his frame like it belonged to a man much larger than him. His wild grey hair stood on end.

Amon had known Reuben for the better part of a decade. In that time, the man had always been slightly overweight, a Jew from New England who loved his carbs and ate when he was under stress, which was constantly. But he'd lost about twenty pounds in the last month, and seemed more vibrant and full of energy than he'd ever been. He'd changed his lifestyle and eating habits after his husband passed away following a difficult and extended battle with Alzheimer's. It was a sad occasion, but also a blessing in disguise, Amon had realized. Despite how his clothes hung loosely on his frame, Reuben had never looked so healthy before. The sudden absence of constant emotional strain had taken ten years off his appearance, though his hair remained the silver of middle age, and uniquely unruly.

"Look who the cat dragged in," Audrey said when she finally noticed Amon standing in the doorway.

He crossed to her, gave her a quick hug, and then knelt down next to the sneakers and began unlacing his patent leather dress shoes. "Forgot I left these here. Mind if I trade you?"

"Sure, if you want to. Leather is a better analog for organic compounds than polyester and plastic anyway." She cocked her head slightly to the side. "Are you thinking about going for a run?"

"Not exactly."

"Hullo, Amon!" Reuben said as he flicked the holo readouts to standby mode and joined them. "I'm glad you stopped by. You should know about this."

"Know about what?"

"The deep learning algorithms are still crunching the data, but it's troubling. It seems like the power of the star shard solution is depleting."

Amon felt his brow wrinkle. "Depleting? How do you mean? The power is pulled from the batteries attached to the particle accelerator, and then amplified through the star shard solution. It doesn't give off any power of its own."

"That's the assumption we've always operated under," Audrey said. "But recent operations have made us question that theory." She pointed the quantum wand at the shoes, whose laces Amon pulled tight and finished tying. He stood up and looked between the two scientists. They both had slight frowns on their faces. Amon took a deep breath. "Okay. Tell me more."

"Over time," Reuben said, "more and more energy has been required to achieve the same effect with the star shard solution. We hardly noticed the first time Eliana ended up on Kakul, because it surprised all of us and we had yet to establish a baseline."

"And then in further experiments you and I conducted," Amon said as he felt himself nodding along, "we chalked up the difference in voltage between transfers to our lack of understanding of how the meteorite channeled the power."

"Accuracy was always an issue, too."

"Now that we have more data, we're starting to see a pattern," Reuben said. "Translocations across the same distance require more power than they used to. I think that means the shards are running out of juice."

"How many transfers do we have left?"

"I can't really tell."

"The solution is all we have left. If it runs out…" His thoughts turned to Lucas, still at large and now certainly in possession of his own Translocator.

What's your end game, old pal? I know you're keeping an eye on me … just not sure where you're watching from.

The others waited patiently. Amon finally noticed them eyeing him warily. He tugged at his collar before forcing his hand back to his side. "The star shard solution is our only real advantage."

"Because Lucas's machine can only hop between stabilization platforms."

"Otherwise the transfer gets scrambled and the bodies come out mutilated."

Audrey shuddered. "I can't believe what he did to himself wasn't fatal."

"He was lucky."

They all recalled how Lucas had translocated himself out of the lab a month ago. He had also tried to steal the star shard, but the alien got to it first.

The sound of Lucas's scream still stung Amon's inner ear.

"He suffered for it," Amon said. "That much I'm sure of. It must go deeper than the scars on his face. But he's still out there, and because of that he's probably even angrier than he was before. He blames me."

"He shouldn't. It's his own fault."

"Regardless, the star shard is our only advantage. We need to maintain it. So give me your best guess—how many translocations does our solution have left?"

Reuben pursed his lips. "Maybe a half dozen more long-range trips? We can send a pair of shoes across the lab a thousand times, but it's taking longer and longer for the solution to become accessible again. After we sent Eliana and her team to Kakul, we barely got it back online in time to receive their first safety signal. And as I said it requires more energy on our end. Our batteries deplete faster and the particle accelerator is working overtime to produce the energy stores we need. Who knows what'll happen if the shard loses its amplification effect mid-translocation, or drains the batteries, or cuts out before the job is done…"

Amon didn't have to imagine. He'd seen enough lab mice and other test subjects shredded, bloodied, and dismembered by a half-baked quantum teleportation to last him a lifetime. Memories of what he'd read about and seen in the declassified Nazi documents from the 1940s sometimes made guest appearances in his nightmares. On those nights, he always woke in a cold sweat and hurried to the lab to check on the Hopper. The sight of its cold, still alloy rings soothed the fears that he would end up like the Nazi fringe scientists, even if the rational part of him knew it was only some old photos and a bad dream.

"And we suspect, too, that a low-power translocation with a depleted solution has other side effects."

"You mean like the space bends?" Amon asked, referring to the nickname he and Reuben had coined for the nausea and sickness that affected a person who had just been through a translocation. The other two nodded. It wasn't a great experience to be translocated even at full power with a molecular stabilization platform on the receiving end, like they had installed for journeys to the lunar base. Nausea and vomiting were common, especially for someone who endured multiple trips in a short time span. Amon had been on the receiving end of that more than once. To think that it could be worse made the little hairs on his neck rise and writhe. "Eliana and her team have another week on Kakul."

Reuben nodded. "I think we need to bring them home early. Just in case."

Amon sighed and wiped his hand down over his face. Apparently troubles came in threes. First Lucas, then the unknown spacecraft, and now this. "Even more reason for me to go get them."

"Ahh," Audrey said, looking down at the brown leather dress shoes Amon had left on the floor. "Is everything okay? You didn't know about this problem with the star shards before you came down here."

"It's…complicated. You know that spacecraft I told you about?"

Both Reuben and Audrey nodded. He'd informed them of the sighting shortly after returning from the lunar base with Enzo when he'd discovered it the first time. Before it had become a matter of national security.

"A Navy general named Joseph Wade arrived by helicopter with an escort of Marines about an hour ago. Enzo and I spoke with him and their…team." He cleared his throat, hoping they hadn't noticed his pause. He wasn't sure how much he could divulge about The Ares Initiative, even to his friends.

"A general?" Audrey said, arching one eyebrow. "In the building? This is a big deal."

"The Marines are planning to shoot the ship out of the sky before it can enter Earth's atmosphere. Since we suspect it's that alien, Xucha's, ship, they want to know if Eliana can provide them any more information that could help us find another course of action. She is, after all, the only person who has had close contact with the alien thus far."

Reuben pursed his lips as he nodded. "It would be safer if her team were back on Earth anyhow. I was going to come up with some excuse to bring them back today even if you hadn't come down to chat. I don't fully understand the star shard solution or how to read its energy levels and would hate to be wrong in our assumptions again and strand them there."

"You read my mind," Amon said. "Er, this goes without asking I guess, but there's enough power to get me there and bring them back, right?"

Reuben and Audrey exchanged a look and then nodded their agreement. "Should be."

"All right then. Spin it up."

Amon strode up the ramp and under two of the blue-green alloy rings positioned like an X, making a gap large enough to step through. He centered himself in the stabilization sphere—designed to be big enough to hold a truckload of supplies, about fifteen by fifteen feet square, and wiggled his toes in his sneakers.

Reuben returned to the holodeck, gave Amon a thumbs up, and made a few gestures. The rings slowly began to rotate.

"Set me down in the old city, if you can!" Amon shouted over the electrical sparks and whining racket of the Translocator's bootup sequence.

"I'll do my best!" Reuben said.

There was a bright light, Amon felt a jolt in his

stomach, like when he gunned his Porsche 911 Carrera over a crest in the road too fast, and then he was standing next to a river under a clear amethyst sky, squinting against the sudden daylight.

The nausea hit him like a freight train. He bent over and braced his hands on his knees as bile splashed on the dirt and splattered his sneakers. Maybe it was good he hadn't eaten dinner after all.

Looking around, Amon took his bearings. He was in the middle of the jungle. The gate into the city was just visible across the river to his left by several hundred yards.

"Tenth a degree off vector, my ass," Amon muttered into the humid jungle air as his lungs struggled to adapt. His ears popped. He grimaced against the nausea that roiled through his gut, and took a step toward the stone archway to find Eliana and her team.

6
———

AMON

"Is that...?" Laskhmi's voice trailed off as she squinted over Eliana's shoulders. The two had been leaning close together, using their bodies to block the sun so they could both see the screen of the Nikon X450 clearly.

Eliana tore her eyes away from a fascinating photograph of the shriveled root system hanging from the ceiling of the cenote, and turned.

She would have recognized the lean cut of her husband's shoulders anywhere. He strode purposefully across the pale paving stones, weaving among patches of waist-high grass. His thick black hair was long enough to curl slightly. He was wearing grey slacks, a blue dress shirt, and...sneakers? They had bright green swooshing highlights, a clownish contrast to his business attire.

A drumroll fluttered through her chest and a fist suddenly squeezed her heart. Something was wrong.

She knew her husband, and as simple as recognizing him, she could see that something was wrong. Apart from the fact that he had no reason to be here in the middle of their expedition, something was definitely wrong.

"Amon," Eliana said, finishing Lakshmi's question even as she left the archaeologist's side and went to meet him.

They came together in the middle of the courtyard. Amon took her hand and let out a soft sigh. "Sorry to drop in on you like this."

She pulled her hand away—a bit too quickly.

A look of hurt passed across Amon's face before he smoothed it away and forced a smile onto his face.

"What are you doing here?" she asked.

For a moment, the familiar tension of unforgiveness rose up between them. She felt herself begin to hold her breath.

"You need—" Amon clipped off the words, hesitated a few times as he tried to decide the best way to frame his thoughts. She recognized the serious expression that pinched his eyebrows together hawkishly when he was working a problem. When he spoke again, it was in the flat factual tone he used with his colleagues when discussing a physics formula.

"Reuben and Audrey are saying that the Translocator isn't functioning properly. The power of the star shard seems to be depleting. You all need to come back to Earth with me before it stops working entirely."

Eliana felt her eyes widen. "What changed?"

Now that the conversation had turned to her team's safety rather than their personal history, the tension between them faded into the background.

Amon put his hands up in a placating gesture. "There's enough power to get us all home, but…" He swallowed and closed his eyes for a moment.

Only then did Eliana notice that he was sweating beneath the collar of his shirt. His skin was clammy. She put her hand on his arm as a shiver passed through his body. "Is everything okay?"

"I may have vomited after I landed here. Space bends are bad today. Reuben thinks it's a side effect of energy depletion in the shard solution. I wish we hadn't lost the rest of the meteorite."

Her mouth went dry. The nausea she felt after the most recent journey to Kakul only lasted fifteen minutes. It sounded like the journey back would be far less pleasant. Given that information, she felt she already knew the answer to the next question, but she asked him anyway. "Why didn't Reuben tell me about this before we hopped back to Kakul?"

"He and Audrey were still trying to make sense of it a week ago. We don't really understand how the star shards work and the LTA had already green-lighted your expedition. Reuben told me he was going to contact you today regardless and ask you to cut things short, but since I happened to be in the lab I offered to bring the message in person."

"Thank you. If we hadn't known the whole story, we probably would have left equipment behind rather than dismantle it." She gazed at the electrical resistance survey, little numbered orange markers, tents and other supplies scattered around the courtyard, as if trying to burn their shape and the place's smell in the mid-day sun into her memory. "Can we have a day or two to finish photographing the site and pack up?"

Amon wrung his hands. "Actually, no. There's something else."

"Jesus, what now?"

"A spacecraft. Enzo and I were on the lunar base five days ago when it was first discovered."

"You didn't think that was important enough to tell me first?" She clenched her jaw as she realized her voice had climbed an octave or two in her shock and anger.

He winced. "One problem at a time. I really was trying not to interrupt your expedition."

She took a deep, steadying breath. She knew that wasn't the real reason. If anything, he probably thought the excursion was a convenient excuse to keep it from her for so long. *Calm down. This is bigger than the two of us.* "You don't think it's…him, do you?"

She didn't need to use the alien's name for Amon to know she was referring to Remethiakara.

"I do," Amon said in a low voice.

"But how? Last I saw him, he was *here*. In that… that place he took me. That terrible tower with the tendrils." She shivered despite the noonday heat and crossed her arms. She had some sympathy for Amon's chills now. In response, she stepped closer to him. Reflexively, he wrapped his arms around her shoulders.

If Remethiakara truly was in a spaceship bound for Earth, they had bigger things to worry about than a jumble of old stones and dead roots. Rationally, Eliana wanted to stay angry at Amon, but their personal differences suddenly seemed insignificant. She buried her face in his chest and inhaled the scent of him, clean sweat mingled with pine and cedar that lingered from his aftershave lotion. He gently rubbed her back.

"I'm sorry we haven't spent more time together lately," Eliana said. "I've been…busy with work."

"No, I'm sorry," Amon said. "I should have told you when we first spotted the spaceship. But I was trying to keep you out of it. To keep you safe. And you were so excited to be able to return here. Your first official LTA excursion." He leaned back to look her in the face. "I was proud of you. And I know I've been like that before. You were always kind to me when I got really involved at work."

She smirked up at him. "You? Get really involved in your work?"

He blushed. "What can I say? One-track mind." He tapped his temple and shook his head ruefully.

So that's why he was here. Because the spacecraft sighting and problem with the Translocator had spooked him. His one-track mind had led him straight to her side.

But there was something else, too. She stepped back out of his embrace and met his eyes again. "So what aren't you telling me?"

He huffed out a heavy breath. "I swear I don't know how you do that. Okay, well…I wish I didn't have to drop this on you, but here it is. The military has gotten involved, some kind of top secret organization. The man who's leading it, General Wade, he asked to speak with you."

She felt her eyes widen into small moons. "What does the general think I can tell him?"

Amon shrugged. "I'm not sure. But what you know could help save lives. He asked for you personally."

"But I don't know anything about a spacecraft!"

"You know more than anyone else does about the alien piloting it."

"Are you sure it's him?"

"I'd love to be wrong, babe. Come speak to the general, see for yourself."

Eliana shook her head. Not that she thought Amon was wrong, just that she found the whole situation hard to believe.

"It's just a conversation," Amon said. "Besides, he already seems to have a plan. A good plan. One that they've been working on for a long time."

"They?"

"The Ares Initiative is what it's called. All they're looking to you for is any last minute information that could make a difference. That's all. It's just a conversation."

Eliana looked up sharply. "What do you mean last minute? When is this spacecraft supposed to be there?"

Amon swallowed and checked his watch. "They tell me it will reach Earth in eight hours and fifty-five minutes from now. Give or take."

"The gear. We have to hurry."

"I'll help. As you can see, I dressed for the job." He gestured to his pressed slacks and green sneakers.

Eliana smiled through the fear that fluttered in her stomach. "We could always use another hand." She turned and waved at Lakshmi, who stood watching them out of her peripheral vision while pretending to study the rubble of the collapsed pyramid. Eliana caught the attention of Ross and the twins, and they began to walk over as well. "We need to tell the others."

Quickly, she summarized what Amon just told her about the star shard. "And, to top it off, Amon tells me a spacecraft has been found. They think it's headed for Earth."

Amon winced.

"What!" Turner said in his always too-loud voice. "Like, aliens?"

"Oh," Eliana said. "Amon, I'm sorry, I…"

"Not your fault," Amon said quickly. "I can explain. Look, we found something, we don't know what it is exactly. I just need Eliana to share her knowledge. These folks are extremely competent. They've got everything under control. This is just a precaution."

"What kind of folks?" Lakshmi asked.

"The kind of folks with security clearances most people don't think even exist. And some Marines. Not sure I should say much more."

"Who else knows?" Lakshmi asked.

"Not the public or the media. I'd appreciate it if you all kept this to yourselves for a while. It's a matter of national security now."

"Sure."

"Yeah."

"No problem."

Ross crossed his arms and nodded.

"Start packing up," Eliana said. "Take any photos

you think you'll need. We may not be able to return." *Sorry*, she mouthed at Amon.

He shrugged, lifted his palms to the sky, and smiled—maybe the first genuine smile she'd seen him give her in a month. The expression melted away as quickly as it had appeared.

Ross had already begun to pull up the metal probes for the electrical resistance survey. Spotting a piece of equipment he recognized, Amon walked over and began to dismantle the stone saw with swift, efficient gestures, packing it into its black plastic case.

Knowing that she might not be able to return to Kakul ever again put things in perspective for Eliana. She still wanted to explore the cenote they'd found beneath the foundation of the great stepped pyramid, but the time constraints made it impossible. They'd taken photographs through the hole Ross had cut. They would examine those back on Earth and then find a new project. That would have to be enough, at least until Reuben and Amon figured out a way to get the Translocator working well enough for a return visit. She wished she'd thought to bring a drone with her. The footage it could have captured from inside the cenote…

She shook off the thought and set to helping pack their gear.

A few hours later, as the sun dipped behind the horizon of Kakul and the two moons overhead faded into view, Eliana poked her head down the hole they cut into the cenote one last time before straightening and shaking her head. She lifted a heavy pack onto her shoulders and buckled it across her chest.

"Is everyone ready?" Amon activated his transponder bracelet and a green light began to blink.

In order for the Translocator to be able to pinpoint the precise location of each individual in the party, they had each been fitted with an identical band. Reuben's latest model of quantum-entanglement device was used to transmit coordinates back to receivers on Earth, and bring them all safely home.

Eliana's hand rose to her own bracelet, but she hesitated. *Should I have said goodbye to Rakulo? He already made his choice not to come to Earth...maybe it's better if I don't.*

At the edge of the courtyard, near one of the carved and vinegrown archways, a thick tangle of vines hanging down from a droopy tree rustled.

Eliana's head snapped toward the movement. "Hello, Rakulo? Is that you?"

She took a step toward the archway. Amon's fingers reached out to seize her forearm. "Careful."

"I'm sure it's nothing to worry about," Eliana said, slipping from his grip. "Probably just a lizard or something."

She set down her backpack and walked toward

the movement. When she got there, she pushed aside the fronds and saw only dirt.

She frowned. The dirt at the base of the bushes was churned up as if by several large feet.

Eliana was comfortable outdoors—years of training as an archaeologist had that effect on a person—but she was no tracker. The marks meant nothing to her. She shrugged, figuring it had been one of the wild turkeys that roamed this part of the jungle, or maybe a few of them given the sight of the dirt there.

She pressed the button on her transponder as she rejoined the group. The others already had blinking green lights on their bracelets.

The indicator on hers flashed for a few seconds, and then they all turned a steady green one by one as the Translocator locked onto their team's position.

After taking one last long look around the court-yard, Eliana sighed. It was time to face the music. She braced herself for the trip.

"All right," she said. "Let's do this."

Moments later she felt a lurch in her stomach, and the whole group hopped back to Earth.

7

PATROL

A branch cracked in the forest, causing Rakulo to spin so fast it brought a white hot pain to his abdomen. The fabric they used to sew up the stab wound in his gut had already been absorbed by his body. A pink ridge of glossy skin had formed in its place. But if he turned too suddenly it caused enough pain to take his breath away.

Ignoring the pain, he clicked the button on the little light-thrower, lifted his fist to his ear, and pointed the bright white beam into the thick tree line where he thought the noise had come from. Rakulo strained with his right ear. Though it seemed to be getting a little better every day, he remained half deaf on the left side.

The light-thrower illuminated the broad fronds, hanging vines, and drooping branches at the tree line, casting stark black shadows into the dense jungle beyond. The hard-edged beam of the light-thrower seemed almost a solid thing compared to the wavering edges of an open flame.

A soft breeze rustled the leaves and a tiny lizard scurried up the serrated bluish bark of an old, bent tree. Rakulo followed the creature up until it disappeared around the dark side of the trunk. Seeing nothing else in forest, he clicked the light-thrower off and let the black cylinder swing from a thong around his wrist as he continued his circuit of the village.

Along with the large metal and wood shovels stacked beside the maize fields, the light-thrower was one of the most useful tools gifted to them by Eliana and her friends. Rakulo had gotten into the habit of taking one with him on his nightly rounds.

Ahead, the cliff's edge came into view. The orb of the orange sun sank into the deep sparkling sea beyond. The clear sky overhead had deepened to violet striped with clouds like green brushstrokes as twilight approached. Pinpricks of stars began to poke through the upper canvas, joining the pale outlines of the two crescent moons.

Things had been strange since he'd driven Xucha away. Never had his people known such peace. The calm actually put Rakulo on edge—he didn't trust it. From the time he was old enough to begin to question the old ways and traditions, he'd learned to live life on guard. His father, Chief Dambu, had drilled the attitude of a warrior into him. His patrols around the village as well as his journeys beyond the Wall were both expressions of that hard-dying habit. Peace or not, Rakulo never went far without the big metal knife Amon had given him fastened tightly at his waist. *Metal.* He rolled the English word around in his mouth, savoring its hard edge.

The light-thrower was called something else in Eliana's language. His mind grasped for the word, but like many of the things they brought from their world, it was hard to remember their names. Many of their words were slippery, and learning them was like trying to catch a fish with his hands.

What does it matter? Rakulo didn't need to know their words because he would never be going to their world. His mother and Gehro had made that perfectly clear.

Rakulo was approaching the village proper now. Kakul was nestled between the cliff's edge and the forest. A hundred huts stood packed close together. Any two adjacent buildings were close enough to lay his outstretched palms along the outer walls of both. There was something comforting about that proximity. Narrow paths wound between the mud daub walls and, as he entered their midst, the quiet voices of his people filtered out of their homes and filled his ears, pushing away his questions, making his restlessness seem less important.

He let the voices push the selfish thoughts of leaving Kakul out of his head, too. His heart yearned to explore, and he had done so—the first warrior in their village to ever see beyond the Wall.

Why isn't that enough?

People conversed quietly with their spouses and children about dinner preparations. He watched and smelled the woodsmoke as cooking fires were lit. Smokestacks rose ponderously into the air. The laughter of children echoed down the narrow paths between houses.

Stepping into the open communal area at the center of the village, ringed by houses, Rakulo stopped short when a gaggle of boys chasing a ball passed in front of him. One or two of them drew up and turned to stare at the scar on Rakulo's bare stomach. He pretended not to notice, and walked on, though he heard them—with his good ear only— whisper in awe behind his back. He couldn't help but feel a strange sense of pride at their reaction, although he tried to keep his expression impassive.

An effusive woman his mother's age waddled up beside him and threaded her arm through his. "Hello, sweetie."

"Good evening, Watiya," Rakulo said "How are your knees today?"

"Little achy in the bones, but nothing I can't

manage. Have you seen how 'dose boys are lookin' at you lately?"

Rakulo nodded.

"Don't pretend as if you don't like it. But pride is only a good thing in moderation."

Rakulo cleared his throat. "Is it that obvious?"

"Not *so* obvious. I see it. But I also remember when you were that age. You're still the sweet little boy who liked to play ball and climb trees in the forest. Even if you are two heads taller than me now, and broad like your father. Did I ever tell you about the time..."

Rakulo smiled. Watiya had been on his side through much of what had happened in the past months, a quiet but stalwart ally spreading ideas her own way. So, she liked to talk. It didn't hurt him, did it? It certainly helped him convince Maatiaak and the older warriors that Rakulo's resistance to Xucha was the right course of action—when half the village had clung to the old ways and been set against him, Watiya had stood up for him. In her own way.

Could he abandon even her? He cared for these people, and owed it to them to stick around...at least for now. They would do as much, or more, for him.

Rakulo nodded and smiled as Watiya talked on and on, telling stories about her friends and family he'd heard a hundred times.

Finally, he managed to lead her back to her own home. One of her daughters was adding sticks to the communal fire and Watiya, seeing that the flame had grown too large for cooking, left his side to keep the food from burning.

Darkness fell suddenly as the sun sank completely into the sea. The only light remaining came from the cooking fires. Rakulo melted into the shadows on the porch of the house he shared with his mother, content to stand and look over his people as another dinner was prepared.

They seemed...happy. With no distant foreboding of a human sacrifice looming over their future, they were different. They looked over their shoulders less. They didn't have dark bags under their eyes, or the haunted looks that were common under Xucha's terrible reign.

I may be stuck here, Rakulo thought. *But it is a cost worth paying to free my people from that madness.*

Citlali joined him, sidling up to his side in the darkness. Her lithe form moved silently on bare feet. Her long, dark hair was pulled back in two braids, and shone lustrous in the flickering firelight. She leaned against him, shoulder pressing against shoulder. Even Maatiaak, Citlali's father, who had never liked Rakulo and always questioned his leadership, nodded and smiled politely in their direction.

When dinner was prepared, the pack of boys who had been playing ball earlier each got called to their own families. He and Citlali chuckled as they watched the boys' parents force each of them to scrub their hands in a wash basin before being allowed to eat dinner. Ulbarro, a chubby dark-haired boy of about ten years old, ignored his mother and swiped a thick leg of roasted turkey where it sat cooling on a clay platter. He was halfway to sinking his teeth into the meat when his mother snatched the bone from his hand.

She was waving the bone angrily over her son's head and berating him when a pale creature, half as tall as a man and several times as long, darted out of the shadows. Rakulo barely had enough time to blink as a gigantic pincher claw snapped around the turkey leg, and took two of Ulbarro's mother's fingers off with it.

The severed fingers fell to the dirt.

Ulbarro's mother screamed.

She clutched her injured hand with her good hand while blood spurted out of the severed ends, painting her legs and the ground at her feet.

The massive creature, its body covered in pale armor-like plates, skittered back into the shadows as quickly as it came. A chittering sound like a baby's rattle wavered in the air as it retreated.

Quen and Citlali grabbed spears from where they were leaning nearby and darted after it.

Rakulo drew his knife and shouted, "Watiya, help her. Warriors, with me!"

A half dozen men and women fell into step beside him as he charged through the tree line.

8

______

RISK

Stepping into the large conference room was like walking into a sauna. Eliana decided this was not the best feeling for someone who was still trying to keep the scant remains of her lunch on the inside.

They'd all spent nearly half an hour hovering close to the bathroom before Eliana gave in to Amon's impatience and let him drag her upstairs to talk to the general, leaving the other queasy archaeologists behind.

The reason for the room's rise in temperature was immediately evident. Computers and other electrical equipment lined the edge of the room. Cables crisscrossed the floor. And nearly a dozen people dressed in crisp military uniforms huddled over a conference table in the center of the room. Eliana felt suddenly self-conscious of her mud-splattered boots and sweat-stained safari shirt.

A barely-audible buzz came from cooling fans and heatsinks, making her whole body seem to vibrate. She wiped a bead of sweat from her forehead with the back of her hand as it threatened to drip, stinging, into her eyes. A digital clock on one of the monitors said it was six in the morning.

Another, bigger display showed a clock that currently reflected 02:33:04—and counted down. She swallowed past the fear and dryness in her throat.

"Eliana," Amon said, "this is General Wade."

A distinguished-looking man with salt and pepper hair crossed the room and took her hand, smiling warmly. "Mrs. Fisk, thank you for coming on such short notice." His shirtsleeves were rolled neatly up to his elbows and his hands were softer than she expected.

"Not a problem," she said, forcing a smile. "Amon said it was very important."

Amon squeezed into the room behind her and stepped to one side to stand by a bank of computer towers while the general gestured Eliana toward the long table in the middle of the room—a table that supported a plane of tinted glass. Eliana sat across from General Wade, the only two people at the table, and studied the hologram which was suspended in the air at eye level. Spheres and oblong shapes of varying sizes shown in crisp blues and greens. One of the assistants dimmed the room's lights, making the semi-translucent holos easier to see.

"I apologize that you had to leave your work behind on such short notice," General Wade said. The holos illuminated his face. "But we have need of your expertise."

"Amon told me about the spacecraft. How can I help?"

"Do you know what it is you're looking at right now?"

Eliana wiped sweat away from her eyes again and studied the holograms, trying to make sense of them.

At first, the shapes before her were just a random array of blue dots and spheres, spread far apart from each other, some as small as a ping pong ball, others the size of a melon.

Behind the general, a very large Marine in fatigues with a vicious scar on his chin took a long, slow breath. A small Asian woman with glasses and a pinched expression cleared her throat.

Waves crashed against the inside of Eliana's skull with a steady throbbing thud. She forced herself to focus. "Oh. It's our solar system."

"That's correct," said General Wade. "We've got the team streaming this down from the SOLARPulse-1 on the moon. It's running about five minutes behind real time. Pretty amazing, isn't it?"

Eliana glanced up. Amon was staring at it and clenching his jaw. Normally he'd be agog at something like this, but she could see how the stress drew frown lines along the side of his mouth. Had those been there a week ago?

She turned back to General Wade as he reached into the diagram with both hands and made an expansive gesture. The hologram zoomed past Jupiter so that the gaseous giant passed between her and the general before receding to her right, near where Amon stood. Then Mars did the same and expanded until it floated directly between her and General Wade. At the opposite end of the table, the curve of a familiar green and blue planet loomed.

Amon stepped forward and put a hand on Eliana's shoulder. She reached back and squeezed his fingers once before letting her hand fall back to the table.

"The scale's a little bit off," Amon said. "The emptiness between the planets has been compressed to make it easier for us to view it. But for our purposes it's good enough."

Between Earth and Mars, several rocks were floating, either in relative stasis or orbiting slowly. The very smallest were labeled with random strings of letters and numbers, like *TZ87* and *AH963*.

Two labels closer to Mars marked larger objects, *Phobos* and *Deimos*, Mars's moons. Eliana recognized the names immediately; her interest in classical mythology was one reason she became an archaeologist. But she'd learned their stories to such an extent that seeing these particular names in this context sent a shiver down her spine.

"In Greek mythology, Phobos and Deimos were the personifications of Fear and Terror," Eliana said, "twin brothers who were said to accompany their father Ares, god of war, into battle."

"You know your history," General Wade said with a hint of admiration.

"It's my job. Amon told me that you call this project The Ares Initiative. Mars was the Roman name for Ares. Some coincidence, huh?"

"No coincidence. The Ares Initiative was named for the guideline that runs it…to protect Earth from external threats. We are under no illusions as to what our role here is."

Straight to the point, wasn't he? Eliana nodded and continued to study the miniaturized solar system in front of her. Halfway between Earth and Mars was a tiny speck, even smaller than the label beside it. But it moved at a fast clip, especially at this miniaturized scale.

The label that moved with it read, *Unknown*.

She glanced over her shoulder again. "Is that it?"

The general nodded. Amon stepped to the side to get a better look.

"My god." Eliana breathed the words as she came to terms with the idea. Knowing the existence of an alien spacecraft was technically possible did not make the effort for her brain to comprehend it any less of a challenge. The human mind has limitations which technology has surpassed, but our brains are still primitive, formed over millions of years of Earth-bound evolution.

Eliana shook her head in disbelief. "That's incredible."

"Yes," said General Wade. "But also potentially dangerous. The scientists on the lunar base haven't been able to identify what's powering this thing. And the pilot either can't receive our transmissions, or is ignoring our attempts to make contact."

"I don't feel like he would have a radio on board…"

"So what does he use? How can we reach him?"

She shook her head ruefully. "I have no idea."

"What do you remember about your encounter with the alien? If you don't mind, I'd like to hear it in your words."

"I wasn't there long. But I know what I saw. The meteorite the alien stole—they're called star shards, he told me—is used as a kind of fuel cell. He was able to draw upon its power at will. So I think it's reasonable to assume he's using the same star shard to power that ship, too. The rest was even stranger. The whole building seemed alive—even the walls seemed to breathe. There was very little in the way of equipment. No buttons or dials or nodes or sockets. It was as if the living, breathing thing had its own electrical charge. Did you know, General, that the human body can be used as a capacitor, to store an electrical charge? It was like that, I guess, but amplified. The way he showed me his history…it wasn't like television or 3D holograms or even virtual reality. It was a full, seamless immersion. These little…"

Eliana shuddered and paused. Someone put a glass of water in front of her. With hands she hadn't realized were shaking, Eliana reached out and took a sip, then carefully set the cup down again. She glanced up at Amon, her ears burning, then met the general's eyes around the red-tinted bulge of Mars between them.

"These little tendrils went into my ears. He used them to show me things. To make me *think* and *feel* the way he thinks and feels. It seemed so real. I had no power to resist it."

Amon put both hands on Eliana's shoulders and squeezed. She closed her eyes and took a deep breath as she pressed the back of her head into his abs, letting the dependable weight of him prop her up for a second.

When she gathered herself again, Eliana said, "He didn't try to hurt me. I know he's done things that are unforgivable, but whatever his failings are he didn't harm me, not really. He was just trying to communicate. To be heard. We should try to do the same for him. His people are obviously highly advanced technologically." She gestured to the ship, which had moved about an inch through the air toward Earth in the time they'd been talking. "But they also have a problem—they're dying. It's very difficult for his people to have children, which they grow in eggs. Gestation takes many years, maybe decades. The mortality rate is incredibly high, too, and due to their long life spans, much time passes between opportunities to reproduce."

"You saw all of that in this 'full immersion'?"

"Some of it. I saw the eggs in person. Other bits I've pieced together since then. But you can tell a lot about a person's culture if you know the right questions to ask."

"How old is he?" General Wade asked. "The alien, I mean."

"Hundreds of years? Thousands? I don't know for sure."

The general exchanged a long look with the Marine leader.

"What?" Eliana said. "What is it?"

"What we do know," General Wade said, turning back to her, "is that this ship is moving fast. If it stays its current course, it will collide with Earth in a matter of hours." He gestured to the countdown clock. "If the spacecraft impacts the planet at its current velocity, it could cause a natural disaster of epic proportions. Earthquakes. Tsunamis. God knows what else. If it continues to ignore the communications we're sending, there are more effective methods to deal with the problem."

"May I?"

Eliana leaned forward to study the 3D hologram of the spacecraft. The general obliged, once again adjusting the viewframe so that she could get a closer look.

At first, the spacecraft was just another oblong rock, like one of those labeled asteroids or one of Mars's moons. But as she studied it further, she realized that the similarity ended there.

This was a sleek aerodynamic ship with a rear fin like a mermaid, and a nose like a hammerhead shark. It had no wings, like you might expect of a ship of human design, and no engines or thrusters that she could identify. Despite the fish-like shape, the hull of the ship reminded her of a beetle, the kind with ridges and bumps and overlapping plates on its armor.

Like she always did when she was studying an artifact or fossil, she began talking to herself out loud. "It's a mystery. The only thing even remotely similar to this that I've seen was the place he took me on Kakul. I can't say for sure, but I'd bet it was him. You know, we've only explored a very small region of the planet. There could be other people or animals living there that we don't know about. And Reme...er, the alien acted very strange, but he never mentioned or showed me any spacecraft. I mean, where would he have kept it? It's not like he had a…"

The words faltered on her lips. She felt her eyes grow wide. She reached back for Amon, who had stepped away and was looking at his cell phone with an anxious expression.

"Amon, what if *that's* what was beneath the pyramid?"

He tore his eyes from the backlit screen of his phone and looked at her blankly for a moment. Then her words seemed to sink in. He paused as he considered it. "How big is the spacecraft?"

The asian woman made a satellite call to the lunar base and conferred with the scientists there for measurements. "About a few hundred yards long, and a third as wide," she reported.

Eliana nodded to herself. She could confirm the measurements with Lakshmi later, but those dimensions *seemed* to be in the right ballpark.

"Those root systems we saw," Eliana said. "What if they were like some kind of power cable? Or…an umbilical cord? If the spacecraft is living biotechnology like the rest of the stuff I saw, the planet could have fed it…and kept it alive." The memory of the tech Remethiakara had used to show Eliana visions of their shared history sent a shudder through her body. She could still feel the way the soft tendrils tickled the little hairs on her ears as they crawled into her aural cavity to send signals directly to her brain.

A soft chime sounded from Amon's cell phone. "Agent Moreno is here." Amon frowned. "I think Enzo is with him now, but I should go to meet them. It's probably important since he's here a couple hours early."

"Is it about Lucas?" Eliana whispered.

Amon nodded.

"Go," Eliana said. "It's okay."

As Amon was leaving the room, the general turned to the big, scar-faced Marine. "Major Bautista, what's your recommendation?"

"Destroy it, sir."

"Now, wait a minute!" Eliana rose from her chair and stared, mouth agape, around the room.

Amon paused, opened his mouth to say something, then thought better of it and left the room without a word.

"Is that really necessary?" Eliana demanded. "What if we could learn something from him? What if we could make peace?"

"Were his intentions peaceful when he kidnapped you?" Major Bautista asked, his face impassive as ice.

She felt herself blush. He was right. Why was she standing up for this alien?

"Our job is to mitigate risk," the Marine continued. "Destroying this spacecraft before it gets too close is the safest course of action."

Eliana shook her head. "I understand your desire for caution, but what if attacking first backfires somehow?"

"Then we deal with that. We have backup artillery systems. And ground crews standing by to clear any debris."

"We can't risk *not* making contact. Remethiakara and his people visited Earth centuries ago. My theory is that that's how the people I met on Kakul got there in the first place. What if Remethiakara could tell us something about our ancestors? Something we didn't even know about our own history?"

"And if he intends us harm and we do nothing?" General Wade said in a soft voice. "What if he has nuclear weapons? A virus? Weapons of mass destruction we don't even know exist yet? Not to mention his own personal power. We have no reason to think his intentions are benevolent. How many of those natives did he execute on that other planet? I'll take your recommendation under consideration, Mrs. Fisk, the same as I do for everyone else in this room. But millions could die if we do nothing, and that's not a decision I take lightly."

Eliana sighed, lifting her hands slightly and letting them fall to slap against her sides. "I'm not saying do nothing. I'm just saying there's got to be another way."

The general stood, and Eliana rose, too. Standing so quickly caused the holograms to waver in her vision, but she took a deep breath and managed to steady herself. Fortunately, the conversation had distracted her long enough that the nausea was finally beginning to pass.

"Thank you for coming, Mrs. Fisk. It means a lot to me, personally, and to this country, that you came when we called upon you."

"Yes," she managed to say. "Of course."

He smiled and turned back to his team as he rattled out a stream of new instructions. "Tammy, get the president on the line. Major Bautista, transmit launch coordinates to our people at Nellis Air Force Base and have them initiate protocol ETX. And then send a message to The Ares Initiative and let them know we're moving forward."

Instead of standing on the sidelines, Eliana pushed her way into the empty, air-conditioned hallway. The door closed and latched behind her, cutting her off from the circle of the general's advisors from which she'd just been politely ousted.

Her recommendation would almost certainly be ignored. She felt deflated. Why did she hurry back here if they weren't even going to listen?

She looked for Amon, but he was long gone.

She took a few minutes to calm herself and splash water on her face in the bathroom. She had no idea what else she could do to help, but, damnit, she had to try.

When Eliana returned to the conference room,

the general was seated at a table with holograms of a dozen people she didn't know. The general had a cell phone to his ear.

"Yes, Mr. President. I understand, sir. Consider it done."

He handed the phone to Tammy.

The countdown clock showed less than two hours now. The general glanced at it. "Less than two hours to launch. Best make your preparations now, folks."

One by one, the holograms faded out of the room, and took with them any hope that Eliana could make a difference.

9

THE TIME TO STRIKE

Amon found Enzo and Agent Moreno standing in front of the headquarters building in the chill, wan light of dawn.

Enzo was wearing the same suit he had on the night before, wrinkled now at the backs of his knees from sleeping in it, probably on the couch in his office. Agent Moreno exhaled a plume of smoke and nervously flicked the butt of a cigarette with a thumbnail. Amon let the glass door shut the burbling waterfall sound into the lobby behind him as he stepped outside.

"I didn't know you smoked, Tom."

"Filthy habit," Agent Moreno said as he sucked the last of the cigarette down to the butt before dropping it to the cement and grinding it under his black shoes. "I'd be drinking, too, if it didn't make my head all fuzzy."

Amon frowned. It wasn't like him to be so cagey. "Should we find somewhere private to talk?"

"Rather stay out here," he said, eyeing the huge structure that loomed over them. "Too many prying eyes and ears."

Enzo narrowed his eyes but didn't object. Amon had no right to. He knew all too well that a history of betrayal checkered Fisk Industries' recent past. "Let's walk."

The three men strode along a paved path that cut diagonally across the broad green lawn, slick with dew. For it to be so cool in the mornings in Texas was a blessing. Amon took a moment to relish the wind. Enzo seemed as unaffected as usual. Moreno glared into the wind like he could stare it into submission.

As they walked, the FBI detective spoke in a soft voice. "I caught Enzo up on what we discussed last time we got together. That the forensic team was able to identify a few of the victims through a combination of fingerprints and dental casts. Several of them turned out to be ex-military. Once we put that together, it was a simple thing to confirm their recent employment at the private security firm, Hawkwood."

Amon nodded. Hawkwood had a checkered past, too. They'd lost their license to operate in the U.S. after conspiring with Lucas Lamotte to impersonate FBI agents and attempting to blackmail Amon into handing over control of his company. Their unmasking drove Lucas to steal the Translocator blueprints and flee the country, which is how Agent Moreno and the FBI got involved in the first place.

Hawkwood managed to continue operations as normal, and even salvaged their contract with the U.S. military. The cover-up was hardly mentioned in the news. War had been part of the fabric of American life for decades, and the military needed its military contractors to continue to operate its endless foreign wars. Amon and Agent Moreno had discussed this development two weeks ago when Amon had driven down to the FBI Field Office in San Antonio.

"Here's the new part," Moreno said. "Hawkwood gave us the run around for a while, claiming that they were protecting the privacy of their employees' families. But we finally got them to admit that not only did several of the victims work for Hawkwood, they were also recently deceased. Hawkwood claims the victims we identified had been deployed to Northern Africa, where they were killed in action. So how did their bodies end up scattered across a vast area in the continental United States?"

"Christ," Amon said. "It looks like they let Lucas Lamotte murder their own people with the Translocator."

"It sure fuckin' does."

"To what end?" Enzo asked. "And why would they lie about it?"

Moreno shook his head. "Don't know."

"But you're sure?" Amon insisted.

"Deadly sure."

Agent Moreno gazed off into the middle distance and didn't speak for several minutes. The trio came to a bench in the middle of the quad and sat in a row so they gazed back toward the elegant steel and glass headquarters building from which they'd just come. Its curved face reflected the burnt orange sun, which rose through a clear sky behind them. Metal letters spelling FISK INDUSTRIES still hung over the entryway. Amon had always liked the way they looked like they were on fire when the sun struck them just right. Now it looked—and felt —as if his whole life was burning down around him.

Amon deliberately turned his body away while Moreno dug another cigarette from a crushed pack in his front pocket and lit the end with a white Bic lighter.

"Got these from my house," he said, the ghost of a smile flowing past his lips and then vanishing in a cloud of smoke. "Had them hidden in the garage, in a toolbox I never open anymore. I forgot they were there. Only noticed as I was packing up the house to move my wife and kids into witness protection yesterday."

Amon felt his jaw fall open, and a terrible crushing weight gripped his torso on all sides.

"What happened?"

"After we got confirmation from Hawkwood, severed body parts started showing up wherever I went. When I opened my car in the morning, a severed foot was sitting on the driver's seat, the black leather covered in dried blood. When my wife went into the shower in the morning, she screamed because she slipped on a severed ear just sitting on the floor."

"Christ. I'm sorry, Tom."

"Worse showed up at the FBI Field Offices. We caught it on camera. No one entered or left the building. An empty room one minute…dozens of twisted body parts in unnatural configurations the next. It was gruesome."

"Is it Lucas? He tried to scare you off this case, yes?" Enzo observed.

Agent Moreno looked like he was going to be sick. Amon put his hand on the man's shoulder and squeezed. They weren't exactly friends, but had grown closer through this horrible experience. It had only been a month since Agent Moreno lost his partner at Lucas's hand—murdered the same way as the victims, through a faulty translocation that reshuffled their internal anatomy in the blink of an eye. The way his family was now being threatened was unacceptable.

"Are your wife and kids okay?" Amon asked.

The detective nodded. "For now. Not even I know where they were taken. Which is for the best."

"We have to find Lucas," Amon insisted. "Put an end to this madness."

"But how?" Enzo asked.

"Hawkwood is out of the FBI's reach now that they only operate abroad," Agent Moreno said. "You know that. What about the Translocator? Are you sure there's no way to, I don't know, triangulate the one he built?"

Amon inhaled through his teeth and sighed. "Not really. Lucas has a MegaPower reactor core from the lunar base, so we have to assume he's using nuclear power to operate the Translocator. You could look for radiation. Or a heat signature."

"Needle in a goddamn haystack," Moreno spat, snapping the half-smoked cigarette in his fingers and throwing its remains to the pavement. "FBI analysts have used satellites to scour every active nuclear reactor site in dozens of countries, and found nothing. If he's devised a way to shield the radioactivity from satellite footage, it's a lost cause anyway."

"There's got to be a way. Some clue. He has the core, which means he has to have a nuclear reactor to use it in. And battery storage nearby. We just need to narrow down our options."

Moreno ground his teeth so loud it made Amon wince. "We're running out of time, Amon!"

Amon bobbed his head in acknowledgement, not wanting to anger the detective. "We'd have better luck trying to lure him out. We just have to figure out what he wants."

Amon's phone buzzed in his pocket. It was a message from Eliana.

"It's happening," Amon said.

They practically ran back inside and up the stairs to the conference room. Raised voices drifted out the door as they drew closer. Agent Moreno's forehead was a mass of wrinkled confusion. Amon pulled him aside as they approached.

"The search for Lucas is not the only hunt taking place right now. Remember the alien you saw come through the wormhole in the Translocator? The one who took the star shard and scared Lucas off?"

A predatory grin spread across Agent Moreno's face, chasing away his exhaustion. "The only good thing that happened that day was Lucas retreating with his tail between his legs."

"Right. Well, here's the thing…we think the alien is headed to Earth again. Instead of hijacking the Hopper, this time he chartered his own ship."

Amon took a deep breath, pulled open the door to the conference room, and stepped into the thick, sweat-stinking air, leaving Moreno to follow him.

Amon stepped into a war room.

"You can't!" Eliana was shouting. "General, please. There's got to be another way. Destruction is not the right answer."

"I'm afraid that it is, Mrs. Fisk. The Ares Initiative voted unanimously, and the attack has been approved by the president himself."

"Amon," Eliana said turning to him. "You agree with me, don't you? We can't just blow the ship up. We can't just kill him. Imagine what we could learn from Remethiakara! Offer him a truce. Please. You've still got time."

She pointed at the countdown clock, which was approaching one hour.

"The time to strike is when the opportunity presents itself," General Wade said. "The decision has been made. No more waiting."

Amon swallowed and looked to the side, away from Eliana's searching gaze, in an attempt to mask his relief. The general had plucked the words from his own mind.

Agent Moreno was staring around the room, dumbstruck. General Wade glanced up at the FBI agent, irritation clear in his face, until Enzo explained in a lowered voice who he was. Tammy blustered up muttering something about a non-disclosure agreement, and led the detective to a laptop. Then she turned back to the holograms over the table, which now showed a close-up of the spacecraft approaching Earth, just inside the orbit of the moon.

"Still no response to the last communication?" General Wade said, glancing at Eliana to make sure she heard him.

"Negative," Major Bautista said.

Eliana's whole stance went cold as ice. She lowered her arms to her side, stalked across the room in front of the general, and put her back to the only wall unoccupied by faintly humming electronics.

"Let's hope I'm wrong," she said. "Or you'll regret this."

"There's no time for regret in a dogfight, Mrs. Fisk," General Wade said. "Only action."

He pulled out his chair at the head of the table and positioned it so that he could see Earth, the moon, and the spacecraft clearly arrayed in front of him.

"Major Bautista," the general said. "Fire the missiles."

The scar-jawed Marine spoke into his communications headset.

At first, nothing happened. Then, two bright-red projectiles lifted from the holo of Earth and sped into the sky.

A seemingly endless instant stretched on as the missiles broke free of the upper atmosphere. The shuttles that had propelled them into space broke away and fell back to Earth. Their secondary thrusters were activated, and they gained speed as they cruised toward the spacecraft.

They made contact. They pierced the hull.

No shields, Amon thought. *No chance.*

The spacecraft seemed to tear and rotate at the same time.

Then it exploded in a riot of pulverized shrapnel.

10

STARDUST TO DUST

Earthlings are so predictable.

Though his mental connection with the mothership was weakened without his helmet to help amplify the power that resided, ever burning, in his blood and bones, Remethiakara projected his thought at the mothership and felt that she received it.

Her response was a keen, bittersweet sense of anxious joy—the anticipation-fear of a coming battle mingled with the satisfaction of fulfilling one's purpose.

A rare and noble emotion, indeed.

My parting gift to you, ancient mother.

Remethiakara had both palms of his gauntleted hands pressed against one translucent wall of the bridge. In response to his truethoughts, a low purr rumbled through her frame and up his arms, and the image of a graceful, six-limbed feline predator from his home world flashed through his mind.

Yes. You have served us honorably for millennia, mother. From stardust you were born, and to stardust I free you to return.

Remethiakara removed his hands from the wall and looked through to the brilliant blue sphere of Earth beyond.

Somewhere lost among Earth's tapestry, two primitive projectiles made their ponderous way into the vacuum of space.

Such slow weapons. If the Earthling's frequent attempts at communication hadn't given him ample warning of their intentions, the mothership's systems would have detected the projectiles before they parted with their planet's atmosphere.

There was no real danger.

Only a risk weighed, an opportunity seized.

He urged the mothership to go faster. To give her courage, he projected a cherished memory from his own childhood aboard her ship, racing his two young brood-kin down the long spine of the craft, from the bridge to the sleeping quarters, laughing with abandon.

Fingers of white lightning flashed out of the star shard's blue beam of light as she picked up speed.

The mothership shot back a cherished memory of her own—the careful coaxing of a young star into supernova, followed by the dangerous hunt for star shards along the hurtling edge of light that surged out across an elliptical galaxy in its wake.

The joy of the hunt thrilled through her.

She was long past the days where she could hunt for star shards. The coming battle was a reminder of that time. She was fulfilling her purpose, and there was no greater joy than this.

Her speed increased, Remethiakara lifted the star shard gently from the beam of blue light, and cradled the space-black meteorite in his arm. Without the shard to power it, the blue light faded, and the bridge returned to its natural dim luminescence.

He left the bridge for the last time, walking slowly along the familiar spine of the mothership the way his youthful self, thousands of years ago, had so often run.

The corridor was now spotted with gouges, filled with cobwebs, littered with the shells of broken biolamps. It had been years since any proper repairs had been completed. The mothership's nervous system was programmed to heal injuries to her own body, but she could only do so much. Pushed long past her life expectancy, it was only natural that time had left scars behind.

The moment for worrying about such things had passed. He had a mission to complete.

At the far end of the spine, the carapace-lined corridor split. The path to the left was closed off with a bulbous, bloated fleshy material that filled the space—the seal of the aft compartment, which had been torn away in the violent shift to hyperspace. Remethiakara took the other fork and soon found his eggs where he'd placed them, just inside an open, circular hatch.

He ducked through the aperture and set the star shard down beside his eggs. He drew on the shard's dwindling energy to activate the equipment inside the hatch and check to see that all systems were functioning properly, then brought the view from the bridge onto one wall.

Blood pounded in his forehead. The mothership's last draught of energy from the shard had done the trick. The projectiles were close now. So close he could almost see the Earthling's letters written along their white length. He was mere moments away from the end of this particular journey.

Remethiakara punched a gauntlet into the wall and willed the circular hatch closed.

It stuck.

He punched it again. The door of the hatch attempted to spiral closed, but it was stiff with age and it stuck open.

A sudden panic fluttered through his body—the flight of fear he once thought he had mastered, but which had recently returned when his progeny had first been threatened.

Mixed with the battle-fear and anxious anticipation the mothership was still projecting to him, now in forceful waves rather than subtle ripples as the moment approached, he lost control of his emotions.

He froze, like the open hatch. He felt his whole body begin to shake.

It was only due to his long years of training that Remethiakara was able to overcome his fear.

Training, and desperation.

Lunging across the cramped space in which he'd ensconced himself, Remethiakara yanked on the stuck hatch. When it didn't budge, panic clenched his throat. He swallowed, forced himself to take a deep breath into the depths of all four of his lungs...

He pulled the top down. He yanked the bottom up.

Slowly, inch by inch, the hatch telescoped close, sealing Remethiakara, his eggs, and the breathable atmosphere into the escape pod.

With his helmet, he would have been able to survive the vacuum of space for several days as the armorsuit recycled his oxygen. Without it? The escape pod was a thin layer between him and sudden death.

It's their last hope, too, he thought, looking at the eggs.

With the hatch closed, he drew power from the shard with his gauntlets, nearly depleting it, and launched his escape pod and a handful of identical vessels, like miniatures of the mothership, from the tail of the ship.

When the force of the launch propelled the pods forward, and the systems indicated that they had been successfully caught into Earth's gravitational pull, his nostrils widened in a smile.

A feeling like a sharpened blade in his heart caused him to turn from his destination and look back at the mothership just as the projectiles collided with her hull.

Primitive though they may be, their destructive power was more than sufficient.

A nuclear blast ripped through the spine of the ship, tearing her ancient body limb from limb.

A great wave of energy ripped her into a million pieces.

The last truethought emotion she sent him, like a faint ripple that surged across the void, was a feeling of gratitude.

And then she returned to stardust.

Thank you, ancient mother. Your sacrifice is seen, and we are grateful. Thank you for saving our lives once again.

Unlike humans with their soft, wet flesh, Reme-thiakara's people did not shed tears. And though it broke his heart to turn away, he had his brood to think about. He looked back to Earth, now a soft curve that took up most of his vision, not in front but *below* him.

The planet was his species' last hope for continuation.

And his only chance for revenge.

It was a planet that would never understand them, but where his brood could finally meet life. It was a planet that had the resources they needed to complete the final phase of their gestation.

He sent truethought directives to the other escape pods. They each adjusted their courses accordingly, drifting away from him on altogether different vectors, toward Earth.

11

LANDFALL

"Target acquired," said Major Bautista, relaying messages coming through a headset connected to Nellis Air Force Base. "Switch to video feed."

The spacecraft's vast, coarse purplish bulk loomed on a single wall of the conference room, the size of a small elephant, every imperfection in the ship's hull visible through the video feed.

Two long white missiles burned a path toward it through space.

Eliana used one hand to hold herself up against the table, the other to clutch at Amon's forearm. The ozone scent of Remethiakara's strange tech came unbidden to her nostrils, sharp and nauseating. Amon wrapped his other hand over top of hers and squeezed.

"Breathe," he said.

She released the tension behind her eyes and felt

air flow in through her nose again.

"It looks like an insect's carapace," Eliana whispered.

"Only far, far bigger," Amon said, swallowing audibly.

Eliana held her breath as the twin missiles dimpled and pierced the hull of the spacecraft, like tiny pins disappearing into a massive pincushion.

For a moment, it seemed like nothing else was going to happen.

But then the dimples erupted outward with dual waves of force that ripped the guts of the ship into the vacuum of space.

The shockwave split the ethereal, elegant spacecraft right down the middle, followed by a starbright flash that blinded everyone in the room.

Eliana squeezed her eyes shut. When the light had faded, countless thousands of incoherent puzzle pieces slowly drifted apart through a cloud of dust where the spacecraft had been.

Her heart wrenched in her chest. She pulled her hand out from under Amon's and into her own lap, and glared at the placid surface of General Wade's expression.

"Status, Major?" General Wade said, not even deigning to notice Eliana.

"Objective achieved, sir," Major Bautista said, equally stoic, with a faraway look as he focused on the voice in his headset. "The spacecraft has been destroyed."

A sigh of relief swept through the room.

Except for Eliana. All she felt was heartache.

Fiery anger rose up in her gut as she continued to glare at the general.

When a sudden rapid beeping pinged into the room, coming through the speakers of several different computers at once, Eliana enjoyed the thin line of irritation that creased General Wade's forehead.

"Nellis," Major Bautista said into his headset, his face going pale like the color of his jaw scar. "Can you repeat that?"

Concentrating hard, Bautista typed on his laptop rapidly until, on the video feed, with the cloud of dust and debris spinning out into space as backdrop, seven red squares were drawn around seven bright specks, like falling stars. The line of specks spread apart as they approached, meandering along different paths.

"Oh no," Amon whispered, his chair making grinding sounds on the floor as he shoved it back with his legs and stood. Everyone else in the room, including Eliana, shot to their feet as well.

"Major, what's the issue?" General Wade demanded.

"Sir," Major Bautista said. "The SOLARPulse-1 has identified seven vessels that are not part of the debris cloud," Bautista said. "They must have separated from the spacecraft moments before the missiles made contact."

"I told you," Eliana whispered, and couldn't keep a half smile from her face as the joy bubbled up in her. She covered her mouth with her hand, but not before Amon turned and looked sharply at her, the expression of worry and shock plain on his face.

"Launch the backup cruise missiles," General Wade said through gritted teeth. "We're too close to the Earth to use more nuclear weapons." Even the general was pacing now, the stress he controlled so well bleeding out into his steps.

Major Bautista sensed this as well and spoke quickly into his headset again. Less than thirty seconds later, new weapons had left their launchpads on Nellis Air Force Base to arc into the atmosphere.

One of the missiles made contact with a smaller vessel in the video feed, snuffing its light out in a shower of sparks. The military people clapped and cheered like they were watching fireworks.

But the clapping died down when the second missile blew up just short of the miniature ships. The smaller craft careened around the rain of fire the missile left behind.

"I want their trajectories mapped," General Wade demanded. "Major, prepare the ground crews for immediate dispatch."

The major ripped off his headset and chucked it on the table. "Yes, sir!" He strode from the room and could be heard bellowing orders to the Marines up and down the hallway outside.

She didn't have to look to know that the rotor blades of the three Blackhawks were spinning to warm up the helicopter for a rapid takeoff.

Tammy had jumped into the major's spot the moment he left, and she was now typing with focus on the laptop. Her head snapped up and she said, "Sir, SOLARPulse-1 reports that the vessels are setting courses for different locations around the world. One will land near Beijing, another in sub-Saharan Africa, a third in mainland Europe...maybe France or Spain? They're not sure. The fourth is aimed at the Pacific Northwest, maybe northern California—no, Oregon or Washington. Number five is currently aimed just off the west coast of South America and will probably end up in Chile. And the last one of the six will land just south of us to Mexico, in the Yucatan Peninsula."

Eliana's heart skipped a beat. *No way that's a coincidence.*

"Time until the first one makes contact?" General Wade said. The action seemed to have calmed him again. He went back to his chair at the head of the conference room table and tapped notes of his own into its reactive surface, pulling up some kind of orders on personal holos.

Tammy relayed the question through the headset. "The one in China will touch down in 30 minutes."

"Reset the clock," the general demanded. "And alert The Ares Initiative reps in each country. I want boots on the ground at each site before landfall. You hear me?"

"Sir, yes, sir!" she shouted loud enough to make Eliana wince, and began relaying the orders through her headset. The rest of the assistants had hopped to join her and the cacophony of talking and typing—a stark contrast to the tense silence they waited through before the missiles made impact—filled the room.

General Wade lumbered over to where Eliana stood, hand still covering her mouth. She had managed to wipe away the smile. Being a civilian in the middle of a war room during battle made her feel small and helpless, so it wasn't hard to look as overwhelmed as she felt. Amon stood next to her, and Agent Moreno had pushed off the wall and came closer to listen in on the conversation.

"There's only one alien, right?" General Wade said.

"So far as I know," Eliana responded, feeling the pressure of the men crowding around her like water closing in over her head. She willed herself to remain calm.

"So the rest of these small ships—I guess you'd call them escape pods—were launched as decoys.

Smart. Even though we managed to destroy one, his odds were pretty good that it wouldn't be the one he was in. You were right."

Eliana snorted. "I certainly didn't know *that* was going to happen. It's a hell of a gamble, don't you think?"

"Depends on your situation," Agent Moreno said. "From his perspective, seven to one are probably good odds."

"When you've got no other choice, even long odds seem good," Amon said. "I'll bet he planned this all along. That's why he ignored our communications."

She nodded her agreement with Amon. General Wade watched her thoughtfully, his mood effectively concealed behind his southern gentleman's perfect poker face.

"If there's only one alien, and the rest of these ships are decoys, which one do you think he's in?"

Eliana pursed her lips. "Which ship?"

"That's right. You heard the lady. China, Africa, Europe, Mexico, Chile, or right here in the good old United States, up in Oregon?"

Her stomach did a somersault. "I don't know."

"You know him better than anyone. You knew he'd make it out of the ship alive, didn't you? You told us so."

She gestured to the video feed, where the bright specks continued to spread apart as they spiraled down toward Earth. One of them, the lowest on the video feed, began to show a burning trail behind it like a comet as it entered the upper atmosphere.

"No one could have predicted this. What I tried to warn you about was that attacking him first would backfire. And it did."

General Wade took one step closer and met Eliana's eyes, which stoked the flames of her anger and gave her the momentary courage she needed to stare back.

General Wade was a hard man, and Eliana had learned that the only way to make hard men back down is to stand your ground.

"You're right," he finally said in his charming accent, smiling at her as he turned away. "Take a break if you need, but I'd appreciate it if you stuck around, Mrs. Fisk—all of you, in fact. We might yet have need of your assistance."

12

PURSUIT

Rakulo gripped the cold handle of the metal knife in his left hand and held out his right, palm open, as he ran. Quen tossed the flint-tipped wooden spear into the air. Rakulo caught it, feeling the grain of the wood against his callused hand. He hefted the spear to his right shoulder, careful to keep the ends from bumping into the tree trunks as crashed through the forest.

Cook fires and the noise of the frightened villagers were smothered by the jungle that thickened behind them. A dozen warriors padded quickly through the trees with him, following the occasional sound of rustling leaves and snapping sticks as the creature they were chasing scurried through the undergrowth ahead.

The huge, pale thing moved rapidly, staying too low to spot clearly in the jungle-dark night, except for the occasional brief flash of pale white that pulled farther and farther ahead.

Rakulo relied on his good right ear and Citlali running on his left to track the creature. It was like hunting wild turkeys in the jungle, which he'd done since he was a kid, except this was no turkey. It was stealthier and faster.

And far more deadly.

They lost the creature's trail at the river, but found damp earth on the other side, the wet track curving away from the stone city.

"Quen, Citlali, check on Eliana's people by the temple of the pretender," Rakulo said, "Maatiaak and Yeli, you two make your way back to the village. Set up a perimeter around the houses with anything you can find—logs, stones, dirt. Keep people away from the tree line, arm the women, and protect the children."

Maatiaak nodded and the two of them peeled away, headed back the way they'd come.

Quen gave Rakulo a grateful look for sending his pregnant wife back toward safety before jogging into the stone city with Citlali. Rakulo waited with the other ten warriors, huddled together in the darkness, eyes fixed on points in every direction, watching and wary.

Quen and Citlali returned a few minutes later, shaking their heads.

"Nothing," Quen said.

"All their stuff is gone, too."

Rakulo sighed. "A relief. Less people to worry about. Let's keep moving. Be silent and stay together."

Rakulo hefted his weapons again, renewing his focus as his eyes swept the darkness for fresh signs of the creature. The spear's obsidian tip glinted in the moonlight that filtered through the foliage.

After moving another two hundred yards, Citlali spotted the creature choking down the turkey bone. Rakulo tiptoed up to within spear-throwing distance, but it noticed them before he could let loose. The creature clicked its giant pincers together menacingly and hissed.

"Gods," Quen breathed, adjusting his grip on the spear and planting his feet in the soft undergrowth.

"Steady," Rakulo whispered.

The creature had three legs along each side of its body that crimped at the bottom into flat feet—feet that he was certain would leave horizontal marks in parallel rows in the dirt. A heavy tail broken into sections curved up over its low-slung body, and ended with a big stinger half again the length of Rakulo's metal knife.

"Now we know what's hiding in those big mounds outside the Wall," Citlali said. "Do you think they've been—look out!"

Citlali turned and hurled her spear across Raku-lo's body and over Quen's startled shoulder with no hesitation. Both men threw themselves to the ground.

Another of the giant scorpions had snuck up on their left side. It snapped Citlali's spear in half with one horrifying click of its claw, and pounced on the warrior at the end of the line, who went down beneath the creature with a piercing scream, his spear tumbling out of his grasp.

The stinger came down once, twice, stabbing holes in the young man's chest with a sickening squelch that made Rakulo's stomach turn. Blood sprayed out of his wounds and spackled the pale armor of the giant scorpion before anyone had time to react.

When they did, it was with ferocity. The warriors converged on the creature and stabbed down with their spears. Flint tips struck the creature and glanced off the pale chitin that coated its body. Four stubby eyestalks swiveled on its head to watch as it was surrounded and assaulted on all sides.

Rakulo feinted left, dodged right, found an opening and lifted his metal knife high over his head. He shimmied back to avoid another thrust from the huge stinger, and came down on the creature's back with all his weight behind the blow. The knife slid into a crack between two overlapping shells and into soft flesh beneath.

The creature hissed and twisted around to bite at Rakulo on his back, but Citlali smashed down on one of its eyestalks with a large stone, granting Rakulo time to roll away and spring to his feet. Quen came down in the opening with his spear, thrusting the flint tip straight down into the creature's open maw.

The spear popped out the other side of the scorpion's head between the back set of eye stalks, and sank into the dirt. Throwing himself on the ground beside Quen, grabbing the shaft of the spear, and adding his strength to his friend's, Rakulo forced the tip of the spear two handspans into wet clay so that it stuck there.

Impaled, the creature's body twitched, but its tail still continued to obey the orders its mind had been giving its body as it died. It stabbed down with its stinger repeatedly in its death throes, striking Quen twice where his shoulder met his neck.

"Agh!" Quen cried out, and fell onto Rakulo.

The other creature, the one that had taken the turkey leg in the village and led them on this chase, had been closing the distance while this fight was happening. It chose that moment to pounce on the tangled pair. Water from the ground soaked his chest as Quen, agitated by his injury and the other attacking creature, pressed Rakulo down into the soil.

Pinned to the ground, he heard grunting, cries of pain, hissing, and the swooshing sounds the creature's stinger made as he struggled out from under Quen's bulk.

Citlali and the others held the creature back long enough for Rakulo to break free, and then drag the injured Quen clear of the one creature they had managed to kill.

Already, the big man's face was drenched in sweat and twisted in agony. Dark veins spread from the stab wounds where the stinger had gone in.

"Keep breathing. Stay with me, Quen. Come on, brother."

Tears filled Rakulo's eyes. Whatever venom the creature's stinger held, it seemed to paralyze Quen's limbs and swell his throat, making it difficult for him to breathe. Rakulo checked his throat for blockages, but found only a swollen tongue as he labored for breath, his eyes wide, white and frightened.

The noise of the others finally pierced through his concern.

"Die, you sick fuck!" Citlali shouted, each word punctuated by a grunt and a crunch, as of shells cracking.

Turning to look, Rakulo saw six people holding back the creature's stinger and claws while Citlali smashed its head in with a large stone, slick with blood. She held it with two hands and drove down relentlessly, only to tear it from the ground and send it plummeting down again.

Finally, she left the stone where it lay on the

pulverized head of the creature and stood over its twitching body, her chest heaving.

The others let go of the creature's limbs and tail and backed away from it, wiping at their bodies as if they were dirty.

"Is it dead?" Rakulo finally asked.

Citlali nodded, smearing dirt and blood across her forehead with the back of her forearm, "I think so."

Several of their own dead littered the jungle around them, too.

"We have to get Quen back to the village. Help me lift him."

"What about the others?"

"They're gone," Rakulo said, "and this battle isn't over yet. Take their weapons. We'll have to return for their bodies later. "

Citlali grimaced, but nodded in agreement.

Rakulo retrieved his metal knife from where it was embedded in the body of the dead scorpion.

Warriors gathered the intact spears from the ground while Citlali and Rakulo supported Quen's weight between them and began to make their slow, painstaking way back to the village.

13

SINKHOLE

Remethiakara started awake.

Smoke and ash filled the cabin. A jagged slash of blue sky was visible through the ceiling. He coughed, fumbling for the star shard with his gloved hands, finding only his sore chest and battered armorsuit.

His head rang and pounded. Not having his helmet was turning out to be a right pain. This planet didn't have enough argon in the air for his species, and without the helmet his suit couldn't regulate what he breathed. Another cough wracked at his chest. He spit bloody phlegm on the floor of the escape pod at his feet.

Where was the star shard?

He looked down. It had been in his lap when they entered the atmosphere. Then he'd blacked out from several gravities of force as fire flared out along the hull of the pod. The pod had incinerated a vast amount of vegetation upon impact, judging by the ash that floated and drifted through the crack in the ceiling.

He must have dropped the shard.

He had to find it.

Remethiakara tried to stand, found himself held down by four thick fastener tendrils that extended from the pod's wall behind him.

He pounded at his chest until the fasteners loosened their grip and receded into the wall. Wrenching himself free, he pitched forward, fell to his knees—

—and nearly smashed his face into the star shard.

It sat on the ground, covered in ash, at his feet.

Remethiakara gingerly blew the ash away. The deep blackness of the geode had receded to a smaller inky core at its center. The desiccated crystal around the core was a misty grey and spiderwebbed with cracks.

The receding of color meant the shard's energy reserves were approaching depletion. He'd been forced to call on it once again to keep his precious cargo alive, by regulating the temperature inside this pod as they entered Earth's atmosphere, so as not to upset the carefully maintained equilibrium of the remaining eggs—or fry himself.

Remethiakara put one gauntleted hand on the shard and pulled on the yoke of the scant power he sensed in its core. The useless crystal on the outside of the shard cracked away, and left him with a small, rough-edged ball that he could hold in one hand.

He dare not use it again. He needed what remained of the shard to keep the eggs alive.

The rest would have to be done the messy, old-fashioned way.

How low the proud have fallen.

First things first: get the eggs to safety.

Humanity was nothing if not predictable; if they weren't already on their way here, they would be soon.

Remethiakara ran the aluminite blade along the base of the interior wall until he was able to peel a large, thin square of skin-like material from the padded floor of the escape pod.

He folded the skin up and formed it like a sack, then placed the remaining four eggs inside. Soft chunks of grass and dirt, picked out of the enormous furrow of churned Earth left by the smoking crash site, served as padding between the eggs, so his movement wouldn't jostle them together. He pressed the skin-like material until it sealed, and watched it meld itself together before his eyes.

Then he cut three more strips for straps, attached them to the egg sack, and slung them over both shoulders and around his waist.

Thus burdened, Remethiakara set off into the jungle, walking his feet very carefully as he steadied the weight on his back.

He'd landed on a hill overlooking a dense, low inland valley that cut into the ground like a perfectly round bowl. Like Kakul, this region of Earth was dotted with sinkholes—perfect hiding places for the eggs.

It had been more than a millennium since he'd been here. It looked vastly different than he remembered. Trees and vines and bushes had grown thickly over the cities of stone and cleared farmland, erasing any signs that a dense human civilization had once inhabited this region.

One thing you realized quickly when you lived as long as Remethiakara had was that time was a powerful force of nature. It moved invisibly yet inevitably, erasing even the proudest of achievements, given enough leeway.

Cutting the skin from the escape pod for the carrying sack was not a coincidental decision, but a deliberate choice. The escape pods were grown from the same seed as the mothership and all his kin were grown. Its cells contained, in a microcosm, all the essential ingredients that his species needed to survive. It could be formed, with a nudge in the right direction, into an incubator that could sustain the eggs and eventually complete their centuries-long gestation, giving Remethiakara enough time to get clear and deal with the humans who would be pursuing him.

Enough time to exact his revenge and gain an influential position among them so that he could find more star shards.

But one thing at a time.

After an hour, using the sensors in his armorsuit to auger below the surface of the muck at the lowest part of the forest, he found what he was looking for.

A small sinkhole in the mud, about fifteen feet deep and several feet wide. Filled with water, perpetually damp, it was absolutely perfect.

He slung off the sack, and pressed the star shard into its surface. Closing his eyes to concentrate, he held the image of an incubator in his mind—if an escape pod was a miniature version of a mothership, then an incubator was a smaller version of the escape pod.

He would just have to hope it had enough power to last. That time would not work against him, as it seemed to have a bad habit of doing recently.

Time and that blasted savage leader. If he ever saw him again, Remethiakara would rip the boy limb from limb and make his mother watch.

He opened his eyes and saw the supple skin of the sack thicken and harden like a protective armor, the better to keep the heat inside.

Then he used his hands to dig a hole in the muck

until he broke into that sinkhole, and carefully lowered the eggs into it.

Finally, Remethiakara did the hardest thing he'd done since he brought the human tribe to Kakul. The hardest thing he'd done since he altered their religion to force them to sacrifice their life energy to feed his eggs.

He used his hands to push the muddy earth back over the hole and conceal it once again.

And he walked away.

14

NOCTURNE

Rakulo's knees were trembling hard by the time he and Citlali, supporting Quen's half-paralyzed and bulky frame between them, reached the ring of fire-light in the village.

Rakulo fell to his knees. A dozen people took the injured warrior from him and Citlali, and laid Quen gently on the ground.

Quen shivered in the warmth of the fire, his body covered with a sweat and wracked by some kind of fever. Yeli was there at his side immediately with a cup of water held to his trembling lips. Ixchel knelt at his side, too, her face a troubled mask, and pressed searching fingertips to his injured shoulder and neck. In the light of the orange flames, veins near the puncture wounds in Quen's neck stood out like a dark cobweb. He choked down a sip of water, then tensed his whole body in agony as a wave of pain washed over him.

Rakulo grunted as he painstakingly regained his feet. He held out a hand and lifted a breathless Citlali up beside him.

At the edge of the village a few strides away, dozens of his people stood in a line and passed loose stones from one person to the next. When the stones reached Maatiaak or one of several other strong men at the front of the line, it was placed carefully along a low barricade that had been erected between two huts closest to the tree line. The barricade already came up to his knees.

"Well done, Maatiaak," Rakulo said.

The old warrior nodded at him and then blew out a breath as he took a particularly heavy stone into his hands, and turned to place it.

The other half of the village not occupied with the barricade was either gathering provisions, or watching the jungle with wary eyes and weapons held tightly in pale-knuckled hands.

Apparently they had run out of spears, for among those that kept watch, some held the metal shovels that Eliana's people had given to them, while others held sharp-edged stones. One small, dark-haired child clutched a jagged piece of obsidian to her chest, and gazed around, wide-eyed and fearful.

Maatiaak finally separated himself from the group of people working on the barricade, and walked over to Rakulo. Gehro joined them, and several older warriors walked within hearing range as well.

"We were taken by surprise," Rakulo said once they had gathered. "But the creature was killed, and one other like it as well. We lost two of our own, and were lucky to make it back with Quen alive."

Maatiaak put a hand on his shoulders. "They died fighting. An honorable death."

"Quen is strong," Gehro added. "He will make it."

"I hope so."

"Are there more of those creatures?" Maatiaak asked.

"There must be," Citlali said. "Hard to say how many."

"The gods have sent these monstrosities to destroy us," Maatiaak said, his voice filled with the old superstitious fear and awe that Rakulo often believed was his worst enemy as chief.

"If that's what you want to believe, then that's your right," Rakulo said, straining to keep his voice level, "but do the village a favor and keep it to yourself."

Maatiaak looked away from Rakulo and spat into the dirt. "Why should I?"

"Because we need people to remain level-headed and focused, and saying this is a supernatural punishment will only cause panic, whether it's true or not."

Maatiaak still said nothing.

"Father," Citlali growled. "Do not dredge up old grudges again. Please, listen to him."

"Fine. But if not sent by Xucha, then where did these things come from?"

Rakulo could see others watching them. He only had one chance to keep this from spiraling out of control.

He glanced at Gehro. The old man nodded encouragingly. Rakulo stepped past Maatiaak into the knot of people so they could all see him clearly in their center. Even those building the low stone barrier paused and turned to listen.

"I take full responsibility for the attack tonight. It is my fault. If you want to blame someone, forget the gods—blame me instead." Silence except for a distant drone of cicadas from the forest. No one objected. But no one lashed out at him either. A leader taking responsibility for something he didn't do was a new thing for them.

"I should have told you earlier, but I didn't want to scare you without good reason. Citlali and I only recently discovered the giant sand burrows in the desert beyond the Wall, where we believe the creatures that attacked us tonight live. They were *not* sent by the gods, but are merely predators native to that land. The desert beyond the Wall is barren. My guess is that they came into the jungle through the holes I cut in the Wall looking for food. We cannot undo what has been done. But we can protect our home. So tell me, are you fit to be food?"

"No!"

"Never again!"

"We should kill them before they kill us!"

Rakulo glanced around at the faces of the villagers. They looked frightened, but determined. Many glanced around at their friends and family with wary eyes and desperation evident in their faces.

Taking responsibility was the right thing to do. They wanted to trust him, but had to know he was on their side.

As he looked around, Rakulo found and caught Gehro's eyes. The wizened old man tapped his chin, gently reminding Rakulo to raise his head and pull back his shoulders like the leader he was supposed to be.

Rakulo straightened, held his head high.

"We need to stick together," Rakulo said. "We are one people. We shall stand and fight. Are you with me?"

Confident nods on all sides. Murmurs of soft agreement.

"Good. Tonight, we will set watch in shifts, care for the wounded, and build a barricade to help defend the village." Rakulo pointed to the low stone barricade. "And when the sun comes up, we take the fight to these creatures. We will hunt them down and make sure they know that this is our home, and we are not backing down."

"Aye!"

"Hunt them down!"

The desperate faces began to nod and glance around at each other, as if to reassure themselves of the presence of their neighbors. The flickering firelight reflected in their dark eyes. Even Maatiaak was grinning fiercely now. Rakulo walked by him and lowered his voice.

"See?" he whispered.

The older warrior nodded. "I'm with you."

To put a final emphasis on his point, Rakulo walked over to a large stone, and though he was exhausted from the pursuit and the fighting, lifted it by himself and carried it to the low barricade, where he placed it carefully. Then he went back for another, and another, and another.

In the next few minutes, Maatiaak and Citlali had split the warriors into three different shifts to keep watch, while the gaggle of boys who admired Rakulo from a distance earlier that day helped him add stones to bolster the barricade.

Once the work had gained a momentum of its own, Rakulo was able to step away for a moment to check on Quen.

Ixchel had given the injured warrior some herbs that seemed to dull his pain somewhat, which put him and those around him at ease. Still, Quen continued to toss fitfully. Yeli held his head in her lap, and pressed a wet rag to his brow.

Gehro clapped Rakulo on the back. "Well done back there. Directing their energy to productive tasks was smart thinking. Keeps them from picking at the scabs of their own imagined fears."

Ixchel rose from Quen's side and came to join the two men where they stood in the shadow of his family dwelling.

"That was always my father's mistake," Rakulo said, pursing his lips as he looked back toward the fortifications. "In times of trouble, his instinct was to stand apart from his people. He thought he was drawing the danger away from the village, but in reality he was abandoning them when they needed him most. I made the same mistake when I was hunting for a way beyond the Wall."

Ixchel nodded sadly. "Which gave Maatiaak the chance to rile up the agitators and turn the double-edged blade of the old ways back against you."

"Precisely. But that's all over now. I won't abandon my people when they need me." He stood tall and turned his gaze upon both his mother and the old forest dweller in turn. "I would never turn my back on anyone here. This is our home."

Ixchel glowed. Gehro nodded approvingly.

"But we need help," he added, lowering his voice. "I fear that even together, we cannot hold these creatures back. They are powerful and dangerous. They move through the forest more silently than any of our warriors."

"We don't need anyone's help."

Rakulo thought of the two dead warriors he'd left in the forest, and clenched his fists.

"What of that codex that Eliana gave you?" Gehro asked.

Rakulo smiled, silently thanking the man for a sly alternative that redirected the fire of his anger. Ixchel meant well, but she and his father had a lot in common when it came to pride. Rakulo had his own pride, true. But he had fought too much, seen the odds arrayed against him too often, to be so stubborn about a thing like that.

"I'll be right back," he said, and slipped into the hut he shared with his mother.

After fishing out the smooth bracelet from the thatch of the roof and tucking it into his tunic, Rakulo picked up the "flashlight"—that's the word for the light-thrower!—from the side of his grass bed and placed the thong around his wrist. Then he grabbed the large, bound codex and carried it back outside.

Kneeling on the grass beside Gehro and Ixchel, he set the codex on the ground and thumbed through the pages, using the light-thrower to help him see the pictures better, until he came to colorful illustrations of a wooden fortification, with men in heavy armor holding sharpened wooden spears while they looked over a fortification and across a pit dug on the other side.

"See these things?" Rakulo said, pointing at the pits at the base of each wall, which, depending on the picture, were either filled with sharpened spears or water. In some places there were two deep pits, dug several lengths apart. In others, traps were hidden there. "We need to dig these to make it harder for the creatures to get over the barricade. It will also give us a height advantage, so we can be out of the reach of the creature's stingers, and throw spears and rocks down on them."

Gehro nodded. "It could work."

Rakulo found Maatiaak, who had one of the shovels, and showed him the picture. Maatiaak studied it, then nodded and began to split the warriors assigned to watch out into digging crews.

Rakulo joined them, taking a shovel himself, and speared the sharpened head into the soft dirt. After some time, Maatiaak was ready to take his turn, so Rakulo handed him the shovel and stepped back to catch his breath. A half dozen strong men had been digging hard, and the new hole was as deep as Rakulo's knees. Standing in it, the low barricade already came up over his head.

He climbed out of the hole and looked up at the sky while he caught his breath. They still had a few hours yet before daybreak. Practically the whole village had stayed up the night, working together on their new defenses.

Rakulo lifted the light-thrower to his ear like he always did on his nightly rounds to survey their progress and swept it across the tree line.

His light passed over a low bush, and reflected off a set of glowing eyes located near the ground. The brush rustled as the creature jerked back and retreated into the jungle.

Rakulo kept the light fixed on the spot the creature had been, and stepped up so his toe touched the barricade. "Climb back up here, quickly," he said to those still digging.

Maatiaak, Citlali, and half a dozen others scrambled up to stand on the stone barricade.

"They don't seem to like that light-thrower," Maatiaak said when he reached Rakulo's side.

Gehro came back to them at that moment, carrying torn-up maize plants in his hand.

"What is that?" Rakulo asked.

"I went to check on the fields. This is what's left of another section of maize at the north end, near the jungle. I think these creatures are tearing it up and eating the roots. That's what's killing the crops."

"Pale skin," Rakulo said under his breath, "they only seem to hunt or feed at night, and they're scared of the light."

"That must be why we never saw them beyond the Wall," Citlali added.

"They're nocturnal," said Rakulo. "Which means…" He looked back at the tree line. "This is the middle of their day."

Rakulo knelt and grabbed a recently sharpened spear—not with flint or obsidian tip, but just a newly sharpened, vicious-looking wooden point.

Lastly, he dug the bracelet out of where it was tucked into his tunic at his waist, and held the button until a green light clicked on.

He saw Gehro and Maatiaak and Citlali and the others all watching him as he fumbled with the bracelet to get it over his hand and on his wrist.

"We need all the help we can get," Rakulo said. "Eyes on the tree line!"

Their heads snapped back just in time to see a dozen of the pale creatures, stingers poised high overhead, as they separated from the trees and came chittering toward them.

15

BOOTS ON THE GROUND

Boots hit the ground in Oregon first.

On a monitor in the conference room, Amon watched bumpy footage streamed from the body cam of the strike force leader. He directed a squad of Marines as they approached a two-hundred-yard furrow along a black sand beach.

Seeing the soldiers approach the crash site from their point of view was like watching a campy horror film. He was just waiting for the squad leader to turn the camera around and speak into it, eyes wild and sweat dripping off his nose.

But that didn't happen.

Instead, the men moved quietly along the column of churned sand, the only noise the squad leader's controlled breathing and the occasional rubbing of his sleeve against his tactical vest as he directed his soldiers with hand signals.

When they reached the ship, the line of soldiers appeared in the video camera's peripherals. They spread out and raised their rifles to their shoulders as they surrounded the craft.

The ship looked like nothing more than a giant eyeball. A dozen tentacles, charred from the heat of atmospheric entry, trailed off the back of the ship. Tendrils of smoke continued to rise from the purplish-black hull. The cornea on the front as the soldiers approached turned out to be some kind of hatch, sealed tight. It took three men to pry the irising doorway open with crowbars, and peer inside.

"Ares 1, are you getting this?" The voice came out of a speaker set on the table in front of General Wade.

"Go for Ares 1," he said, his voice booming confidently into the rapt silence of the room.

"All clear on the Oregon coast, sir."

"Good work, Sergeant. Secure the area. Ares 1 out."

Next to Amon leaning against the wall, Eliana chewed her nails. She listed toward Amon and whispered, "What do you think they'll do with the ship?"

"Destroy it, I hope."

She smacked her lips. "What a waste."

Her interest in the alien worried Amon. It almost seemed like she was *fond* of him. Was that considered Stockholm syndrome? Rather than tear open a fresh wound and get roped into another argument with her, he grunted noncommittally.

The science team appeared on the feed a moment later and rapidly began to erect a white tent over top of the ship. Someone muted sound from the feed, and then switched off the video.

Amon wondered how Agent Moreno was doing next door. Without a good lead on Lucas to chase up, or a home to return to, he had asked for the use of a quieter conference room nearby, where he now worked from his laptop rather than make the long drive back to San Antonio. Enzo was in there with him, reviewing case files and satellite imagery, hoping another clue that would lead them to wherever Lucas was hiding.

General Wade glanced at the clock on the wall, which now counted up instead of down. He walked across the room and marked an X on a white board, the third in a row of six boxes—one site to clear for each pod.

The first pod had crash-landed about an hour ago, in France. Like the pod in Oregon, the one in France had been empty. Chile came second, and that site had also been marked clear.

As for the remaining crash sites, the U.S. military were *en route* to the border of Ethiopia and Kenya. That ship had come down near a wildlife reserve. It would take them another hour to reach their destination.

China, on the other hand, seemed to have created a public relations nightmare. When it began to look like the pod would come down in a populated area near Beijing, the Chinese defense forces blew the ship out of the sky with anti-aircraft lasers rather than evacuate the neighborhood.

Eliana pulled out her phone for the thousandth time and flipped through a news feed. She groaned audibly. "The major U.S. news networks are reporting that China is now *mis*reporting the crash as a meteorite."

"I supposed that's easier to grok than 'alien spacecraft,'" Amon said. "They have people there already?"

"It's been contained," General Wade said, casting an irritated look in their direction. Amon began to get the feeling that they had overstayed their welcome.

"Except for what's leaked online," Eliana shot back.

"Listen, I don't like it either," General Wade said, "but it was up to the PRC to handle the situation how they saw fit."

"Doesn't that upset your little covert operation?"

The general padded slowly across the room until he was standing close enough to lower his voice so that only the three of them could hear it. "Because I know you've been through a lot, I'll chalk that last comment up to nerves. This is a complicated situation." General Wade's eyes skipped from Amon to Eliana and lingered there until he turned away.

No one else made a comment, and the room settled back into troubled silence.

Amon fidgeted and checked the time. If his estimations were right, Major Bautista would converge on the landing site in the Yucatan Peninsula any minute now.

He watched Eliana chew her nails to the nub while they waited. He twirled his own phone in his hands. Reuben and Audrey had been texting him hourly with updates on their attempts to quantify the star shard solution's remaining energy. He refrained from giving them too many instructions while he was stuck in here, though his mind buzzed with questions and more ideas for tests to run.

You're not in the right state of mind for that kind of work. Just let them do their job.

His phone vibrated in his hand. He answered it on the first ring. "Yeah?"

"Is Eliana still there with you?" Reuben said.

"She is. One sec." He put the phone on speaker. "Okay, go ahead."

"We received an incoming signal from Kakul. Rakulo must have activated his transponder. Any reason you can think of he might do that?"

Eliana looked up at Amon with wide eyes. "He must be in trouble."

Amon pressed his tongue against the inside of his bottom teeth.

Reuben sighed through the phone. "That's what Lakshmi said too. I guess it was too much to hope his transponder was activated by accident?"

"We have to check in with him," Eliana said. "He wouldn't have sent a signal unless something was wrong."

"I'll tell you what I just told your friends here," Reuben said. "We're in no position to send anyone back to Kakul right now. Just look what kind of shape you came through in."

Amon silently sent up a prayer to the man for saying the words for him. *Thank you, Reuben.*

"Maybe they're just wondering where you went?" Amon suggested gently. "We left in a hurry, and you didn't have a chance to say a proper goodbye."

"I don't know..." Her fingernails settled back between her teeth.

"El," Reuben said in a voice that brooked no negotiation. "I cannot in good conscience send anyone else through right now. You could get seriously hurt. I would never forgive myself if that happened."

Amon swallowed. "Me either."

"Ares 1, this is Red team leader," Major Bautista's voice came over the radio. General Wade gestured at Tammy, who pulled the video feed up on the wall again.

"Reuben, we'll have to get back to you," Amon said, and hung up the phone.

Beside him, Eliana turned to face the video feed, clasped her hands together, and held them to her chest.

Agent Moreno opened the door and pushed into the room with an excited expression on his face, *his* cell phone pressed to his chest. His entrance went largely unnoticed because everyone's eyes were now fixed on the video feed. Moreno sidled up next to Amon and said in a low breathless voice, obviously aware of the tension in the room but unwilling or unable to hold his tongue, "I just got a lead on Hawkwood. Air traffic control is getting reports of Blackhawks crossing the Gulf of Mexico. The old Air Force tail number of one of the hadn't been repainted, and someone caught it on camera. Guess who bought the helicopter in a military auction six years ago?"

"No way," Amon breathed.

Agent Moreno nodded fiercely. "Hawkwood."

"Shh!" someone hissed from across the room.

Moreno lowered his voice to a whisper. "Have they found anything?"

Amon shook his head. "Not yet. All the ships are empty so far."

"Craft spotted. Top of that hill," Major Bautista's voice came through the video feed, drowning out

Moreno's whispers. He spoke in terse sentences. "Going radio silent during the approach."

The squad moved up a winding dirt path that dwindled to nothing after a few dozen yards. Going two at a time up a tree-thickened hill while those in the back covered for their comrades, the Marines moved carefully, gaining ground.

They finally crested the hill and spotted the ship in a clearing down the other side, resting on top of a few felled tree trunks.

This one no longer smoked. It was the same dark purple color as the others. Long, charred tendrils trailed out behind it.

The major motioned for his men to surround the ship. He approached the hatch himself, putting it in full view on the video feed on his tactical vest.

It was wide open.

Inside, a large square of the floor had been cut out and peeled away.

Other supplies littered the single-room interior cabin. A sac filled with liquid that might have been water. Amon gasped when he saw a cup and a plate nearby with crumbs on it. Some kind of wrappers littered the floor. Next to him, Eliana made a choking sound as the camera swept across several skinny tendrils extending from the wall and drooping limply across the floor.

"Ares 1, are you seeing this?" Major Bautista asked. "*Ocupado.*"

He made a hand motion of some kind behind the camera, and the soldiers put their backs to the ship and paced outward, searching.

"There!" someone shouted.

A figure cloaked in black crashed through thick brush at the edge of the crash site and disappeared into the jungle.

The video feed shook hard enough to make Amon nauseous as the major and his soldiers gave chase. Tree trunks and leaves and vines and bushes flashed past. Men shouted. A flock of birds beat their wings as they took flight.

Judging by the way his wife trembled and hugged her arms around herself, he could tell she recognized the alien in spite of the jarring camera movements.

A distant revolving *whumf whumf* noise came through the video feed and rose in volume.

"Inbound, nine o' clock. Take cover!"

Major Bautista's camera flipped and rolled, sky changing place with ground, as he dove behind a large tree.

Then the video feed was filled with thick smoke.

Gunfire sounded. The *whumf whumf whumf* grew to a deafening volume before Amon recognized the sound as the beating blades of several helicopters.

His own heart started hammering in his chest. Eliana moaned.

"No way," Agent Moreno whispered as a white silhouette outlined on the matte black body of a helicopter flashed across the screen, just visible through the smoke.

Major Bautista raised his rifle to his shoulder and fired into the treetops. Someone threw a rope out the far-side door of the helicopter, and a squad of black-clad mercenaries jumped down. The camera jarred even more as the major switched targets.

Though Amon was overcome with nausea at both the content and the visual of the scene, he forced himself to fix his eyes upon it. *It's just a campy horror film* he lied to himself.

A man stood up from behind a bush to the major's left. Bautista turned and fired, and Amon finally saw it clearly—the bright white horse's head, drawn in the war-horse style of a chess piece.

"Un-fucking-believable." Agent Moreno's jaw went slack. "Hawkwood."

"Lucas," Amon whispered.

16

A MATCHING LAUGH

When the soldiers spotted him, Remethiakara turned and sprinted downhill through the trees, searching for cover among the thick green brush from which he'd just emerged.

At least his eggs were safe. That was all that mattered. His armorsuit could deflect or heal almost anything their weapons could do to him, as long as he avoided a head shot. Had he not lived through worse?

In the event of his capture, he felt the calmest confidence that he could outlast the worst form of torture they could devise.

As long as he could be certain that his eggs were safe.

And now they were.

This thought freed him.

Solid projectiles from the human warrior's hand

weapons whizzed by his head, cracked into tree trunks, pinged off rocks. Using the forcefield built into his gauntlets and pulling some energy from his own body, Remethiakara caught one of the solid projectiles in the air and bent it around a tree, sending it flying sideways through the neck of a particularly swift soldier who was running ahead, trying to flank him on the left.

The man collapsed in a heap, mid-stride, rolling several times before bumping into a cactus.

Their weapons spat another volley at him. Remethiakara cast up a forcefield to deflect the bullets, then turned and sprinted for a large rock twenty yards away.

A cluster of those solid projectiles bounced off his armorsuit as he ran, and he felt a stinging pain where they struck his lower back. They didn't penetrate his armor, but the force sent him careening and stumbling down the hillside.

He struck the large rock with his bare head, and managed to crawl around to the other side as a geyser of smoke arced overhead, released from a small cylindrical device that was thrown up the hill by someone from the cover of the trees.

Remethiakara was momentarily confused. How did they get around him that fast? Why the smoke screen? Didn't they need to be able to see him to capture or kill him?

He tensed and struggled to his feet, balling his

fists as he readied for the melee to fall on him. He expected one of the soldiers to step around the rock he was using as cover and try to bash his face in at any moment.

When that didn't happened, Remethiakara frowned and reconsidered his position.

Peering uphill around the rock, he saw that two lines had been established. Two rows of weapons fired through a curtain of smoke, one uphill, the other down. The smoke continued to spread like a thick curtain between the opposing lines. More canisters were added to the mix. The group that had been pursuing Remethiakara a moment ago fell back to a more defensible position while the smoke dissipated in the open air.

In his experience, humanity liked to make war upon their own kind. That was one reason that Remethiakara's elders had determined them to be savages when their planet was first discovered.

The obvious conclusion here was that there were now two factions of human soldiers in the area. He peered around from his hiding spot. He spotted a soldier uphill as he leaned out and fired into the smoke. He wore a camouflage uniform. The other group that had appeared suddenly from his exposed side had on armor that was all black with the head of a white animal on the chest.

Leaves rustled from that direction. Out of a thick stand of trees, a man with a clean-cut black beard, wearing a crisply-pressed grey linen suit, which seemed laughably worthless as far as utility or defense were concerned, pushed aside a curtain of thick vines and stepped into the open not ten strides from where Remethiakara took shelter behind the rock. He showed his open hands and walked forward.

The only concession he made to self-defense was a vest strapped over top of his crisp suit. And even that was carefully arranged.

The white animal head was on his vest, too.

The only thing that wasn't symmetrical and perfect about the man, Remethiakara saw as he came closer, was his face—the left side of his face was paralyzed, so that when he smiled it was not a full grin but a grimacing sneer. His skin there was mottled, as if by a burn, or maybe some kind of acid. A horrible accident.

The man said something in his human language, and Remethiakara remembered belatedly to turn on the translation device in his suit.

"—help you."

"Help me what?" Remethiakara thought, and after a moment's delay heard the suit project the human-language sound through the chest of his suit.

The man blinked. "You didn't move your mouth."

"I don't have to."

The man glanced around the large rock they were sheltered behind. "You can tell me how you do that later. Right now we have to go. I'm here to help you."

"Why?"

"We can discuss that later. Hurry," the man insisted.

"I remember you. You were after the star shard, too."

"Ah, star shard. Is that what you call those meteorites?"

"The phrase will suffice for the limits of your conceptual knowledge. I thought you were killed."

A burst of bullets pinged off the boulder near his head. Remethiakara flinched, and studied the neat man standing before him.

Even under duress, he couldn't suppress an intense curiosity about this race of aggressive, hair-less apes. What was it about some of them that held his fascination so endlessly?

That woman, Eliana, had fascinated him in a similar way, but she hadn't been open-minded enough. This one seemed different somehow. More resilient than most. More open-minded, perhaps. He could be useful.

"Do I look dead to you?" That sneering grin lifted the right side of the man's face again, although not the left. The skin seemed like it was drooping, although the muscle beneath had hardened and perhaps begun to atrophy underneath.

"That looks fairly permanent," Remethiakara said.

"A temporary inconvenience." The gunfire increased in volume and was joined by the screams of men. "We're running out of time. We have to go."

"Why should I trust you?"

"What if I told you I know where to find more of those star shards you seem to prize so highly."

The man began to jog with a loping gait into the jungle.

Remethiakara hesitated only a moment before following close behind him.

After a short walk away from the firefight, they emerged into a clearing in the jungle, where a flying machine was waiting, its blades beating a racket above. They climbed in.

"What is your name?" Remethiakara shouted over the roar of the machine.

"Lucas Lamotte."

"This place has changed since the first time I visited your world, Lucas Lamotte."

He cocked his head to the side. "How long ago was that?"

Remethiakara considered the question. How could he put it in a way that the human would understand? "Well over a thousand rotations of your Earth around your Sun."

Lucas began to shake with uncontrollable laughter. "I'll say."

"You'll say what?"

The active side of the man's mouth gasped open, and out of that jagged maw came a grating laughter.

The flying machine parted from the ground and tilted away from the direction of the fighting, carrying them into the air.

17

MESHUGGENEH

Everyone in the sweltering conference room had come to their feet during the gunfight, blocking half of Eliana's view of the video feed. She had never sat down—couldn't sit. She was too anxious. Though sweat ran down the back of her neck, she felt a chill course through her body like a fever. The pulse of her blood beat out of time with the buzzing, humming, beeping, and blinking of the computers set up around the room—the clocks, the monitors, the projections, the holos, all closing in around her.

"No sign of our target," Major Bautista finally reported, after the whirring of helicopters had receded into the distance. "Four casualties, and six of our own injured. Of theirs, eight dead. They left no wounded behind."

Agent Moreno punched the doorframe at his shoulder. "Damnit!"

Eliana glanced sharply at the detective, who clenched his phone so hard in his other hand she thought the glass screen would snap in half. "You have to follow them."

"Satellites tracking, sir," Tammy said.

"General Wade, sir," Agent Moreno said. "Request to hand pursuit off to the San Antonio field office. Lucas Lamotte is a fugitive wanted by the FBI. This case is mine."

"Not over international waters, it's not. Request denied, Agent." General Wade didn't even turn around, he just stood staring at the video feed and breathing evenly, though his crisp uniform was now soaked beneath his arms as well.

"I told you," Eliana said.

The general snapped around to look at her. "What did you say?"

"You should have listened to me. Next time you want to ask for my advice, don't."

"El, please—" Amon began.

She pushed her husband aside as he tried to embrace her, her sweat-slick arms slipping easily out of his grasp.

In the hallway, she gulped down two mouthfuls of cold air, and then she was moving again, swerving through the beehive of the building's corridors and stairwells until she made her way back to the cavernous lobby on the ground floor.

There, alone, with the high ceilings expanding far

above her, and only a few stoic Marines standing guard at the front entrance, she finally felt like she could breathe again.

She sat on the low marble bench that edged the pool and listened to the white noise of the water crashing down behind her. Eliana couldn't explain why her heart was rooting for Remethiakara, but she felt in her bones that humanity should act as ambassadors for peace, not fire missiles at the first alien life form they'd ever encountered.

Imagine what we could learn if we exchanged ideas instead of injures.

But they hadn't listened to her. She seemed to have no influence over the general's opinion despite him seeking out *her* advice.

She gazed up toward the soaring glass and steel ceiling high above and whispered, "So go where you can make a difference."

Eliana was up and running again before the words had finished tumbling off her tongue, leaping down the stairs two and three at a time.

She reached the sub-basement level of the Translocator lab at the same time as the elevator dinged. Its polished steel doors slid open, revealing her husband, who wore an anxious expression.

"There you are. Eliana, wait." Amon hurried out of the elevator and chased her down the hall. She could hear his sneakers squeaking on the tile behind her.

"Rakulo needs my help."

"I knew you were going to say that. El, please, slow down."

He caught her arm at the edge of the open blast door. She twisted around, yanking out of his grip as her jaw trembled.

"So you can try to stop me again? How'd that go last time?"

"Babe, I'm sorry. Okay? I'm sorry I tried to stop you from going back to Kakul before. But this is not my decision to make. The Translocator is unstable. If it's activated with the star shard giving off such low power readings, you could come out the other end in pieces! Or—"

"Or dead. Or not at all. I *know*."

"So why do you insist on doing something that could get you killed?"

"Because I promised I would send Rakulo help if he ever needed it. And I don't break promises I make to my friends."

Reuben and Audrey, as well as Lakshmi and Ross and the twins, stood silently in a knot by the Translocator platform. When she glanced in their direction, they looked away and pretended to be focused on whatever Reuben was looking at on his computer screen. She couldn't blame them. If she were in their shoes she wouldn't want to get involved in this argument either.

Amon sighed and rubbed his eyes. Eliana turned

to walk across the room, determined to make Reuben see her side of things.

"Wait," Amon said softly.

She did, standing halfway between Amon and the monstrous Translocator rising like an elegant modern art sculpture at the far end of the lab.

He crossed to her side, and took her hand. Looking her in the face, he raised his voice so the others could hear.

"Have you been able to quantify how much energy the star shard solution has remaining, Reuben?"

"Not in any meaningful way. We've attached two additional backup batteries that were delivered this morning, and have been running the particle accelerator constantly to keep them charged up. I'm hoping they can fill any energy gaps if we do need to use the Hopper for an emergency."

"And you haven't activated it since we came back from Kakul, right?"

Reuben nodded.

"Giving it time to cool off between activations *does* seem to help," Audrey added.

Amon's eyes never left hers. "I wanted to save the star shard solution in case we needed it to chase Lucas down. But seeing as we still can't track him down, and that Hawkwood just slipped out of our grasp, if this is that important to you to risk your life...then you can use it instead."

"Thank you."

"But Amon," Reuben insisted. "If we chase Lucas across the world, at least the odds are good that they'll end up on *Earth* somewhere. If Eliana goes back to Kakul, she could get stranded there. Or worse—"

Amon held up his hand. Reuben reluctantly clamped his mouth shut, though he continued to mumble under his breath.

"He's right, Eliana," Audrey added in her quiet voice. "If you go through, we can't guarantee your safety. The consequences could be even worse than we theorize."

She pursed her lips and looked toward the ramp that led up into the sphere of concentric rings surrounding the transfer platform. Amon squeezed her hand gently.

"One condition," he said. "I need you to promise me something. That you won't lie to General Wade again."

Eliana blinked. "What…what do you mean?"

"When he asked you which of the escape pods the alien was in, you said you didn't know. But I think you did."

Eliana felt her cheeks flush. Despite the differences of opinion they'd had lately, Amon really did know her better than anyone. "I couldn't be sure."

"You suspected. That should have been enough."

"I didn't want to be responsible for his murder."

"A sentiment I understand. Instead, Hawkwood ended up getting to him first."

"They would have anyway."

"Maybe. But now, whatever technological innovations or cultural knowledge the alien possesses is, very likely, in the hands of Lucas Lamotte."

Eliana scowled as her anger returned, white hot. She hadn't thought that through, and she was mad that he was right. But her anger was not aimed at Amon this time, it was anchored by him and directed out at the forces and people who kept disrupting their lives. "I never trusted Lucas."

"I know you didn't. I should have listened to your instincts about him years ago...and I'll have to live with that forever." He didn't say it in an accusatory way—it was simply a matter of fact that he was stating, plainly, for the record.

Eliana swallowed, any words she was holding back suddenly evaporated.

"If The Ares Initiative needs your help again," Amon said, "can you promise me you'll tell them the truth?"

At first her heart urged her to lash out in anger. But there it was again—her instinctive defensiveness at everything that had to do with Remethiakara. Why was she so protective of him? What Amon was asking was reasonable. And she knew, even if The Ares Initiative didn't agree with her recommendations, they were just doing what they thought was necessary to protect themselves and the people of planet Earth.

They were supposed to be on the same side.

"Okay, I promise I'll tell General Wade the truth from now on...*and* tell him where to stick it when he ignores my sensible recommendations."

Amon laughed and seemed to relax. "Good. I know you're good for your promises, which is why I won't keep you from this one. But I'm going with you."

"What? No way. We can't put *both* our lives at risk."

"I won't risk getting separated from you again. Not now, not ever. Reuben, spin it up."

Still grumbling, Reuben nonetheless made his way to the holodeck and began to activate the controls as he typed in the coordinates for Kakul. "You're both *meshuggeneh*, you know that?"

Now that she didn't have anyone to fight, Eliana had the freedom to worry about what she was about to do. She wasn't used to this—she was a hard charger, a take-action-now-and-think-about-the-consequences–later type of person. The sudden gap where she was given time to reflect made her nervous. "Is there enough energy for it to send both of us?"

"From what I can tell, the star shard's energy usage functions a lot like a car engine," Audrey explained. "You'd expect a car to use basically the same amount of fuel, with only small variations, whether it's carrying one person or four people over the same distance, right?"

"Right."

"It's the same with the Translocator. Distance is the variable that has the biggest impact on energy consumption. That's why we could do so many small-scale tests, and also why they turned out to be a poor indication for estimating long-range translocation capacity. Whether one or two people are sent through at a time has a much smaller impact."

Eliana licked her lips. That was logically sound, but it didn't do much to calm her sudden flight of nerves.

Reuben made one last gesture, and she could almost feel the air crackle with electricity as the arch came to life, channeling the power stored from the particle accelerator. "Basically, your odds of getting killed are more or less the same whether you go through alone or with a buddy."

"Reuben," Amon said in a chiding voice.

Eliana reached out and gripped Amon's warm hand tightly in her own. They walked up the ramp and began to move toward the platform.

"*Meshuggeneh*. Mental. Crazy. You know, I could refuse to send you if I wanted to."

"I know, old pal," Amon said. "But there's no one I trust more at the helm than you. You'll bring us home in one piece."

Reuben cursed under his breath.

Once they were standing together on the platform, the blue-green alloy rings began to spin around them so fast they were a blur, and a stiff breeze whipped their clothing tight around their bodies.

Eliana squeezed Amon's hand and closed her eyes, felt the bright light shine against her closed eyelids. There was a jolt in her stomach as she and Amon were whisked away from Earth—together, for a change.

18

HOLD THE LINE

Rakulo let rip a war cry that would have curdled his father's blood. He hurled his spear down over top of the waist-high mud and stone barricade, impaling the top of the sharpened wooden stake into the bent neck of the attacking scorpion as it tried to climb up out of the half-dug trench.

The pale creature snarled and twisted as it fell back into the pit, wrenching the spear out of Rakulo's raw hands. He hissed as a large splinter as long as his middle finger drove itself through his palm. His pain must have been dull compared to the monstrous creature, who landed on the blunt end of the spear, driving the stake through its own neck and finishing the job Rakulo had started.

"Hold the line!" he shouted as he caught his breath.

Another of the giant scorpions broke from the

tree line and sprinted toward him. Unlike the one that attacked his position moments ago, this one didn't climb into the trench first, but instead jumped off its back legs in an attempt to clear the wall in a single leap.

With a curse, Rakulo ripped the split piece of wood from his palm, and ignoring the sting, lifted another spear from the dwindling pile.

The flying scorpion tilted its tail down and extending its six spindly legs as it reached for the lip of the barricade, at the height of Rakulo's chest. With two hands firmly wrapped around the spear, Rakulo thrust forward and up at the creature's exposed white belly.

The sharpened point once again broke the pale flesh and caught in its hard exoskeleton. This time, Rakulo had to brace the spear against his body. It bent precariously, pushing the supple fresh-cut branch to its limit. The spear held, but Rakulo was unable to rip it out of the scorpion. The drooling, stalk-eyed creature came down on the barricade, leaving fresh indentations in the wet clay.

Rakulo screamed with effort, twisted the spear, and finally yanked it out of the creature's gut.

With mandibles clicking in anger, hissing, and seemingly unaware of the wound Rakulo had just inflicted, the scorpion curled one huge pincer over top of the barricade and levered its body up. In the blink of an eye, the creature dashed forward and rammed its weight into Rakulo's knees, sending him stumbling back.

Citlali jumped in front of him and stabbed down at the creature from its blind spot on the left. Rakulo rolled away and came to his feet right as Maatiaak stepped in from the opposite side and swung a wooden club sideways at the sharp tail that bent toward his daughter. The older warrior strained his neck to keep the poisonous tip of the stinger from coming into contact with her flesh.

Maatiaak managed—barely—to keep the stinger away. As a result, he drew the scorpion's ire toward himself. The creature redirected its stinger's slash and Maatiaak was forced to fall backward, dropping his club and stumbling as he scrambled away.

Rakulo hopped back to his feet and lunged into the opening the pair had created for him. He stabbed down at the spot on top of the neck where two armored plates left a crease. The spear went clean through, popping out through the scorpion's saliva-coated mandibles. When he yanked the spear back out, a spore of black blood sprayed onto the ground, and the scorpion died with a gurgling exhalation.

With help from Maatiaak and Citlali, they managed to heave the hard-shelled body of the dead creature over the barricade. Rakulo watched with grim satisfaction as the limp body crunched into the bottom of the trench.

Their position secured for the moment, Rakulo

glanced across the barricade to his right and left. The rest of the warriors, maybe twenty on either side of his center, were recovering with hands on their knees as the most recent wave of scorpions retreated.

"What was that, the third wave?" Citlali asked, panting heavily.

"They're strong. It takes four or five or us to hold back just one of them."

Maatiaak shook his head. "Too many."

These were not good odds. Rakulo had never so keenly yearned for the solid strength of Quen at his side. He glanced behind him, toward the center of the village. The children were huddled in the biggest hut there, with the older women who were too weak to fight.

Two of his warriors had been hit by a stinger during the melee. They writhed on the ground apart from the others, a short teenager no older than fifteen, and an older man far past his prime. They each clutched at their bleeding wounds and jerked spasmodically as the poison spread into their veins.

Hurrying into the momentary calm, Ixchel directed four pairs of women. They lifted the injured warriors, and carried them back to the shelter where the young and injured hid.

"Why do they wait?" Maatiaak asked.

Rakulo cast his gaze at the jungle. Dozens more

sets of quadruple eyes watched from the tree line, lurking in the shadows.

"If they charge all at once, they have a good chance of running us over," Citlali said.

"They must know that. The way they coordinate these attacks, surely they're not stupid."

Rakulo did not doubt their intelligence for a moment. "They're testing us. Probing our defenses," he said. "We've killed a few of theirs, so they know we're not harmless either. If we can just hold the line until dawn, the sun should scare them back and buy us the time we need to build better defenses."

Maatiaak shook his head. Rakulo forced himself to meet the old man's eyes. Words didn't need to be exchanged. Rakulo knew exactly what the old cynic was thinking.

We'll never make it.

"What about Eliana?" Citlali said. "Her people have more powerful weapons."

Rakulo glanced down at the bracelet, and wiped a drop of black blood off the blue light, which had continued to blink a steady pulse since he'd activated it.

He shook his head. "I don't know."

A scream came from the far right of the line, where a warrior clutched an open wound above his right knee. The man fell against the outer side of a hut, to which the barricade had been connected with wet clay.

A scorpion scurried horizontally up out of the trench, along the roofline of the hut, holding itself sideways by digging its feet into the mud daub and using its tail as a counterbalance. Five warriors surrounded the creature, trapping it. The scorpion held its ground, snapping with its pincers to keep the warriors at bay.

Rakulo felt himself growl in his own throat. This bloody dance had been going on too long. Citlali was right. They couldn't hold them forever. But he had to try.

Rakulo dashed toward the cornered scorpion. When he came within spitting distance, he hurled his spear, which the creature easily dodged. The spear twanged and wobbled where it embedded into wall of the hut, cutting off the scorpion's retreat. The creature rotated itself, leaning its tail to the side for balance, and launched over the heads of the five warriors surrounding it, to fall on Rakulo.

Rakulo drew his metal knife from his belt. As the creature came down, he let his feet slide out from under him. He slashed upwards as he fell.

A squirt of hot liquid painted his face.

At the same time, a flash of lightning behind him lit the darkened night.

The creature screamed and averted its eye stalks from the sudden brightness. Still trailing droplets of blood, the creature stumbled back and crashed into the barricade, taking a chunk of stone with it down into the trench. Then it scurried up the other side and across the open field to the safety of the shadowed jungle, where it disappeared into the darkness.

A great hissing came out of the jungle like a nightmare chorus.

"Hold the line!" Rakulo shouted as he struggled to his knees. He wiped the metal blade of the knife in the grass and tested the movement in his throbbing left arm, which was raw from where he'd slid through the dirt. It was painful, but nothing seemed broken.

When the flash of light, like a sun in the night sky, faded, two figures stood in the village. A tall man who was bent double, holding himself on his knees as he puked into the dirt. He was pale and shaking. The other, a dark-haired, bronze-skinned woman Rakulo recognized, did not look well herself. Yet Eliana, at least, managed to hold the contents of her stomach in.

Amon spat in the dirt, wiped his mouth, and said something in their language to Eliana. She grimaced and nodded. The rest of the warriors stood looking on in stunned awe at the two people who had materialized out of nothing in their midst, while also keeping one eye on the jungle, where the nightmare chorus slowly gained in pitch.

"Rakulo," Eliana said. "What's happening? What is that noise?"

"I'm sorry, I don't have time to explain. Did you

bring any of those long-range weapons? What are they called?"

Eliana shook her head in disbelief, looking around. She sucked in a breath as she noticed the quadruple sets of glowing eyes at the tree line. "Guns? No, we didn't bring any guns. What in the world is going on, Rakulo?"

"We're under attack," he said.

"By who?"

"I'd advise you to pick up a weapon."

Two dozen scorpions—nearly four times as many as had been involved in the previous waves of probing attacks—stepped slowly out of the jungle, advancing in a row. One or two of them nursed wounds, Rakulo noted. The one whose belly he'd sliced open with the metal knife limped at the front of the pack. It used one of its six legs to hold its guts in. Saliva dripped from its mandibles.

"Oh, fuck," Amon said.

Rakulo didn't know what that meant, but he appreciated the sentiment that shivered through Amon's voice.

"What *are* those things?" Eliana asked.

He turned to her and gripped her shoulders. "No time. There are children and women hiding in the center of the village. I need you to get them to safety."

Eliana gritted her teeth and nodded. "Got it."

"I don't know how long we can hold them back,"

Rakulo said. "It takes at least four of us to fight one. Get the children to safety, and bring us help if you can."

She nodded. "Where are they?"

"Citlali will take you."

Citlali shot daggers at him with her gaze, but obeyed.

"Rakulo," Eliana said, "come with us."

"We'll buy you some time. Go."

Eliana's face darkened. "Give me the transponder."

"The what?" he said. "Oh." He slipped off the bracelet and handed it to her.

Citlali looked between him and the row of oversized scorpions advancing slowly across the open ground, singing their hissing, clicking nightmare song.

"Go!" he shouted at them.

Citlali broke into a run. Eliana and Amon jogged after her.

Rakulo picked the light-thrower up off the ground where he'd set it by the barricade, and shone the bright beam along the slowly approaching row of predators. They hissed and averted their eyestalks.

Yet this time instead of retreating to the shadows, they grimly advanced.

19

FINDING THE FLOOR

Amon blinked back the black splotches that threatened to overtake his vision, and pressed his fist to his chest. His breath was coming short and heavy, like the asthma attacks he had as a kid. Fortunately, Eliana seemed less affected than he was. She was engrossed in a low muttering conversation with the lithe brown woman as they moved between dark, close-packed huts with thatch roofs and clay walls. Amon wiped sweat from his brow and hurried after them.

The two spoke in the native language, full of harsh fricatives and soft shushing sounds. Citlali—which is what Eliana called the young woman—was barely more than a teenage girl, but she had deep-set, haunted eyes that told of experiences beyond her age.

To their rear, in the direction of the group of

thirty or so bare-chested and tattooed warriors, shouts rose up, and Amon pictured that those pale, mutated monstrosities with tails like giant scorpions were now approaching their poorly defended line with the three-foot trench filled with cracked and bloody white exoskeletons.

He choked down another urge to puke, and picked up his pace.

"She's taking us to find the children and the old women," Eliana explained when he caught up. "Citlali wants to take them to a cave in the jungle where they can hide. Amon, are you okay?"

He shook his head and clung to reason. "Is she mad? Didn't those things come out of the jungle in the first place?"

Eliana exchanged a word with the young woman. "She wants to take them down the cliff to the beach, then move south and loop around back around from that direction. The forest stretches for miles. She says she can keep them safe."

Amon's mind was still clear enough to realize that hiding would only delay the inevitable. The warriors did not balk at the fight, but those scorpions were obviously deadly and poisonous besides. He feared the natives might be outmatched, despite their foolhardy courage.

"Damn, but I wish I brought a gun," he said, pausing every few words to catch his breath, "If those scorpions...kill the ballsy young chieftain...

and his friends, they'll catch up to the women and children sooner or later."

Eliana bobbed her head from side to side. "What are you suggesting we do?"

"Take them back to Earth."

Eliana bit her lip. "Rakulo made it clear that his don't people want to leave Kakul. This is their home."

"Better alive on a strange world than dead at home, don't you think?"

"He did ask for our help."

"This is their best chance."

The cliff's edge came into view and they approached a dark hut. Citlali knocked an offbeat pattern, obviously a code of some kind. Something heavy shifted on the other side of the door before the curtain could be drawn aside.

Amon peered over Eliana's shoulders into the dim hut, lit only by two candles but crowded with dozens of cherubic faces of children, and a scattered handful of wrinkled, weary-looking older folks. Their expressions were hard to make out in the complete darkness, but the stench of all those fear-filled bodies packed into such a tight space choked him and enhanced his nausea.

A groan came from somewhere behind him. Amon turned and peered at the doorway of another dark hut opposite this one, on the other side of a firepit that lay cold and ashen between them. Eliana brushed past Amon and swept aside the curtain to reveal five injured men writhing on the ground inside.

"My god, Quen!" Eliana said.

She turned and exchanged sharp, accusatory words with the young woman Rakulo sent to guide them, then turned to Amon, exasperated, and said, "Citlali tells me that they were going to try to take these injured people with them. Look at Quen, he's writing in agony. This is suicide. We have to take them back to Earth. It's their only hope."

"Convince them, not me."

"Damnit," she said, running her fingers over the smooth top of her dark hair, strands of which had come undone while they ran and now hung to frame her high cheekbones and sharp chin.

The shouting coming from Rakulo's direction grew louder and more frantic. Someone screamed in pain. Amon heard a gargling hiss cut through the racket, a sound that no man could make.

"We're running out of time."

Eliana turned to Citlali, and began to argue with her in a heated voice. The girl looked distressed but shrugged. *It's out of my hands*, her gesture said.

An older woman, probably a matriarch, approached and pushed Citlali gently behind her. Amon recognized her as Rakulo's mother.

The matriarch negated what Eliana was asking her with firm gestures with the blade of her hand.

Though elderly, she was a stout woman, obviously deferred to and respected by the others. People looked on but remained silent while the matriarch spoke. They seemed scared to disagree with her and kept their distance from the argument she was having with his wife.

When Eliana gripped the matriarch's shoulders, so worked up she was apparently going to shake some sense into the old woman, the matriarch pulled back with one hand and slapped his wife.

"Hey," Amon shouted, putting himself in front of Eliana. "Don't you dare. We came here to help you!"

The stern woman, a foot shorter than him but no less intimidating for her height, stood her ground and glared up at Amon.

Eliana caught his wrist before he could strike her.

"My own mother has slapped me harder than that. Please, just let me talk to her." He saw the earnestness in his wife's face. "Trust me," Eliana whispered.

He finally relaxed his hand, and she turned back to the matriarch. Her nostrils were flared and she stood stalwartly with arms crossed over her bare breasts. In the background, faces stared out silently from the relative safety of one of the huts. From another came the moans of sick people in pain.

How many people could be hiding here? Fifty? A hundred? Amon did a quick calculation. The Hopper could translocate a dozen people at a time if they were all making skin-to-skin contact. More, perhaps, if the adults held their children in their arms.

Could it be that was all of them? The entire village, every last one?

"With or without her, we have to hurry," Amon said.

"She is still refusing." Eliana lowered her voice and spoke in calm but matter-of-fact tones to the matriarch, opening her hands in a gesture of invitation.

The matriarch shook her head in stubborn refusal.

An old man approached then. His hair looked like a single tangled dreadlock, and he had long dirty nails as if he'd been digging in a garden. This man got down on his knees next to the matriarch and beseeched her as if in prayer.

The old man gestured in the direction of the fighting at the opposite end of the village.

Finally, a young woman with short-cropped hair came out of the hut where the injured Quen lay. Below a strip of cloth bound tightly and deftly over her small breasts, this young woman's belly bulged slightly.

She must have been only a few months pregnant.

Eliana said something to her. The woman smiled, then glanced fearfully, but in the direction of the hut containing the injured warriors, not in the direction of the battle.

"Yeli says the baby belongs to Quen," Eliana translated, her face going very pale.

Amon felt queasy. He turned discreetly behind a bush and spat, then dry heaved, trying to mask the sound but failing miserably.

When he turned back, Yeli, the pregnant woman, had approached the matriarch and gently placed her hands on either side of her wrinkled cheeks. The old woman's stout face crumpled as she dissolved into tears. She put her hands on Yeli's curved brown belly and cried openly, eyes shining a brilliant green.

Then the matriarch said a single word to Eliana.

"She agrees. Let's go."

"Don't need to tell me twice," Amon replied.

Eliana and Citlali collected the youngest children and the oldest, bringing them all out into the open.

"Let me take the first round," Amon said. "Teach Citlali how to use the transponder. She can take the second set, while you gather the rest in groups of a dozen." He nodded to Citlali who, even holding a child in each arm, looked at ease and stood lean and strong and balanced like a gymnast.

Eliana nodded, fit the third bracelet on Citlali's wrist, and began to explain how she had to hold the button for five seconds to activate the signal.

Amon ran into the hut where the injured warriors were located.

"Hang on." Although he knew they didn't understand his words, he hoped they understood his signals. He beckoned them all close with his hands, took a deep breath, and activated his transponder.

Seconds later, the blinking light went solid as Reuben locked on, and every person in contact with him stepped *across* space and time, to be reassembled inside the stabilization platform of the Translocator on Earth.

The blue-green alloy rings spun down. Amon clenched his now empty stomach and swallowed a spout of bile that lurched up his throat and twisted his tongue with its sour taste.

"Somebody find a doctor!" he managed to say when he found his voice again.

While Amon trembled, the team of archaeologists, who had been resting and recovering in the lounge, sprinted up the ramp and helped carry down the injured men and the women who had been caring for them. Amon leaned his forehead against the cool surface of the metal rings.

When the last of the natives had been moved clear of the platform, Amon raised his voice and shouted across the lab. "Send me back before the next one comes through."

"I'm trying, I'm trying," Reuben muttered at the holodeck.

Amon lurched and then he was back in the village, mere feet from the edge of the great white cliff. Overhead, a white and a red moon shone down over the softly crashing violet waters far below.

He staggered away from the cliff's edge and rejoined the others for the second time. Older folks stood watching him warily, as if he was sick or crazy or maybe both. How had this man disappeared before their eyes, only to come back again from a different direction?

He did his best to ignore them. Citlali stood with a tight-pressed group of the remaining children, who clutched her legs and held onto the younger children.

Amon squinted into the light of their dissolving molecules as the Hopper transferred them in invisible streams of encoded data all the way to Earth.

"Come here," Amon said, gesturing to a mixed group of older men and women. The children were almost gone now except for a few teenagers. Eliana had sent the rest of the young ones with Citlali. Now, the old and middle-aged who couldn't fight made up the remaining three groups—only three? There must have been fewer people left alive than he thought.

"That's it?" Amon asked.

He gestured at the pitiful figures, huddled in groups.

Eliana nodded. "They must have numbered in the thousands once. Xucha decimated their population year after year for generations."

Eliana cast her eyes down at her feet. Amon waited for the rest of the group to place their hands on his body. One old woman grimaced as she put her hand on Amon's clammy forearm.

"Amon, no," Eliana said as she finally divined his intentions. "It's my turn."

"It's my machine that's malfunctioning. It should be me who suffers."

He activated his transponder. Eliana looked irritated, but the button locked on in less than thirty seconds and she couldn't very well pry the frightened people who clung to him away to take his place.

She had already begun to gather the next group around herself when his surroundings shifted again.

Amon's whole body convulsed as his muscles knotted. He gritted his teeth and managed to hold his ground as this group of people ducked out of the stabilization sphere before the rings had fully come to a rest. The ducked and dodged, frightened even to touch the metal edges of the rings, looking around at the array of holograms and vaulted, steel-strutted ceiling above like bewildered tourists as they were ushered down the ramp by the others, directed to gather against the far side of the lab.

"Again!" Amon called.

"Are you out of your mind?" Reuben called, his wild hair standing on end as the air filled with the electrical charge thrumming through the power-arch of the Translocator. "Send someone else."

"You know I can't, Reuben. Just do it."

Reuben cussed loudly, but activated the Hopper anyway. A moment later, Amon was standing on Kakul with wobbly knees while a group of men screamed with hoarse voices behind him.

He shivered as his skin excreted a thin layer of cold sweat.

Amon braced himself on his knees to catch his breath. Someone yanked him back to his feet as they ran by, pulling him out of the range of a snapping pincer which closed on the air where his ankle had been a moment before. Someone kicked the head of the Scorpion as their comrade stabbed it with a wooden spear.

"Go! Run!" Rakulo said, using the English words.

Amon looked over his shoulder and saw that the pale monsters were just now swarming over their hastily assembled earthworks.

One warrior stabbed out with his spear. The scorpion snapped the tip off, and then jumped on him. The young man went down wordlessly. The pale creatures climbed straight over top of him. Several stingers stabbed down into his body, almost as an afterthought.

Amon sprinted back to the village right as Eliana re-materialized in the center of it.

Only one group left in the village, plus the warriors who were falling back in that direction—maybe ten of them in total, rallied around the fierce chieftain who kept the scorpions at bay with a spear in one hand and a metal knife—Amon's knife, he saw—in the other.

"Rakulo!" Amon called. The young man parried the downward slash of a stinger with the spear, and stabbed down at the head of another creature. "Rakulo, to me! To me!"

He jumped up and down, once, twice, then bent over panting from the exertion.

Eliana gathered the last group of villagers to her side and activated her transponder bracelet. A group of frightened women, that dreadlocked and feral-looking older man and the matriarch among them, gripped her arms, and linked arms with each other.

"I love you," Eliana mouthed, as she disappeared with her group.

The group of warriors slammed into him, lifting Amon from the ground as he activated the transponder.

They retreated, Amon clutching their arms to keep them close to him, as the scorpions surrounded them. They shuffled away, spears extended, with Amon at the center of the group, until they had their backs to the cliff's edge.

Finally, the transponder light went solid as Reuben got a lock. The scorpions lunged as they began to dematerialize.

Amon felt one of them clip his side, and then pass

through his disintegrating body and plunge down into the crashing waters of the roiling sea below.

Amon and the forms of the remaining warriors reassembled in the lab.

As the warriors ran down the ramp and into the embrace of their families, Amon looked down at his hands, which shook uncontrollably and burned. Could he see the floor beneath or was he hallucinating now?

He tried to clutch his shaking left hand with his trembling right. He felt his own mouth fall open as his hands literally passed right through himself.

A shudder seized his body.

The tightness that had been squeezing at his chest turned into a tearing, ripping sensation.

Amon screamed as his molecules threatened to pull apart.

His knees buckled and he fell.

He lost consciousness before he hit the floor.

20

A BARGAIN

It was a longer ride than Remethiakara expected.

When the sun had reached its zenith, they landed somewhere on the coast, climbed out of the propeller-powered vehicle and into a much larger, silver-skinned suborbital craft. A dozen padded seats filled the interior of the passenger compartment, lavishly decorated with animal leather and non-functional gold filigree, which Remethiakara found completely frustrating and pointless.

The dual-winged and bulky craft seemed to be powered by two combustion engines. It was steered manually by two men sitting inside the nose at the front fuselage, which Lucas referred to as the "cockpit."

Remethiakara shook his head at the inefficiency of such a mode of travel. These Earthlings may have made significant technological advancements since he first discovered the Mayan tribe and insinuated himself as their god, but they were still savages in his eyes.

"What kind of fuel is used to power this craft?" Remethiakara asked of his groomed host, who sat across from him sipping heady, golden liquor from a broad-rimmed glass.

Lucas Lamotte kept a napkin in his left hand and used it to mop up any liquor that dribbled out the drooping, burned-looking side of his lips. He was obviously embarrassed and keenly aware of his impediment, and yet striving, simultaneously, not to show it.

Remethiakara's people were not fond of cripples, even among their own species. Such people were returned to the ancient mother upon their birth, as their existence threatened the longevity of the entire race. As a result of this conditioning, he couldn't keep his contempt for this human out of his thoughts. Why had he not offered himself as a willing sacrifice, for the good of his people's survival? Such an instinct was only natural.

Since Remethiakara didn't know where he was being taken, however, he cautiously concealed his truethoughts, and was glad the mothership was not nearby to hear or respond to them.

"Airplanes are fueled by a carbon-based substance called petroleum," Lucas said.

"And where does the substance originate?"

"From deep within the crust of the Earth."

"You mine your own planet? That seems highly inefficient, not to mention harmful to your species' longevity." Remethiakara's cautious visage cracked as his tongue licked out to wet his teeth, an expression that commonly indicated disgust among his people, though Lucas did not know this. "Do your leaders know that they are unlikely to achieve a truly symbiotic relationship with their mother planet if they continue to ravage her for fuel?"

Lucas smiled his crooked smile. "I suspect they hardly care."

Did the armorsuit lose that phrase in translation, or was the human speaking truthfully? Remethiakara frowned and looked out the window, down over the vast ocean that churned on the planet's surface far below. The Mayans he had brought to Kakul had known more about living in harmony with nature than their more technologically savvy counterparts, it seemed.

Several hours passed. His human host began to fidget in his seat. After Lucas had drained three glasses of the golden liquor, he set his glass aside and rubbed at his eyes.

Remethiakara was not tired. In fact, he enjoyed the man's obvious discomfort. His own people, with such long life spans, learned when they were relatively young how to endure stillness without complaint. Humans, however, obviously never got the chance to internalize a skill such as patience. And this one had expended nearly half his short life already.

Below their flying craft, the vast darkness of the ocean gave way once again to undulating swathes of hilly land. An hour later, his sharp eyes took note of the snow-capped mountain ranges in the distance. The mountains rolled below them, their peaks poking through the cloud cover illuminated by the light of a single silver moon.

It reminded Remethiakara what had drawn him to this world in the first place—its natural beauty. And to think that these ignorant Earthlings were destroying it to power primitive combustion engines! It was laughable yet sad. He clamped down on his lower lungs to keep his abdomen from shaking.

"Almost there," Lucas said, mistaking Remethiakara's withheld laughter for discomfort. The craft tilted downward and began its descent.

The plane finally landed on an icy black strip of runway secluded deep within the mountains. From here, they climbed into another of those rotor-blade crafts and flew into the snow-covered crags over which they'd just passed. A short time later, they touched down again in a howling gale. Lucas donned a fur-lined coat he retrieved from a storage compartment in the plane. He handed a second coat to Remethiakara, and sprinted for cover.

Remethiakara simply activated the internal temperature regulation of his suit, ignored the stinging wind on his exposed head, and walked calmly after Lucas, who gestured urgently for him to follow as if welcoming a guest to his chambers. Remethiakara paused so that his suit could take a bearing. They were entering this mountain on its eastern slope. On the other side of the mountain, far to the southwest beyond the ocean they'd just crossed, his suit made brief contact with a signal from the womb, hidden deep and warm in the jungle. Knowing his younglings continued to be safely hidden made the cold weather—a climate his species would never choose as the default, but which they could withstand in small doses with the help of their armorsuits—bearable.

Remethiakara rejoined Lucas. They passed through a massive metal door—which cut off his suit's contact with the womb, as was to be expected —then through a chamber enclosed at both ends where men examined them with scanning machines and wands and other electrical equipment. His suit set off several different alarms, whose meaning he could only guess.

They asked him to remove his suit. He refused to comply, of course. He would not be fool enough as to be left defenseless this deep in enemy territory, even if the enemy seemed to want something from him bad enough to bring him all this way in such a lavish and inefficient manner.

When Remethiakara shrugged and turned to leave, Lucas waved the security men off and ushered him past the checkpoint, completely ignoring the alarms and their objections. They were detained again, and contact was made with some kind of authority. At this point, Lucas himself had to get on the line, and only after much time had passed were they allowed to move farther into the facility.

Alone now, the two of them walked deep into the mountain, down a long hall that had been cut roughly out of the stone, and then down a gradually sloping ramp to a vaulted chamber in which they found one of the massive molecular Translocators.

For the first time since Lucas had waylaid Remethiakara in the jungle, he looked upon the scarred human male with a grudging admiration.

"I was under the impression that your people only had one of these machines."

"Yes," Lucas said, sneering, "Amon Fisk would like to think he's the only one smart enough to build such a thing. Another functional Translocator? Impossible." He spat on the cement floor and quickly raised his sleeve to his mouth to wipe away the strand of drool that slapped down on his chin.

"Most fascinating," Remethiakara said, barely managing to keep his tongue from his teeth. "Where is its power source?"

"I think you'll find this far more sophisticated than the jet engines."

It was a long shot from what Remethiakara would have called "sophisticated," but that didn't mean he wasn't interested in the technical capability of any power-generating machine he could exploit for his own ends. Lucas led him into an adjacent chamber.

"These are the batteries," he said.

"How does it work?"

Lucas explained how a massive nuclear reactor continuously captured energy from the natural decay of radioactive substances, and piped that energy into these batteries for use later.

People wearing polymer suits with clear masks squaring their faces walked around the room, taking readouts and tapping notes into devices they carried in their gloved hands. He didn't think those suits could provide much protection from an attack or self-repair damage like his, but defensive, cross-functional, and self-repairing garments obviously weren't a priority for them yet.

Remethiakara lay his gauntlets along the battery, and then took his own readings on the radioactive isotope they'd isolated, using a function built into his armorsuit. "And this is the same kind of nuclear power source than is used to power the other Translocator?"

"No. I was forced to modify it after our first plan

was…altered" Lucas lifted his chin. "I believe I have you to thank for that."

Remethiakara turned back to face the human. "You wish to thank me?"

"When you removed the star shard as an option, I had to seek an alternative. Which has borne fruit, as you can see." Lucas gestured expansively to the nuclear reactor venting smoke into the ceiling, where broad ventilation screens pulled it out of the vast cavern, which echoed with Lucas's slightly slurred voice—whether from his injury or the drink, Remethiakara couldn't tell. Those ventilation systems must have been difficult to drill, this deep within the mountain. Impressive.

"Not to mention that it caused Amon some consternation," Lucas said. "Enough to set the Lunar Terraform Alliance back by several months."

"Does this bring you pleasure?"

"It does."

Do not underestimate these Earthlings, Remethiakara reminded himself. *And certainly don't place your trust in them.*

"But I wish to finish what I started," Lucas went on. "Without the meteorite you took, we are confined to Translocations only between platforms painstakingly constructed in specific locations. By harnessing the star shard's properties, Amon has been able to cut the platforms out of the Translocation, without any adverse *loss*." He sneered the last word as his fingers brushed unconsciously across his scarred cheek. "So where is the star shard you took from me?"

"The shard I recovered was, unfortunately, depleted during my journey," Remethiakara said smoothly.

"I know for a fact that Amon's is still functional. I suspect he is also hiding more somewhere in Fisk Industries. You got into his lab by creating a wormhole through his Translocator once before. Can you do it again?"

"Not without an adequate power source."

"Use the nuclear reactor."

Remethiakara growled in his throat. "You misunderstand. What you are asking me to do cannot be done with that primitive toaster. I need a *real* power source—a star shard."

Lucas clenched his jaw and turned away from the reactor. "Very well. In the absence of certainty, I have developed a backup plan, with information provided by our benefactors at Hawkwood. This way is perhaps better, and doesn't require another conflict with Amon. Come with me, please."

Remethiakara reluctantly followed him to a sparsely furnished office. Lucas produced a small cube with a hole in one flat surface and placed it on the desk. Then he took out a thick folder full of papers.

When activated, a cone of light produced a blue-white model of a planet. It took a moment for Reme-thiakara to recognize it, for the model rotated upside down.

"This is your planet. Why is it upside down?"

Instead of answering him, Lucas said, "There are other things the Translocator is capable of."

He opened the folder and began spreading diagrams and sketches out along the table. The diagrams revealed a particularly twisted, if concrete, logic.

"If you agree to help me modify the Translocator to accomplish our goals," Lucas said, "then I will show you where more of the meteorites—star shards—can be found. Once I have what I need, they are yours for the taking."

Remethiakara went very still, like the reptilian and lacertilian ancestors from which his people descended. If the mothership were here, her blood would have pulsed with hunger.

Once more, he was grateful that his truethoughts couldn't be interpreted by Earthling technology.

Remethiakara met Lucas's eyes. They glistened hungrily, and in them Remethiakara thought he saw something of his own ancestry echoed, despite the human's obviously mammalian origins. What were the odds that the weapon he needed to reconquer this planet was to be handed over to him?

"I'm listening. How many additional star shards do you have access to?"

"None yet," Lucas said. He manipulated the desktop hologram projector with his fingers. A red dot began to blink in the center of the great continent capping the southern pole of the planet. "Our analysts don't know how much of the meteorite is left down there, but they believe there are unrecovered samples beneath the ice of Antarctica. We just have to dig them out."

21

———

PRESS

Eliana had been torn from Amon's bedside to attend this damned press conference. Although her own nausea from back-to-back Translocations had receded, it seemed like nothing could undo this twisted knot of sickness in her stomach.

Her mind dwelled constantly on Amon and all the things she was sorry she ever said to him, or even thought in his direction. It all seemed so trivial now that he was lying unconscious and on the brink of death in a hyperbaric chamber tuned to prevent his atoms from flying apart.

You stupid, brilliant, idiotic, brave, hardheaded man. I hate you. I love you. You can't leave me. Don't you dare leave me. Please, God, let Amon come back to me and I promise I'll be a good Methodist again.

With these thoughts running through her head, it took her whole effort to keep her cool and focus on the director's words. His forehead glistened with nervous sweat where he stood front and center before a huge crowd of reporters and camera people, vans with bright spotlights mounted on top, and not a few members of the public all gathered in front of the closed gate to the Austin Lunar Research Center.

General Wade and his assistants stood in a row flanking Director Badeux, with Eliana at the left end, as far from the center as she could get. She blotted at the tears that threatened to fall from her eyes, and sniffed—too noisily, she thought. She couldn't seem to help but draw unwanted attention from the nearest reporters in the crowd. Good thing that what Enzo was saying was so captivating that it soon absorbed everyone's attention.

"On the night of November the second, astronomers at the SOLARPulse-1 lunar observatory detected a large asteroid on a course bound for Earth."

The director gestured to the portable hologram projector that appeared beside him. As if on cue, a large asteroid, rendered as a 3D model for just this occasion, popped into the air.

"This information was intentionally but temporarily concealed from the public," Director Badeux said. "The Lunar Terraform Alliance, in conjunction with the leaders of the United States military, including the President himself, agreed unanimously that it was in the interest of national security to keep this information classified until such time had elapsed that the threat had been eliminated. We wanted, least of all, to cause a widespread panic, especially concerning a problem that was completely out of the control of the general public."

He pressed his glasses up on his nose and took a sip of water before continuing.

"Throughout the course of the last week, a contingency plan was executed with tactical precision, and ultimately, with success. Put into place decades ago by the Lunar Terraform Alliance and the U.S. Air Force, with cooperation from governments around the world, this plan was designed to protect the planet from inbound Near Earth Objects —NEOs—such as this asteroid, that were potentially life-threatening to our world."

General Wade nodded his approval. The general's stoic expression was hard to read, especially from this angle down the row of people and in the harsh glare of the light. Eliana thought she sensed a momentary tension in his stoic face, a half-second where his expression grew more taut. Even the general knew that the real threat to Earth's safety remained at large.

Ultimately, this impromptu press conference was not about safety, but about control. Control of the narrative.

Six hours ago, Eliana would not have objected to perpetrating such a miscarriage of the truth. But after what she'd promised Amon and what happened to him, the thought stewed in her gut.

Don't people deserve to know the truth?

General Wade cleared his throat and stepped up to the microphone as the director moved aside.

"On the night of November the seventh, after the identity of the asteroid and its trajectory had been thoroughly analyzed and ultimately confirmed, the U.S. Air Force, under my orders with authorization from the commander-in-chief, launched a super-atmospheric missile at the NEO. The missile delivered its payload successfully, breaking the asteroid into several much smaller—and less harmful—pieces. This mitigated the potentially disastrous environmental and existential threat the larger asteroid posed prior to payload delivery. However, pieces of the asteroid still entered our atmosphere and fell to Earth. We've identified seven separate crash sites, only one of which is in the continental United States. Strike teams, with LTA scientists attached, were dispatched to attend to the piece of the asteroid that fell in the pacific northwest. Other countries have done the same."

"Thank you, General Wade," Enzo said. Then he addressed the crowd again. "Once the sites have been cleared of any extraterrestrial contamination, the Lunar Terraform Alliance will commence study of the asteroid pieces that end up in our custody here, at the Austin Lunar Research Center. Now, we'll take a few questions."

The crowd of reporters all spoke at once, drowning out each other's questions in a wave of shapeless noise. Eliana winced and looked down at her feet.

"Yes, ma'am?" the director said. "With the CNN badge and red shirt."

The crowd shushed attentively. "Can you respond to the allegation by Chinese media outlets that are reporting that the so-called asteroid that fell near Beijing was actually an alien ship of some kind?"

"Rumors not supported by fact," General Wade snapped. "Next question—"

"But the fact is that the Lunar Terraform Alliance found an alien planet when the Translocator malfunctioned at the gala last year, yes?"

Eliana felt all eyes in the crowd dart to her, then look away, almost as if they were embarrassed to be caught looking.

"I can assure you that these two incidents are completely unrelated," Enzo interrupted. "Next question please. Yes, you sir."

"Why is Mr. Fisk not in attendance? I heard he was involved closely with the LTA in making this discovery."

Eliana recognized the voice and looked up to see

a big, jowly fellow with camera straps crisscrossing his shoulders and a notepad balanced on his paunch.

Carter, investigative reporter and photographer extraordinaire had interviewed Amon personally after Eliana returned to Earth following the first Translocator accident. Though it had been over a year since her safe return, she knew Carter recognized her, as he glanced intently between Enzo, the general, and herself.

"Mr. Fisk is deeply focused on a project with the Translocator," Enzo said, "and could not—"

"Oh, just tell him the truth, Enzo," Eliana said.

General Wade glared at her down the row.

Eliana sighed, walked over to the microphone, pushing herself unapologetically between General Wade and Enzo.

"My husband was injured in an unrelated incident." She took a deep shaky breath. Her first deep breath since Amon came back through the Translocator unconscious, she realized. *Amon was right.*

"Is this related to your LTA-sanctioned expeditions to that alien planet?" Carter asked.

"Yes," Eliana said. "I'm not a physicist like my husband, so I can't explain exactly what happened to him. What I do know is that the mechanism that sent me to Kakul for the first time, which we discovered by accident, was damaged somehow, and that's what put Amon into a coma."

"Is he going to be okay?" Carter asked in a small voice.

The crowd was hushed except for the rapid typing of a thousand pairs of hands on their phones.

Eliana sighed. She could see the genuine concern creasing Carter's round face. "We don't know yet."

"Will you be going back to Kakul?"

"Look, I don't know what the future holds, okay, Carter? I'm not an oracle. I'm just a woman trying to get through the day. But I will say this: If Amon was right—and he usually is—my expeditions to Kakul are over. The way to that world is now closed to us. Forever."

Eliana turned and strode across the pavement to the gate. Someone inside the gatehouse must have seen her determination, for the gate slid open a few feet to allow her re-entry. A furor of noise rose up behind her. Flashing camera lights cast her shadow ahead of her in flickering, sharply angled silhouettes.

Eliana focused on the sound of her shoes striking the pavement, the grass, the marble tiles. The sound of the waterfall receded behind her and then her shoes struck the rubber-edged stairs.

"That was fast," Reuben said after Eliana placed a palm on the security scanner, and the blast door hissed open to allow her into the lab.

"It was to the point."

"How did they take the news about the 'asteroid.'" He used air quotes around the word.

"Well enough. I didn't mean to, but I think I provided a reasonable distraction."

She finally reached Amon's side. Eliana set both hands down on the curved glass of the hyperbaric pressure chamber. Amon's soft breath fogged the clear plastic that lay an inch or less above his mouth. Reuben had explained that the confined space was intentional, as it provided less area over which to maintain the pressure.

The hyperbaric chamber was literally pressing him together at a molecular level.

But without you here, who's to keep me *from flying apart?*

22

GRIEVING

Rakulo stood apart in the vast metal cave, crowded with wooden crates and storage containers, and watched as his people grieved.

They grieved the loss of their village to the poisonous monsters that had attacked, suddenly and without mercy.

They grieved for the dead and the wounded.

They had been forced to abandon those who had fallen in the fight with the scorpions. There had been no time to gather the bodies. They had barely gotten out alive. The black blood of the scorpions he'd killed still matted the hair on his arms.

The wounded half dozen that Amon had brought back—before the scorpions broke through their defensive position—were laid out on small, narrow cots lined up against one side of the metal cave into which his people had been shepherded after the journey. The beds had wheels and stood as high as his waist.

Quen was laying on one of the cots, being attended by a redheaded woman in a white coat. Ixchel stood on Quen's other side, watching the woman carefully, and arguing with her in her own language aided by expansive gestures.

Several other white-coated people had been called in from somewhere above. They too pored over the wounded people and poked them with prodding devices, exploring the webwork of veins that spread beneath their skin. The wounded sweated and thrashed in pain from the venom that infected their bodies until the white-coated redhead had injected some kind of drug into the thick muscles of their legs.

Rakulo closed to his mother's side and put his hand on her shoulder. She looked back at him, exasperated.

"Will you be able to save them?" Rakulo asked the woman.

She glanced up at him, then to Ixchel, and then to the rest of their people, who had spread out a few blankets over the hard stone floor.

The doctor pursed her lips and shrugged. Not that she couldn't save his people, simply that she couldn't understand what he was asking.

Rakulo struggled with some of the slippery words Eliana had taught him during her time on

Kakul. Like the name of the light-thrower, they evaded him. And then he caught one—a hard-edged word that felt solid to him.

"Doctor, yes?"

The redheaded woman's face lit up, and blossomed into a wide smile. She nodded enthusiastically.

He turned back to his mother.

"I'm sorry, mother. I don't know enough of their language. But Eliana said these people—these doctors—are like medicine woman of their people."

Ixchel's jaw set as she pressed her lips into a hard line.

"I trust Eliana," Rakulo said. "If she says these people can help, then we need to leave them alone so they can do their work."

She shook her head gravely, and tears welled up in her luminous brown eyes.

Rakulo put his arms around his mother's shoulders. He knew how much this woman cared. She was not harassing the doctors without reason, but out of fear and a sense of helplessness—he knew, because he felt it, too.

But he shoved that feeling back down, and put a smile on his face. A short walk around the precisely square edges of the cave-like room they were in seemed to ease his mother's distress somewhat. She was breathing more deeply when they returned to the rest of the villagers. Gehro stood and came to join them.

Ixchel reached down and squeezed Gehro's hand. He went very still for a moment, then slowly relaxed his hand into hers. Rakulo tried to pretend like he saw nothing, and fought to keep his smile down.

"Is everything okay?" Gehro asked.

The tears had dried on his mother's weary face. She nodded and smiled sadly.

"How are you?"

Gehro nodded. "I've lived in different parts of the forest—I'm used to sleeping in different places. To carrying what I want with me, and taking what I need from the Earth. I can't say this cave is to my liking, but it is not uncomfortable. The others, though, many of them have never gone farther than a day's slow walk from the village. They are having a more difficult time adjusting."

"Not to mention the nausea we all had," Ixchel added. "Though that has abated, at least for me. I am particularly worried about Yeli. Has she been drinking enough water?"

"She has," Gehro said. "I've been keeping an eye on her."

Silence fell between them like a blanket. His mother took a deep breath and started to speak, then stopped. Rakulo fidgeted and looked around. Where was Eliana? He had so many questions to ask her.

When could they go back to Kakul? Would they help him reclaim their village?

Ixchel finally spoke. "Go," she said. "I can see you want to."

Rakulo shook his head vehemently. "My place is here. With our people."

"You are with us." She reached out and laid her palm on his chest, so that her callused fingertips brushed across welts of the patterned tattoos that marked him as their chief. "Besides, now is the time that we grieve for those we lost and give support to those who are still fighting for their lives." She cast a pointed glance back toward the line of cots against the far wall. "Who better to help our people walk the dark road of grief and loss than me?"

Rakulo felt his eyebrows shoot up. "None better, mother. You are the strongest woman I know."

"Damn right."

He chuckled slowly and grinned at Gehro. "You've got your hands full, old man."

"I'm young in spirit."

"I won't be gone long," Rakulo added. "I just need to—"

"Enough. No need to explain yourself. Do what you need to do. We'll be here, watching over things while you're gone. Make us proud."

Rakulo embraced his mother, and then Gehro, the old cave-dwelling nomad to whom he was closer, in many ways, than he ever had been with his father.

Rakulo waited as the two walked hand-in-hand back toward the villagers and settled slowly down on a thin blanket.

After taking the time to make the rounds and talk to the rest of the villagers, Rakulo found a room where water ran miraculously from a metal fountain into a polished white bowl, and cleaned the blood off his arms. Then he went searching for Eliana.

It didn't take long to find her. She was in the adjacent cave-like room, where the gigantic machine that had brought him to Earth twice hung like metal vines from the ceiling of a cenote.

The sphere of concentric rings centered between its feet sat empty. Nearby, where one foot of the machine met the floor, a dozen people of varying complexions and heights, wearing artificially colored clothing from the brightest reds to midnight blue to bright-white like the doctor's coat, examined an exposed complex. Apparently there was more of the machinery beneath the floor. Did it run beneath his feet where he stood near the door, too?

Now that he had been familiarized with some of this world's technology, this scene did not surprise him as it once might have. Nevertheless, he found the exposed wiring and the crowd of scientists unsettling. As if someone had broken the machine's chest open and was peering inside at its heart.

It didn't hold his attention long, however, for his eyes were drawn to a lone woman sitting beside what looked like a metal tube on the other side of the room.

He walked over to Eliana, careful to swing around and approach her from the side so as not to startle her. As he did, he walked up beside the metal tube and he realized that it was Amon lying inside, unconscious. He lay beneath a curved sheet of transparent glass, fogged slightly by his breath.

Unlike Quen and the other warriors who'd been wounded in the fighting, no sickly-looking purple veins spread out from a wound. In fact, no wound of any kind was visible.

Everyone had seen Amon faint after he materialized with Rakulo and a dozen other warriors clinging to his weakened frame. Rakulo had picked him up and laid him out on the floor, but then had departed as Eliana and her own people crowded around and tended to him. Rakulo had been so concerned with the safety of his own people since then, and so confident that their own medicine people would know what to do to help him, that he neglected to realize that Amon hadn't simply fainted from exertion.

Something else was terribly wrong.

Something, he suspected, that had to do with the exposed wiring and pried up floorboards behind him on the other side of the room.

"Is this my fault?" Rakulo asked, knowing as he said it that were he to do it over again, he would change nothing in his actions. He'd have done anything to save his people, and would do so again.

"Of course not."

"I'm grateful you came to our aid. You and your husband. I would trade places with him if I could." Rakulo also meant that.

She set her hand on his shoulder. "Thank you for saying that, but even if you could, it's not your burden to bear. The *Translocator* did this to him."

"Translocator," Rakulo said, testing the word and committing it to his memory even as he peered nervously over his shoulder. "Is something wrong with this Translocator?"

"Yes. It's not working correctly."

"Does that mean we cannot return to Kakul?"

Eliana grimaced. "I was hoping you wouldn't ask that, but...no. Not right now. But I promise, if they can fix it, I will do everything in my power to make sure your people get home safely. And in the meantime, you're more than welcome to stay here. We'll find your people a better place to live. We'll make sure they get clothes, and food, and water. It's the least I can do."

"Thank you. They are okay right now, just worried about those that were injured."

"If anyone can save Quen and the others, our doctors can do it."

"And what about your husband? Can they save him?"

Eliana sniffed and looked back at Amon, wiping her cheeks with the back of her hand. "I don't know," she said very softly.

They stayed together in silence for a time. Finally, Eliana said, "There's something else you should know."

He looked at her.

"*He's* here. On Earth."

Rakulo didn't need her to explain who *he* was. The disturbed look in her eyes told him quite clearly.

"The god-pretender," Rakulo whispered. "But how?"

"He had a ship. While you were fighting those scorpions, he came here and crash-landed on our planet. Our warriors are hunting for him, but he's managed to evade them so far."

Rakulo clenched his hand into a hard fist and pressed against the cold blade of the metal knife, which he'd somehow managed to hang onto in the fighting. "I should have killed him in the tower. I must finish what I started."

Eliana nodded. "I understand how you feel. And

were it my decision to make, I would honor that for you. But first we have to find him and figure out what he's doing."

"Whatever it is," Rakulo said with conviction in his voice, "he always wants more power, more control. And I'd be willing to bet that it has something to do with those eggs. The only reason he didn't kill me when he had the chance is because he wanted to protect them. They are more important to him than anything else."

"I remember how he reacted when you destroyed some of those eggs in the tower. You think he brought them here?"

"I know he did. I saw him remove them from the tower, through a doorway to somewhere dark and safe."

"Beneath the pyramid."

Rakulo blinked in surprise. "I…suppose it could have been. You think?"

"It's just a theory, but I think that ship of his was hidden below the pyramid." Eliana nodded slowly as if coming to a decision. "Okay. That's a good start." She glanced back at her husband, laid her hand on the sheet of glass as if to reassure him that she was there beside him. "Let's introduce you to the others. I promised Amon that I would tell them the truth, and I intend to do so. They're all looking for Xucha and would be glad to have your help. If they're going to find the god-pretender, they probably need it."

23

NEW EXPEDITION

"So you're telling me this alien lays eggs?" General Wade asked from the head of the conference table.

Eliana grimaced. "Sort of. I think it's probably more accurate to say that he *grows* them, since his species has been incapable of natural reproduction since they ventured into space."

"And he told you this?"

Eliana nodded. "According to the history I was shown, it was an adaptation forced upon them by the low gravity of space. Over time, it became the only way they could reproduce. I believe his race is also descended from reptiles, so it seems a natural evolution when you realize that they never gave live birth like mammals would have."

"Nothing about this makes sense," General Wade grumbled, swiveling in his chair so that he could stand and pace across the back of the room.

Someone had finally adjusted the air conditioning so that the conference room was no longer a sweltering sauna, but Eliana's palms were still damp with nerves. It was hard to talk about this stuff—she felt a deep instinct to conceal the information on Remethiakara's behalf. But she had made a promise to Amon, and since it might be the last promise she ever made to him, she didn't intend to break it.

Eliana looked over at Rakulo, then around the room. Her eyes moved past Director Badeux, Reuben and Audrey—who she'd insisted join them from the lab below—to Major Bautista, who had just stepped off the chopper from Mexico, and the other military aides and personnel manning the surveillance equipment set up around the room. Even Agent Moreno had returned, at Eliana's insistence, and stood just inside the door.

"What about Lucas Lamotte?" General Wade asked. "What's he after? And how did he know about the alien in the first place?"

"Last year, the alien came to Earth through a wormhole in the Translocator to steal the star shard we had," Reuben said. "Lucas saw him then."

"What was Lucas Lamotte doing here?"

"He kidnapped an FBI agent and blackmailed Amon into letting him into the lab," Agent Moreno added.

"They were both after the star shards," Audrey said. "Lucas was forced to translocate himself out of the lab. It scarred his face and caused him permanent damage, almost like a stroke victim, from what we can tell."

"Why wasn't I informed of this?" General Wade demanded.

"Don't look at me," Audrey said.

"The FBI and the LTA agreed to keep the information quiet, on a need-to-know basis," Director Badeux said. "We didn't think it was important after the ship was spotted. The alien had the star shard already, so the damage had been done."

"And it's my job to track down Lucas," Agent Moreno added. "Not yours."

"Do you have any leads, agent?" General Wade asked. He was all business now. Eliana appreciated that. Were she in his shoes, she suspected she would have continued to hold a grudge. The general had this ability to set his personal feelings aside and assess the problem logically. It reminded her of Amon, which doubled her resolve.

"We managed to track Hawkwood's plane across the Atlantic this time," Moreno said. "They were obviously bound for Europe. We lost their trail in the Swiss Alps. My people are working on narrowing down the exact location. We're searching the mountains for any radioactive heat signatures or concealed bases."

The general pursed his lips and paused, bracing himself on the back of his chair with both hands. He took a deep breath. "We didn't find eggs, or see the alien with any. Are you absolutely certain he brought them to Earth?"

"I'm sure. Rakulo saw him take them out of the tower. He wouldn't have left without them. But that doesn't mean that's the only thing he wants."

"What else does he want, then?"

"Power. Control. That's what he always made sure to maintain on Kakul. He seemed to get some pleasure out of controlling those people. And I think, ultimately, he used their life energy to grow his eggs."

"Creepy," General Wade said.

Eliana snorted. "You don't know the half of it."

"So, if he wants power, how does he get it?"

"The star shards."

"Does Lucas have access to more of those meteorites?"

"No," Eliana said. "At least, I don't think so."

"Agent Moreno?"

"Can't be sure," he said.

"Well, if he doesn't have them," Audrey said, "I'm pretty sure he knows where he can find some."

"What do you mean?" General Wade asked.

Audrey glanced at Reuben, who sighed and then said, "Last year, when Lucas first became a fugitive, he stole the Translocator plans from the lab. We have to assume he also knows about the carbonado, which was originally discovered and dug out of the ice in Antarctica."

"Antarctica?"

Audrey nodded, her face bright now that they were talking about her favorite subject. "The carbonado meteorites have been buried deep in the Antarctic ice for hundreds, maybe thousands, of years. The sample we had was only one of many that are still buried under the ice."

General Wade nodded. He glanced over at Major Bautista, and Eliana could see that they shared some unspoken thought.

"Does that mean you're on board?"

"The hunt for Lucas Lamotte is our first priority," General Wade said. "Agent Moreno, that's your first priority. Find where Hawkwood is hiding him, and figure out what the hell their endgame is. I don't believe that a private security company known to operate in a mercenary capacity is in this for the compliments Lucas is giving them. They have to have some kind of ulterior motive." He turned back to Audrey. "In the meantime, Doctor Murphy, do you think you can help us locate more of these star shards?"

She bobbed her head, sending her red hair bouncing around her face. "Yes."

General Wade inclined his head at her, and then turned to Major Bautista. "The Major and his strike team will provide protection and operational support on the ground." Then he glanced at Eliana and Reuben. "You two stay here and provide operational support."

"I'm going with you," Eliana insisted. "With my expeditionary team, and Rakulo as well." The bare-chested warrior had been silent the whole time. Eliana was already thinking about where to find him some cold-weather clothes. "We'll work with Audrey to put together supplies for the dig. We'll also need machinery that will help us retrieve the star shard once we locate it."

The general gave her a sour look. "Fine. But you and your team are under military supervision. You'll report to Major Bautista and follow his orders, is that understood?"

Eliana wanted to spit, but instead she forced a smile onto her face and said, "Yes, sir."

"All right. You all have your orders. I want wheels up in twenty-four hours."

24

COLD WINDS

An icy wind sliced across the frost-covered landscape, burning through Remethiakara's exposed nostril-slits as he inhaled the cold air deep into his top set of lungs. He waited a minute until his body and the thermoregulator built into his armorsuit could warm the air before letting it pass into his lower set.

He glared around the barren plain. He, Lucas, and a team of mercenaries were deep into this icy continent now. Their search had begun at a point near the coast and spiraled inward as they dug for signs of the shards.

The coast lay far behind them now. Dark mountains lined the horizon on all sides. Nearby, nestled in the shadow of an exposed black bluff mottled with turquoise ice, Lucas and the other men manhandled a red tripod from which a silver tube hung suspended.

Remethiakara stood to one side and watched as they lowered the drill to the ice and activated its engine. The drill bit ground an even, crunching cadence that crashed across the frosted plains toward the distant mountains.

Shivering, Remethiakara sent a truethought to his suit to increase the internal temperature. His already short temper flared when it didn't respond. He turned away from the others and furtively banged a fist against the receiver near his chest. It started up again with a jerk as more heat was imparted.

He knew that humans had inhabited Earth's colder regions, but this was starting to get ridiculous.

Once, on his millennia-long journey through the stars, Remethiakara's clan had found a planet where a rift had been torn open to another dimension and sucked all the moisture and heat out of the atmosphere. By the time they managed to close the rift—by creating a wormhole with an opposing magnetic resonance that caused the rift to implode toward its origination point—the planet had already been turned into a desiccated, ice-bound world.

He'd lost three of his kin to that interdimensional disaster. Antarctica reminded him of that place, and put him in a sour mood.

His race was naturally cold-blooded, which meant that they evolved in humid environments with a high heat index. Cold, dry places like this were not only unpleasant, but also potentially lethal.

Not that he'd let any of his human companions in on that little gem of a secret. Remethiakara would never have lived as long as he did without learning that weaknesses were best kept to oneself when staying among strangers.

Fortunately, Lucas had the foresight to provide extra layers of clothing for Remethiakara before they made the journey here. The synthetic parka and waterproof pants they gave him fit on over his tight, breathable armorsuit without issue. He even donned a pair of the heavy boots, which he never would have dreamed of wearing in a warmer climate.

The churning roar of the drill veered into a lower range as its chipping teeth parted the ice far below the surface, spitting the churned particles out the top of the hole to form a chipped-ice pile.

Finally, the drill reached its desired depth and stopped. Two men put their gloved hands on levers and used the tripod to lift the drill out of the hole it just dug.

Lucas took a knee next to the opening, which was less than a few handspans wide at its mouth, and beckoned him over. As he'd done a dozen times already, Remethiakara held his gauntlet over the hole and felt for the low pulse of power a half-frozen star shard would emit.

He felt nothing. Perhaps it was buried deeper than they had suspected. He shook his head.

"Nothing in this one either," Lucas announced. "Let's move. While we have daylight, people!"

The mercenaries grumbled and frowned, but immediately began to dismantle the drill and tripod for transportation.

Remethiakara felt a grim satisfaction that he wasn't the only one not enjoying this journey. Nonetheless, Lucas drove the men onward, and Remethiakara said nothing for he knew that once he had the star shards, he wouldn't have to take orders from anyone anymore. Out of habit, Remethiakara reached out with his armorsuit's signal and tried to get a read on his younglings in their hidey hole. Instead of the soft ping that would let him know they were there, he felt nothing but the bite of the wind. Either they were too far away, or his armorsuit was acting up in the cold again.

"We must be getting close, Remy," Lucas said, smiling his twisted smirk at Remethiakara before turning away to answer his satellite phone, which had begun to ring from a pocket of his thick coat. He pulled the phone out and lifted it to his ear under his fur-lined hood, and walked out of earshot.

Lucas had recently begun using that shortened moniker to address him. He thought ignoring it would make it stop. It seemed, however, to have the opposite effect.

However, silence was safer. Speaking to them would only encourage them, and he didn't need that kind of attention. He just wanted to get the shards and get out of here.

Remethiakara stared at Lucas's back while the others packed the drill onto the automated hover-sleds. He ignored the caustic glances the mercenaries shot in his direction when they thought Lucas wasn't looking. He didn't blame them. The feeling of mistrust was mutual.

He especially didn't trust Lucas. For one, he treated his men poorly, and seemed to get off on ordering them around. The worm was always on his phone, always dabbing at his face, which covered his mouth and made him seem like he was planning something.

Oh, Lucas had been nothing but pleasant to him, but that just made him even more suspicious. He had known conniving humans in his time. They could smile to your face while their hand reach around behind you to stab you in the back—both physically and metaphorically.

And if one thing was certain, this one wanted something.

Was he telling the whole truth? That he just wanted Remethiakara's help modifying the Translocator, and that he could keep the star shard afterward and be on his way?

Or did he have some ulterior motive?

Remethiakara shivered, but refused to hug his arms about him. He pushed the armorsuit's thermoregulator up another half a degree. It didn't help.

He resorted to clutching the parka about himself in the spiteful wind.

25

MOLECULAR INSTABILITY

"Can you hear me? Blink if you can hear me."

The voice came to him muffled, as if someone was knocking on the window of his Porsche. Amon tried to obey. His eyelids fluttered down through what felt like a reef of coral, hard-edged and gritty. He squinted in pain and took a deep breath—or tried to—and then realized it felt like a crate of wrenches had been set down on his chest. Why was it so hard to breathe? Was this an asthma attack, or the heart attack he always feared would one day come to take him unawares? He opened his mouth and gulped as he tried to sit up.

"Wait wait, Amon don't—"

His forehead smacked into a solid sheet of glass. That's when he panicked.

"Help!" he croaked "I'm trapped! I—"

A hissing sound came from near his left ear, and the pressure on his chest suddenly eased.

Oxygen.

Amon inhaled gratefully, sighing.

"Amon!" Reuben said. That's who the voice belonged to. "Amon, are you all right?"

He finally wiped the grit out of his eyes and looked through the sheet of glass at the exposed steel crossbeams in the ceiling directly overhead. He could just make out the tip of the conductive silicone arch that soared over the Translocator. He was laying in some kind of bed...

A shiver went through him. Was it a bed? Closer to a coffin.

"Is this...Reuben, am I in the hyperbaric chamber?" he finally asked, struggling to keep his voice level.

"My god, am I glad to hear your voice," Reuben said, dropping the Rs from the ends of his words as he instinctively reverted to the New England accent he'd managed to smooth out over the years. It always came back when he was worried—interspersed with yiddish slang. "You're what my filthy-mouthed Aunt Elly woulda called—and I'm quoting here—'fuckin' *meshuggeneh*,' you know that? You scared me half to death, you son of a bitch. And yes, you are in the hyperbaric chamber. I had to pull it off a top shelf in the warehouse. Good thing you hung onto it."

"It was from the early days of our molecular

reassembly experiments. I couldn't just get rid of it. Cost me a small fortune to buy from the hospital, you remember that?"

"I do. And it's a good thing, too. It saved your life."

"Last thing I remember was activating the transponder and being pig-piled by a bunch of sweaty, half-naked warriors. What happened? Where are the others?" Panic suddenly seized him and his throat constricted again. "Eliana! Did Eliana make it?"

"Relax, man. Relax. Eliana's fine. The two of you managed to bring about seventy-five of the natives back. They're camped out in the warehouse. The LTA docs are looking after the ones that were injured. They're trying to synthesize an antivenom from—"

"Reuben!" Amon shouted. "Enough bullshit, I'm trapped in a glass coffin and my temper is short. Where is my wife?"

He grimaced. "Well, here's the thing, boss…"

"Spit it out."

"Okay, okay. She joined an expeditionary team to Antarctica. To search for more of the carbonados—I mean, the star shards."

Amon felt his eyes widen. "Of course! Holy shit. That's what the alien is after. And I'll bet Lucas wants to get his hands on them, too."

"Yeah, that's what we figured as well. It was Rakulo's idea, actually."

Amon shook his head. "Strong enough to kick my ass and smart, to boot. Remind me to give that kid a pat on the back when I see him. Have they reached Antarctica?"

Reuben checked his watch. "Yeah. About two hours ago. I lost track of time."

"Well get me out of this thing. I need to talk to Eliana. Surely they took sat phones with them, yeah?"

"They did. I've got the number right here. But I'm not letting you out of the hyperbaric chamber. It's locked from the outside."

"Reuben…"

"It's for your own good! You're not molecularly stable yet. The high pressure in there is keeping you together. I wasn't even sure you'd wake up, to be honest, but I wanted to try."

The full implication of the hyperbaric chamber hit him like a punch to the gut. A cold sweat broke out along his forehead. Amon's felt suddenly dizzy and had to relax his head against the bed and close his eyes. He focused on inhaling through his nose as he got his nerves under control.

"How long?" he said an interminable time later.

"How long what?"

"How long do I have to stay in here?"

"Until you're stable. Doctor's orders."

"You're not a medical doctor."

"I'm the only goddamn doctor you've got. It's not like you can find 'molecular instability' in the medical texts, you know."

Amon inhaled through his nose and blew the breath out through his mouth.

"Can you at least get my wife on the phone?"

"Yes, of course." He placed a cell phone on the glass over Amon's head. It was already ringing.

The phone call connected and Amon heard static. Then Eliana's voice came over the line with a gale of wind howling behind her.

"Hello?"

Amon sighed. "Hey. It's me."

"Amon, thank god. Are you okay?"

"Hanging in there. Wish I was there with you, but Reuben is taking good care of me."

"Don't worry about me. General Wade sent, like, a freaking platoon of Marines. I don't know how many Marines a platoon *actually* is, but there are enough armed men carrying automatic rifles to storm a fort."

Amon felt himself smile. "You're worth even more than that, I assure you."

"We have to get moving soon. Audrey is leading us to the drill site where the meteorite piece that you made my ring out of was first discovered."

"Be careful, El. It could be dangerous."

"I know. But we need to find those star shards

before they fall into the wrong hands. The major tells me that the general has 'eyes in the sky', whatever that means, looking for signs of Hawkwood. I don't see any scram jets, but…"

"Maybe they're using satellite footage."

"Could be."

Amon wiped his hand down over his face. His palm came away wet, but his brain was working and his heart was regulating its rhythm now that he was hearing Eliana's voice and knew she was okay.

"Oh!" Eliana said. "You'll be interested to hear this. Agent Moreno said at the briefing that the FBI tracked the Hawkwood planes back to Europe. They lost the trail in the Swiss Alps somewhere. But that means—"

"Lucas is hiding the Translocator in the Swiss Alps. I knew it!"

He could hear the smile in her voice. "Agent Moreno said you'd say that. He told me to tell you that they still need help finding where he's hiding. He asked if you had any other clues…and it got me thinking."

"Yeah?"

"When Lucas stole the Translocator blueprints, maybe he took information, research, or old data of some kind? You know me, I'm obsessed with historical research. Maybe whatever is in there would give you some idea where he's hiding and what he's planning to do."

"And why he needs Remethiakara's help."

"Exactly."

"Well, it doesn't look like I'll be going for a jog any time soon, so I can start digging back through the archives. I wonder if my old hard drives are still in the building, somewhere…"

"Keep me updated on what you find. What?" Her voice grew more distant as the wind noise howled through the speaker, even muffled as it was through the glass of the hyperbaric chamber. "Okay. Amon, I have to go. We're moving inland now."

After a hurried goodbye, she was gone again.

"Reuben," Amon said. "I need to get my blood flowing, can you tilt this thing up?"

"Hm. They have two of those small forklifts to move supplies around in the warehouse that we could use. I can probably rig something up."

"Great. Oh! And bring me my laptop."

"How are you going to use it?"

"I dunno, can't you get a wireless mouse and keyboard I can use? Or cast a hologram keyboard on the glass here."

Reuben rolled his eyes. "You're impossible. Okay. I'll try. Meantime, try to get some rest, would you?"

The backs of his eyes throbbed as his adrenaline-boosted pulse hammered through his veins. In fact, he was kind of tired.

He fought to keep his eyes open until Reuben came back, but he lost that battle.

26

FROZEN CONTINENT

They drove into the heart of the cold continent through most of the day, encountering nothing except frost covered hills. In the distance, the clean white sheet of snow was broken only by the jagged teeth of black bluffs biting into a pale blue sky.

Eliana shivered on the back of a snowmobile, and latched her arms more tightly around Audrey's waist as they speared ahead into the biting wind.

Lakshmi and Ross rode together on a second snowmobile, and the twins shared a third. They followed close behind Audrey like a team of *Tour de France* cyclers, sheltering in their wind stream.

Each of the archaeologists was bundled up tightly in cold-weather gear that Major Bautista had procured from some military surplus storehouse in the harried twenty four hours in which they had to prepare. The parka she wore was heavy and covered most of her body and face. Only a small patch of skin around her eyes was exposed to the air, which burned her eyes and chapped her lips.

Eliana didn't need to explain to anyone how dangerous Lucas Lamotte and Remethiakara would be as a pair if they got ahold of another star shard. It would be bad news. She shivered, and not from the wind, at this thought.

Major Bautista and a small squad of armed Marines rode identical snowmobiles abreast of and behind them—their protective detail. A mile or so back toward the coast, the rest of their supplies trailed with the rest of the platoon and larger—but slower moving—SUVs outfitted with tractor treads. Somewhere out of view overhead, a pair of fighter jets circled deeper into the heart of Antarctica, searching for any sign of Lucas and Hawkwood.

None had yet been reported.

Throughout the day, the wind howled into their faces in fits and starts. At its height, the gusts were strong enough to alter the course of the heavy-treaded snowmobiles.

Audrey, at the helm, determinedly redirected the craft to the correct bearing, and shouted back into the wind as she pointed to a spot in the distance. Eliana nodded her agreement and the team pulled off at one of the old drill sites for which Audrey had provided the coordinates. Eliana stared at the snow-covered ground as Audrey double checked her GPS.

"Here we are, at last," Audrey said.

To Eliana, it looked like nothing more than a slight dimple in the snow. "Should we check if there are any pieces remaining down there?"

"No need. The first carbonado meteorite was discovered here, and I can personally assure you that we could find nothing else in the immediate vicinity. However, our search ended here. We'd been digging for months, and with the meteorite finally in hand, we decided to call it quits. There were, however, two other places we hypothesized that fragments of the meteorite could have made impact."

She pulled out a tablet and opened up a topographical map of the area on which two red spots pulsed slowly. One was located in a patch of open ground about twenty miles to the northeast of their current location. The other was centered just inside the jagged teeth of the mountain range on the horizon to the northwest.

Eliana nodded. "All right then. Let's get moving."

In the late afternoon, they reached the second site. The vast white tundra stretched out in all directions.

"Anything?" Eliana asked after Lakshmi, the twins, and Ross had drilled holes, set probes, and conducted an electrical resistance survey that could penetrate the snow-covered ground. The hard ice was unforgiving, and the sun had already begun its descent by the time they got any usable data.

"Ice for days," Talia said. She stared at a small tablet she held in her mittens, where an application translated the electrical resistivity read from the probes into different material types.

Turner reached over his sister's shoulder and brushed a few flurries off the tablet's screen. "Looks like we've got some dirt about twenty feet down. Some soft stone, maybe clay. Nothing dense or hard enough to be the carbonado meteorites that I can see."

Eliana studied the screen for a minute before agreeing with their analysis. She turned away from the survey gear to gaze out over the frost-covered hills toward the black bluffs, behind which the third site was located. They might not have enough light to reach that one today. "Never realized how vast and empty this place was."

"This is the warm season. You should see it in the middle of the winter," Audrey said. "Makes my hometown in Grand Rapids, Minnesota, seem like a tropical paradise."

Eliana snorted.

"No thanks," Lakshmi said as she and Ross yanked up the metal probes from the ice and set them down in another section of the grid they were creating that would give them a full picture of what lay underneath. It would be another couple hours before this area was fully mapped. "I'll take a humid jungle over this any day."

The rest of the grid yielded nothing either, so they packed the gear and continued inland. Now the black bluffs loomed high overhead, and the setting sun cast long shadows across the crust of the continent toward them.

As she suspected, the major gave a signal to stop near sundown. "I assume you can't operate in the dark," he said.

"Afraid not."

"Then we'll wait here for the supply train to catch up with us, and make camp for the night." The group of vehicles arrived shortly, and circled up in a protective ring. Marines unloaded and began to set up tents and patrols with practiced efficiency.

Major Bautista stood just outside the ring of SUVs watching the sky above the bluffs and talking into a handheld radio. As Eliana walked over to join him, he pulled the radio away from his mouth.

"What the matter?" Eliana asked.

"One of the pilots said they spotted something. They missed it the first time because of the way the sun was casting the mountain's shadows. I asked them to take another pass."

"Is it Lucas?"

"Either that or a colony of penguins. The pilots are coming in lower this time to get visual confirmation."

A moment later, one of the jets burst out of the clouds from the left, and curved toward the ring of mountains. The tightly contained roar of its engine cut through the sky.

"If it is Hawkwood over there, aren't you worried they'll see the jet?"

"There's no element of surprise in a place like this. If we approach on foot or in these vehicles, they'll see us coming from miles away. Better to scare them off with the jets if we can manage it, rather than risk the lives of your team, or my men."

The radio in Bautista's hand crackled. "Major, I definitely see people on the ground here. They look to be operating some kind of drill."

Eliana gasped.

"Affirmative. Feed me the visuals."

Major Bautista looked at a tablet in his hand. Images began to appear.

On the screen, a small group of people clad in heavy winter gear much like their own, stood in a semi-circle around a jagged scar in the ice.

"What in the hell..." Major Bautista said.

Eliana looked up in time to see the fighter jet pulling a sharp U-turn and driving down toward the jagged fang of the black mountain nearest to them.

"Mayday!" the pilot's panicked voice came over the radio. "I've lost control. Repeat, I've lost control of my plane."

"Eject, Captain!" the major shouted into the radio. "Get out of there!"

The top of the plane popped off and a small speck shot into the air moments before the plane careened out of sight behind the mountainside.

Moments later, the echo of an explosion drifted across the icy tundra.

27

LEVERAGE

Pieces parted from the fuselage and a black speck was thrown upward as the pilot ejected.

Remethiakara relinquished the power he was pulling from the star shard at his feet. The jet plane continued to spiral downward. Gravity did the rest of the work for him.

The plane slammed into the black face of the mountain and exploded in a gout of flame.

"Well done, Remy!" Lucas hollered, his greedy lips parting into the broad, half-cracked smile Remethiakara was now all too familiar with.

A column of greasy black smoke drifted skyward from the ruins of the fallen aircraft. Remethiakara flexed his fist and felt the weight of the power in the shard at his feet. Some of the mercenaries nearby, who had been gaping at the crash site of the small aircraft, took several involuntary steps back when he activated the shard's power. Steam rose into the air, and turned the ice encasing the shard into water that flowed off the oblong, jagged-edged meteorite. The liquid water reformed into a frozen puddle on the ground in the sub-zero temperatures.

Once exposed, he could see that, although it was a small shard—just larger than the size of his fist— waves of invisible power pulsed from within the meteorite. Short of creating another interstellar wormhole through which to transport a dying mothership, this shard would do just fine.

"That's not my name." Remethiakara's tongue darted out to wet his teeth. "I've had enough of you."

He made a fist, sending his truethoughts thrumming through his armorsuit. He latched onto the seething, writhing knot of power in the shard and gathered it into himself, concentrating it until it would make a blade of raw energy in the cold, dry air.

"Ah, ah, ahhhh." Lucas's smile widened into the lopsided grin, and something about the look he gave Remethiakara brought him up short.

There was not nearly enough fear in his eyes.

"Wouldn't do that if I were you," Lucas said. "Or you'll never see your precious eggs again."

Remethiakara pulled his tongue back into his mouth in shock, biting the tip with his sharp teeth. He hissed in both pain and surprise.

"Oh, yes. I knew you would land in the Yucatan

Peninsula. Given the Mayan influence Eliana detailed in her interviews about the people of Kakul, it seemed the logical place for you to go once our spies heard that the U.S. military had discovered an alien spacecraft bound for Earth. Hawkwood's executives didn't believe me at first, but they came around to my way of thinking when reports of the so-called "meteorite crash" drifted out of China. After we evac'd you from the jungle, it was a simple matter to search the jungle for whatever you were looking to find there—or rather, what you left behind. Luck comes to those who reach for it, I always say."

Remethiakara released his hold on the shard's power with a shudder of ineffective rage. As he did so, the cold that permeated the air seemed to slice into his lungs.

"What have you done with them?"

"The eggs? Don't worry, Remy, they're in a safe place. Unharmed. And they shall remain that way as long as you keep your end of the bargain and modify the Translocator to do what we need it to do. You see, I had to have some kind of leverage. Otherwise, what guarantee did I have of your cooperation?"

Remethiakara went very still and glanced around. Lucas wasn't wrong. He had underestimated this one.

The mercenaries fanned out and surrounded Remethiakara in a half circle, rifles raised and loaded. He exhaled through numb nostril slits and stared at Lucas through the cloud of frozen breath that hung in the air. Remethiakara's suit translated his thoughts into human language for him. "How do I know I can trust you?"

Lucas just laughed. "Oh, Remy. You don't have a choice."

Though his mind scrambled for another option, he didn't find one. He could easily kill all these men with a swipe of his hand, now that he had the shard, but would certainly endanger the lives of his progeny. He couldn't risk it.

Instead, he fell back on an old habit—patience.

"Very well," he said.

"Good. Very good. You may lower your weapons, gentlemen. He will not harm you."

Remethiakara inclined his head ever so slightly. He would accede to this treacherous human, for now, but he would never give him the satisfaction of groveling. He would rather take his chances with the sub-zero cold than beg.

The mercenaries lowered their rifles, but he noticed that they kept two hands on the guns and did not let their fingers stray far from their triggers.

"Now, where is our ride? Ah," Lucas said.

A helicopter with a white Hawkwood logo—a horse's head—painted on its tail came down out of the sky from the south. "Here we are. Time to get moving, fellas. That was a U.S. Military aircraft, and

I'm sure it wasn't traveling alone. I would prefer not to be here when the good old boys come looking for whoever broke their toys."

Remethiakara consoled the anger that seethed within him by bending down and picking up the star shard.

He drew another stream of power from the stone and used it to warm himself completely, recharging his suit at the same time as he banished the biting cold.

No telling when the opportunity to escape this predicament would present itself. It was best to be prepared.

28

URANIUM CLUB

"Oh, thank God," Amon whispered when Eliana walked through the blast door and into the Translocator lab. He pressed both his palms against the glass lid of the hyperbaric chamber, which was at this moment propped up vertically against a wall. He could almost stand on the seam where the lid met the metal base of the bed without discomfort.

His lovely wife looked around the room, her tanned brow creased with concern. Then she spotted him through the glass and hurried across the lab, her green eyes shining with joy and obvious relief.

Reuben, who had been digging through old molecular reassembly research files on a worn and busted-looking Fisk Industries laptop, cleared his throat, closed the computer, and walked a polite distance away to greet the rest of the expedition crew who were straggling down the long hallway.

When Eliana reached him, she pressed her hands flat against the other side of his pressurized glass cage. "You're awake."

Guilt spilled the words off his tongue. "I promised you I'd be there. That I wouldn't risk us getting separated again."

"It's okay."

"When I heard about the plane—" He finally choked off his guilty rambling. An unbearable ache pushed its way from his gut into his throat, causing his vision to blur. He blinked back tears.

"I'm fine, Amon. Look at me. I'm fine."

"'Not now, not ever.' That's what I said. Already, I broke my promise." He let his forehead fall heavily against the glass pane again. "What kind of man does that make me if I can't even keep the promises I make to you?"

Eliana rested her forehead against the glass on the other side. He couldn't slip his hand around her waist, he couldn't kiss the warm skin of her cheek, but something about the proximity of her, the way she stayed present with him through the pain, the way she didn't flinch when his eyes locked with her luminous green emeralds...it calmed him. Amon took a deep breath. The tides of his pain began to ebb away again.

In his anxious mind, while he had been waiting

for her to return from the dangers of her expedition, he had imagined that *she* would be the one crying.

Instead, he was the one with tears streaming down his cheeks. Amon sniffed and wiped at his eyes. He took a deep shuddering breath and blew it out. A thought that had been buried in his mind but not fully formed until now struck him.

"We go through life like distracted drivers, so fixed on our destination that we miss the all-important details standing right in front of us. I've been that distracted driver. I took you for granted and for that I am truly and eternally sorry."

She sighed and shook her own head. "I'm not without fault, either. I was holding onto a stupid grudge. I know that everything you've done has been to try and keep me safe. I shouldn't have stayed mad at you for so long, and for that it's my turn to be sorry. So maybe we can just call it even?"

He shook his head. "I don't deserve it."

"You do." One side of her mouth twitched up into a wry smirk. "You risked yourself to save Rakulo and his people, and to spare me this." She knocked on the sheet of glass separating them. "And for that, I think you deserve a second chance."

He swallowed. "I just want things to go back to being normal between us."

"We don't lead normal lives, Amon," she said. "That may be asking too much.

A bitter chuckle rolled up out of his belly. "I suppose you're right about that."

And just like that they were on the same page again—on level ground.

Eliana sighed and undid her hair from the messy ponytail it had been held in, pulling the elastic free and slipping it over her wrist. She ran long fingers through her thick hair to brush the tangles out, twisted it and set it down over her left shoulder.

"There's something else I've realized," Eliana said. "On the plane ride back, I was trying to figure out why my first instinct lately has been to try to help Remethiakara. I *still* don't think it's right that General Wade attacked the spacecraft. Shoot first and ask questions later goes against my nature. I'm an anthropologist at heart. Imagine how much we might have learned if we'd just taken a different tack, but after the escape pods landed on Earth and I suspected where he was heading…the only excuse I have is that I empathized with him. Selfishly, I wanted to give him a head start, on the off chance there would be an opportunity to learn more about him later. Hell, even in Antarctica, when that fighter jet hit the mountain, you know what I thought? Not, 'Oh god, I hope that pilot survived,' but 'Oh *good*, now Remethiakara has a chance to escape.'"

Amon's eyebrows shot up. He waited in silence, sensing that she had more to say.

"Something happened to me while I was on

Kakul. Remethiakara changed the way I feel about him. It made me…empathetic to his cause. Like it was my job to assist him." She shook her head. "It's weird. Almost as if he planted the thought in my subconscious mind so deep that I didn't even know it was there until just now." She tilted her head slightly and stared off into a middle distance.

"Are they true thoughts?" Amon asked.

Her head snapped back. "What did you say?"

"Those subconscious thoughts he planted, are they true?"

"I…I don't know. I feel like they are true, but at the same time, I know they're not *mine*. They didn't originate with me. Does that even make sense?"

Amon leaned his head back against the padding back of the hyperbaric pressure chamber's bed. "I think so. Who knows how the alien tech works? If he could get into your head to show you visions of his history, it's logical to think he has the ability to plant some other thoughts and impulses in your mind as well. After all, impulses and instincts are just electrical signals your body sends to your brain."

She nodded enthusiastically. "That's it. That's exactly it. It's like an impulse I can't control. But I know it's not true—I mean, it feels true, but it didn't come from me. I think I'm beginning to be able to tell the difference."

Amon looked past Eliana and realized that the rest of the expedition team, along with General

Wade and his cadre of assistants, were gathering around Reuben and watching the two of them whisper at each other from across the lab. Eliana turned to see what Amon was looking at, and pulled back her shoulders slightly. Amon wiped his eyes and took another deep breath.

"How are you doing?" Amon said.

"I'm fine. Are you okay?"

"I will be once I get out of this glass coffin. Reuben says I need another couple days to stabilize before I can leave the hyperbaric chamber. In the meantime, we've been searching through the old files as you suggested. I think we may have found some information that might help. Let's get everyone together." Amon shook his head. "Some of it is hard enough to believe. Better if we don't have to explain it twice."

Due to Amon's predicament, General Wade and his crew had moved their gear downstairs, and set it up on one side of the lab so that the operation could be run from a single location.

If I'd known, Amon thought, *I'd have built a command center here when we remodeled the lounge.*

As it was, they took over the lounge and then some, spreading their gear across an entire wall of the lab adjacent to the stage on which the Translocator was mounted, careful to keep the access ramp up to the stabilization sphere and platform clear.

The expedition team had shed their winter gear and changed back into regular clothes.

Agent Moreno stood patiently with his hands clasped in front of him, wearing the same suit he'd been wearing since this all began upstairs. It was more wrinkled now.

Reuben and Audrey were present, and even Rakulo—who had stayed behind during the expedition to Antarctica to take care of his people—stood stoically silent and surprisingly calm on the other side of Eliana. Amon envied the tall, broad-chested young warrior's ability to be appear so blasted calm. He exuded the kind of an inner stillness and confidence that Amon had always envied in athletes. In fact, looking now, he saw that despite their differences in choice of clothing, Rakulo and Major Bautista shared that quality.

Amon himself still stood inside the hyperbaric chamber feeling highly self-conscious. The machine was still propped up vertically. Eliana hadn't left his side. The group of people gathered around them.

Major Bautista began by debriefing them on the events that had transpired in Antarctica.

"Unfortunately, by the time we reached their location," Major Bautista said, "Hawkwood, Lucas Lamotte, and the alien known as Remethiakara were long gone. Our satellites tracked the helicopters which evacuated them. Intelligence confirmed that the aircraft are registered to Hawkwood. We tracked them through Argentina, but lost them at the Venezuelan border. We assume they switched aircraft to leave the country undetected."

Major Bautista nodded at the FBI detective.

"However," Agent Moreno said, picking up the thread, "we can assume that from Venezuela they were bound once again for the Swiss Alps, where we tracked them before. While our reconnaissance there continues, with aid from the military satellite surveillance provided by General Wade's intelligence team, we've yet to mark an exact location."

"And that takes the conversation back to us," Reuben said. Since he was not stuck inside a glass cage, Reuben spoke for both he and Amon. Reuben held up the battered laptop in his hands. "Eliana gave us the idea to dig back through the research that Lucas stole for clues. Fisk Industries keeps most of its data backed up onto a proprietary cloud storage server, only accessible via two-factor authentication, plus a valid FIID—Fisk Industries Identification number—of an active employee. That was how we knew Lucas had accessed the Translocator blueprints in the first place. The rest of the old research is on this laptop and several external hard drives—files that Amon and I didn't think we needed any more, but kept out of habit. Our operating theory is that if we can figure out what Hawkwood is trying to do with the Translocator it might give us a better idea how to stop them.

"So Amon and I began by doing a thorough analysis of our access logs. As we already knew, Lucas took the Translocator blueprints and details of the experiments we ran, dating back about ten years. However, as it turns out, that was not *all* he stole. He also grabbed all of the declassified experiments on molecular disassembly and quantum teleportation—foundational data on which the Translocator was originally based."

Reuben walked over to the holodeck and plugged the old laptop in. A hologram of a grainy sepia-toned photo appeared in the air over the deck at several times its original size.

The photo showed three scientists holding a cage of lab mice between them. Two of them wore thick-rimmed black glasses. One was balding, his forehead wrinkled, with upshot eyebrows that matched his proud smile. Each of the scientists was wearing signature white lab coats. Each coat had a single identifying marker: A black and red Nazi swastika sewn over their hearts.

Amon recognized and knew this photo well.

"This photograph was taken in *July* of 1942." Reuben paused, obviously waiting for a reaction from the small crowd. When he didn't get one, he said it again, this time with a rising inflection that made the statement into question. "July of 1942?"

Blank looks were all he got in return.

Amon smiled. "Reuben, most of the people here aren't physicists, or even scientists. You have to give them more context."

"Very well, here it is, in brief: the discovery of nuclear fission—man's ability to split the atom—was first made by German scientists in December of 1938. In January 1939, the Nazi *Wehrmacht* kicked off a program that was nicknamed the *Uranverein*, or uranium club—a scientific effort to develop and produce nuclear weapons. This is what really started the famous nuclear arms race of the 20th century.

"Later that year, after the German invasion of Poland, the Nazis drafted a whole bunch of Polish physicists and expanded their nuclear program. It's common knowledge that they broke it down into three parts: the *Uranmaschine* (nuclear reactor), uranium and heavy water production, and uranium isotope separation. What's not common knowledge is that there were several other aspects of the program that were run secretly—experiments in bomb making, cloning, human/animal hybridization, genetic mutations caused by radiation, quantum teleportation, and much more.

"But that didn't pan out for them, either. In early 1942, after three years of slow progress, the directors of the program concluded that nuclear fission would not contribute to the war effort in a meaningful way, and direction of it was handed over to the Reich Research Council. The number of scientists working on applied nuclear fission diminished rapidly.

"Except," Reuben added, pointing back at the sepia-toned photo suspended in the air above the holodeck, "for one project that was continued in secret. This photo was taken in July of 1942. The cage full of lab mice they're holding in their hands? Cloned, albeit imperfectly. If you zoom in a little, you'll see how mangled the mice are. Limbs in the wrong places, or deformed in other ways. These men look way too happy to be holding a cage full of dead, mutilated lab mice. A few months after this photo was taken, the program was shut down. We don't know why."

General Wade frowned. "How is this going to lead us to Hawkwood?"

"This is just one of the experiments they conducted in that secret project, which coopted the nickname of the original nuclear project, *Uranverein* —the uranium club. What we don't know, and what people have been speculating about for years, is where they conducted these experiments. We got this information when the Germany declassified the remainder of the Nazi experiments fifteen years ago. That's around the time Amon and I first met, and we began the work that eventually led to the construction of the Translocator."

He didn't have to point or gesture, but the eyes of

everyone in the room unconsciously tracked up to the massive electrified arch that towered overhead.

"And?" General Wade said, drawing everyone's attention back to Reuben.

"Well, two things. For starters, now that we know that Lucas has all of this old research, we might be able to narrow down what, exactly, he's trying to accomplish with his copycat Hopper. Lucas was never one for original ideas. My guess is that whatever he's trying to do has its origination point in this research."

Major Bautista and General Wade were both nodding along now.

"If we know what he's trying to do, we can figure out how to counter him," Major Bautista said.

"The second thing," Reuben said, "and more important than the first, is that if we can figure out where the Nazis conducted these experiments, maybe that will give us a lead on where Lucas and Hawkwood are hiding."

Agent Moreno said, "We know the Nazis had several secret bases in the Swiss Alps."

"Precisely. You can even see mountains in the background of this photo."

Over the shoulders of the white-coated Nazi scientists, shrouded by mist and distance, a row of mountain peaks jutted into the sky.

"If we can figure out where their base of operations was—where the so-called uranium club conducted their nuclear experiments—I'd bet money that it will lead us to Lucas."

"Well," Eliana said. "If archaeologists are good at one thing, it's making sense of ancient history. Let's start digging."

29

CRADLE

Remethiakara picked up the large clay pot full of dark soil, and carried it across the room.

According to Lucas, the cavernous atriums of this underground facility had been carved out of the mountain over a century ago, during a great war. Then it had been lost to the annals of history, only to be rediscovered by Hawkwood, the mercenary organization Lucas served.

The couple dozen people who haunted this vast facility were all members of Hawkwood. Of those, half of them were fighting men that served double duty—they were both the security force and Remethiakara's prison guards. They protected the clandestine location from outsider intrusion, and they kept him from finding an exit. He was given his own room, but even while he slept he was under heavy guard. Everywhere he went, they followed him—with their guns and their eyes and their cameras.

He used to be the one running the zoo. Now he found himself living in one.

Admittedly, the facility didn't seem to be in need of much protection from the outside world. During the trip to reach the mountain lair from Antarctica, which had taken place in the daylight, Remethiakara had finally been afforded the opportunity to see for himself how remote the place was—located deep in the mountain range, far from even the smallest population centers.

No more overt displays of force had been made against him since the confrontation with Lucas in Antarctica. Remethiakara had also been careful not to provoke the fighting men. He just wasn't desperate enough to try anything rash yet.

Lucas needs you. That's the key.

As Remethiakara carried the large clay pot toward the stand of several computers and a holodeck that controlled the Translocator, Lucas watched him from the far side of the room. He was standing among a group of men, none of whom had introduced themselves to Remethiakara. Some wore formal suits. Others looked like veteran warriors— aging, but still bulky and scarred and full of swagger.

"So how's this work?" Lucas called across the room.

"You'll see," Remethiakara said.

The other men cast irritated glanced in Lucas's direction. He shrugged and dabbed at the corner of his mouth with a wadded up handkerchief, affecting disinterest.

Remethiakara had observed that Lucas drooled more when he was excited. It was disgusting.

Ignoring his anxious audience, who obviously suspected foul play since they themselves were taking that approach, Remethiakara stopped by the computer and set the clay pot down next to the night-black star shard, which he'd placed there earlier in anticipation of this task. Mere feet away, the glass and metal machines Lucas used to operate the Translocator hummed and whirred and flashed with little lights.

It had taken him years to learn how to direct the power of the star shards—now, it was second nature. How many times in his life had he built a new cradle? How many times had he started a new colony? How often had his people been forced to begin again?

Since they lost their homeworld and became a race that wandered among the stars, his people had learned to thrive wherever they found themselves. That was their biggest advantage—an ability to grow new life on any blasted hunk of rock.

Remethiakara slowed his breathing and focused his mind. This drew impatient coughs and throat clearings from Lucas's direction. He tuned them out like the background noise they were.

Everything else narrowed to unimportance—the echoey atrium, his impatient audience, the danger he'd inadvertently dumped his offspring into…all of it faded to a distant hum.

Then, slowly, dipping into the black well of energy contained in the star shard with his truethoughts, Remethiakara began to draw power out like a thread.

He forced the air out of his lower lungs. When he breathed back in, he filled them with raw power. Energy pulsed through his body, conducted through his blood and bones. It tingled the tips of his fingers and the narrow slitted nostrils through which he drew in yet more oxygen.

Remethiakara held his breath, and focused on his body which seemed to thrum with sparkling energy.

It had taken some effort to get the balance of chemicals in the soil right.

Will this work again?

He smiled at the familiar thought. It was always this way in the moment before he began. That's how it was with truethoughts. When you're creating something from nothing—or combining a million disparate atoms and compounds into a sum that is greater than their individual parts—there is always that moment of self-doubt before you begin.

And then you lean into it.

You move through it.

Remethiakara exhaled and directed the power within him to flow like a river into the nutrient-rich soil, where a piece of his own flesh, cut from his arm, had already been buried.

At the same time, he raised his right hand and rolled up the flexible sleeve of his armorsuit, exposing a cotton bandage that covered the self-inflicted wound. Using the star shard's power, he made a blade of the air and sliced through the bandage and into his flesh a second time, drawing a line of black blood through which the excess oxygen bubbled out.

As he exhaled, the power flowed out of him and Remethiakara shivered with the pain of its exit.

The stream of black blood soaked into the dirt, creating a conduit through which the shard's energy could leave his body and catalyze the nutrients in the soil.

It provided the seed of organic life he'd planted there with an impetus to grow. And a bond which could only be broken by the shard's destruction.

When the soil was moist with black blood, Remethiakara stood and pulled his arm away as he re-secured the bandage.

Then he placed the star shard on top of the soil.

"Is that it?" Lucas said in a low voice.

Remethiakara glanced over his shoulder. Lucas had crossed the room to stand only a few feet away behind him. The others hung back, flanked by wary soldiers hugging their automatic rifles to their chests. Even the tough-looking grizzled veterans clenched their teeth and gazed warily from beneath their brows.

Lucas wrung his damp handkerchief in his hand and peered around Remethiakara toward the clay pot. A trickle of blood dropped down the side of the red fired clay. Lucas raised his eyebrows expectantly.

"Patience," Remethiakara said.

Several minutes passed. A few people began to grumble. Their interest wandered.

Suddenly, there was the sound of clay cracking. Small shards of pottery began to snap off and careen across the floor.

Three micro-thin tendrils shot out in different directions and slapped out along the sides of the computer towers and holoprojector screens. They glommed onto the oblong, rough-edged meteorite, squirming hungrily as they squeezed the rock and found purchase in imperfections along its surface.

"Incredible." Lucas dabbed at his mouth. "How does it work?"

"It is similar to the brain that powers your computers, the...what did you call it?"

"The CPU?"

"The cradle serves a similar function in our biotech, but even more than that: it is the brain as well as the heart. We shall know shortly if it will be able to integrate with your machines."

Remethiakara bent down next to the pot and carefully removed the pieces of clay that had not been forced free by the sudden expansion within the soil. He brushed aside the dirt and traced the tendrils back to the raw nerve center of the living organism he'd just shocked into life—the cradle. It was exposed, at risk now more than at any point in its life, as its root system had not been fully established. This new 'central processing unit' would give him the ability to give Lucas what he wanted.

And much more.

"As it grows, the cradle will provide a method to siphon power from the star shard," Remethiakara said, "and a system through which we will be able to channel the shard's wild power into the Translocator."

"Impressive, Remy."

Remethiakara gritted his teeth at the nickname he despised.

Instead of reacting to it, he turned away from Lucas and floated his hand over the soil. He felt a pulse through his armorsuit. Already, the organ had swallowed the star shard. It was now big enough to fit in his palm. It pulsed out of time, spasmodic, like a fish out of water, beating its raw existence desperately into the cold air.

Through his palm, Remethiakara sent a

truethought that exuded warmth and safety—the same emotion he sent to his egg-bound offspring in times of stress—to reassure the creature, to connect to it.

A perception of relief and gratitude pinged back into his somatic senses. The emotion was faint but present, and he knew its ability to communicate would evolve as it grew. The organ's contractions slowed to a more even, steady rhythm, and Remethiakara turned back to Lucas.

"When will it be ready?" Lucas asked.

"Soon." Remethiakara gestured Lucas to come closer. "Watch."

He placed his open hand over the organ and massaged it gently, using his truethoughts coupled with the star shard's well of power to manipulate the organ's shape without touching it.

Its edges rippled.

Its volume smoothed out and rounded.

Then it flatted and spread its roots into the vents in the computer towers, over the holoprojectors, across the floor, growing before their eyes as it slowly consumed the machine.

Lucas pulled the handkerchief out of his pocket and dabbed at a strand of drool that dribbled down his chin. "This better work."

"Don't worry," Remethiakara said. "It will work. As long as you hold up your end of the bargain."

With an involuntary twitch, Lucas's eyes shifted

toward the knot of men on the other side of the cavernous room. He lowered his voice and whispered, "Are you threatening me?"

"Of course not." Remethiakara pulled back thin lips to show his teeth to Lucas, in an imitation of the human smile. "We need each other."

Remethiakara licked his teeth.

The cradle pulsed under his hand.

30

MANHUNT

The screen of the laptop blurred. Eliana closed her eyes, leaned away and rubbed her neck, which was sore from hunching over the screen for hours, reading the tiny typewriter font they printed lab reports in circa 1940.

Her faint memories of undergrad classes in German had been put to the test as she joined the others in rifling through the archived scans of research notes from Nazi scientists, hoping that some scrap of information would give them a clue as to Lucas's plans and whereabouts.

"Here," she said. "Someone else take this for a while. I stopped at Müller, Hermann. October 14th, 1940."

"I'm pretty sure these words have no meaning anymore," Lakshmi said as she took the laptop into her lap. "Even with the computer translating most of the German for me."

"Then look through the photo archive instead."

She groaned. "More disfigured mice?"

"They used frogs in several experiments," Agent Moreno supplied from across the room.

"Egh."

Agent Moreno paced back and forth as he stared at a large digital map of the Swiss Alps that he'd projected onto the wall. Sections of it were highlighted in red and yellow, indicating where satellite scans for signs of life or the heat signature of an active nuclear reactor had already been conducted.

She patted Agent Moreno on the shoulder. "Have they been able to pinpoint where the July 1942 photo was taken?"

"Not yet," he said. "The FBI pattern recognition search on the mountain range came up with a few possibilities, but nothing concrete. Director Badeux got me access to NASA satellite photographs, and General Wade has his aides scouring through those an inch at a time."

"I'm going to go check on Amon," Eliana told her team. "There's gotta be something. We'll find him. Just keep looking."

Eliana exited the lounge. As she crossed the lab, she saw that she wasn't the only one who needed a short break. Through the glass of the hyperbaric chamber, Eliana saw Amon close his eyes and take a deep, steadying breath through his nose. His voice was muffled by the glass, but he tended to enunciate more clearly when he was angry, and she could hear the way he bit off each word as he spoke.

"Reuben," he said. "I can't take it anymore. I need to *move*. Let me out of this damn thing."

"Look, this isn't like a normal case of decompression sickness," Reuben said. "The rashes on your skin have started to heal, but it'll be at least another twelve hours before the air pressure regulates back to sea level. We don't know how your body will react if I let you out now."

"He's right," Audrey said. "Anywhere from seven to fourteen percent of divers who recovered from the bends using hyperbaric oxygen treatment experience ongoing symptoms."

"Not to mention that when you last went through the Translocator, your particles came together all mixed up with the weapons the natives were holding. That and the low-powered Translocation both contributed to your molecular instability. We've been monitoring you for heavy metals poisoning, blood embolisms, ongoing neurological sequelae..."

"And have you found anything yet?"

"Not yet, but I'm still running some—"

"Great!" Amon interrupted. "No symptoms. Now let me out!"

"I can't do that."

"Reuben. Listen. I've been in here for days. I'm tired of pissing into a bag. My own body odor is starting to make me gag. I desperately need a shower, and nothing would make me happier than to shit on a real toilet instead of inside this glass cage. Otherwise, though, I feel perfectly fine."

Eliana snorted with barely contained laughter. He really did seem to be better. She hoped it was true. Amon's guiltless grin following his words caused Audrey to blush and turned away.

Reuben, however, did not seem to think it was very amusing. He glared at Amon.

"Fine. Fine! But if your molecules fly apart when you step out of the chamber, you've only got yourself to blame. If not, you can shower, but after an hour you'll report right back. You hear me? You'll come straight back here so I can take your vitals."

"Fantastic. Deal."

Reuben heaved a deep sigh, then rolled his baggy denim shirt sleeves up to his elbows and entered the code that would release Amon from the hyperbaric chamber.

Eliana gritted her teeth in nervous anticipation.

There was a slight hissing sound as the pressure equalized. Amon worked his jaw and shook his head to ward off the sensation of discomfort he was obviously experiencing. When the glass lid hinged open, he eagerly clambered out.

Amon staggered with his first step, but Eliana

was already at his side. He grabbed at her shoulder to steady himself and she felt a chill there where his hand pressed. There was a brief moment of pressure, and then it was gone as Amon fell forward. Instinctively, she caught him around his waist and pulled him back against the solidness of her body.

Amon leaned into her. He flexed his hand, opening it and then making a fist a few times. For a brief moment, she thought she could see the floor through his hand.

But then she blinked and it was solid. She touched his palm to be sure of it.

"Are you okay?"

"Yeah, I'm fine. It just tingles a bit."

"What's wrong?" Reuben said.

"Nothing. Look. Solid as a rock."

"Bah!" Reuben said as he turned and stalked away. "Back here in one hour, Amon! I mean it."

"Yes, sir, boss, sir."

"Lean on me," Eliana said.

When Amon wrapped his arms around her, she was assaulted by a particularly strong odor.

"You weren't kidding," she said. "You really do need a shower."

He laughed. "Yes, that's true. But first—have you found anything in the archives?"

"Not yet. But we're still looking. We'll find something."

"Show me."

She nodded and led him, slowly, one shuffling step at a time, toward the lounge.

They didn't make it. The dark-haired Tammy, General Wade's aide-de-camp, intercepted them before they got there.

"I think we found something. Quick."

Eliana nodded. "I'll take him. Get the others from the lounge."

"I think I can walk on my own," Amon said. "My muscles were just stiff, that's all."

She nodded as Amon shook out his arms, rolled his head around in a circle, and bent at the knees, testing his balance.

A minute later they had all gathered around Agent Moreno's map in the lounge. It had been switched to satellite imagery, and it showed the entire region of Europe through which the Alps stretched.

"You're all looking at an aerial view of Switzerland," General Wade said. He circled one massive ridge with a laser pointer. "This is the Eiger, a rather distinctive mountain peak in the Bernese Alps. The computer identified it as one of the peaks from the photograph that Reuben showed us. A NORAD search algorithm mapped possible locations of where that photograph was taken to within a hundred miles of the peak. Our best guess is that it was taken here."

A circle was circumscribed the Eiger mountain.

To the west was a dot labeling the city of Lauterbrunnen. Criss-crossing roadways could also been seen on that side in the satellite photos. To the east, however, it seemed to be nothing but foothills and mountains.

"I was skeptical at first when we began the heat scans. But we kept looking. And then we found this."

A red splotch appeared at the edge of the hundred-mile radius circle on the map. It covered an unlabeled mountain, much smaller than the Eiger.

"This is a remote peak. It doesn't have an official name."

"There's no town for miles in any direction," Agent Moreno said. "Are there any other power plants labeled there?"

"Not that we found."

"Got you," Agent Moreno said, baring his teeth like a wolf.

"How can you be sure?" Amon asked.

Eliana noticed he was still clenching and unclenching his hands unconsciously. She resolved to watch him like a hawk and take him straight back to Reuben to check his vitals as soon as possible. But she didn't want to interrupt the conversation now that they had a real lead on finding Lucas.

"Remember how we said one of those mountains in the background of Reuben's photograph was the Eiger?" Tammy said. "Our computers were comparing the photograph with digital imagery of the mountains today—it didn't find a match because, we realized, about 20 years ago there was a rockslide that changed the shape of the peak. If you compensate for that adjustment…"

Tammy fed something from her tablet into the projector. The old photograph of the Nazi scientists popped up, and a grid appeared over top of over the mountain peaks of the photograph.

Another image popped up superimposed on top of that, a modern photograph of the Eiger taken from the same angle that they'd sourced from the internet.

The lines automatically adjusted as they measured and compensated for the changes in the famous mountain peak's shape from the old photograph to the more recent version.

A blue dot appeared on the mountain range, inside the hundred mile radius.

"That's how we got a location."

The photographs disappeared as the satellite map appeared again. Tammy zoomed in until the mountains around the blue dot filled the holoprojector's entire view screen.

"And then we used the satellite's infrared view to look deeper."

A red highlight appeared once again. As the satellite zoomed in farther, the edges of the glow slowly came together, into what Eliana's mind at first saw as a kind of root system, entwining its fingers deep into the center of the mountain.

"Is that real?" Eliana asked.

"Live satellite imagery," said General Wade. "You're looking at an unmarked facility dug into the side of a mountain—you can thank Director Badeux and the SOLARPulse-1 telescope array for that. They obviously don't keep the whole place heated. We started looking at temperature fluctuations over the last 72 hours. The area around there changes, but this area remains at a level temperature."

The root system's edges hardened further, and the visual changed to resemble more of a floor plan. There was the entrance, there a series of long hallways, there a kind of thick chamber at its heart. The red highlight extended into another large chamber that must have been even bigger than the underground Translocator lab in which she now stood.

"Sir," Major Bautista said. "It's confirmed. The location maps to the trajectories of the Hawkwood aircraft we originally followed to Europe. I think we've found our man."

Eliana's heart threatened to beat out of her chest. She forced down the sense of elation that rose up from her gut, and as she did, recognized that this feeling wasn't a compound native to her body. It was a foreign invader. And as she recognized this, the joy twisted and sickened and turned.

Her throat constricted. Eliana almost threw up

on her shoes. But she managed to keep control of herself, and instead, swallowed against it, tasting bile on her tongue and burning in her throat.

Eliana remembered a time she got food poisoning from eating undercooked tuna steaks in college. With severe food poisoning, your body's reaction to it is visceral, instinctual, entirely beyond a person's conscious control. She spent that whole night praying to the porcelain gods. Her stomach regurgitated its contents and then some, entirely without direction or conscious effort on her part. Long after the bad food had been purged, her body continued trying to heave it back out again.

That was how she felt about her sympathy for the alien. Like a poisonous food had been planted in her gut, and though it was gone, the symptoms still lingered. Her body still wanted to purge it.

Eliana practically spat the words out of her mouth. "And our alien. He's there, too."

Amon reached back and gently squeezed her suddenly sweaty palm.

"I'll coordinate with the Swiss," General Wade said. "Major Bautista, prepare the strike team."

Major Bautista snapped into a sharp salute. "Yes, sir."

"Amon and Eliana," General Wade said, turning to her. "The two of you together know more about what Lucas and this extraterrestrial are capable of than anyone else here. I need you there, on the ground."

"I'm in," Amon said, nodding once.

"Reuben won't like that," Eliana pointed out.

"I don't have a choice. I'm responsible for whatever Lucas is planning to do with that Translocator. I can't let him hurt anyone else."

Eliana gritted her teeth, and squeezed Amon's hand even harder. He didn't flinch when her nails dug into his skin.

"General," Eliana said, "there's one other person who knows the alien even better than I do."

31

FOR BOTH OUR WORLDS

That morning, two more of Rakulo's warriors had succumbed to the poison and died in agony. He watched them seize and thrash, and then take their final breath mere minutes apart.

Ixchel lost her temper when the white-coated medicine people attempted to wheel the beds, on which the dead bodies of those two warriors lay slack, out of the room. It took Rakulo and Gehro and Yeli all together to hold her back from physically assaulting the poor people, who had shown no malice or ill will.

It was difficult to communicate with the medicine people without Eliana there to translate, but Rakulo lucked out when Reuben wandered into the large metal cave, saw them, and rushed to his aid. Rakulo managed to convey to the wild-haired man, whom he trusted, that the bodies must stay put until the proper prayers and offerings had been made. When Reuben relayed the message, the medicine men left empty-handed.

Just a few hours later they had returned bearing good news, with Reuben at their lead to smooth the approach.

Now, Yeli held one of the Quen's cold hands in both of hers, her round belly pressed up against the raised bed, as one of the white-coated medicine people pushed a large needle into Quen's neck and injected a greenish-yellow liquid into his body.

The big warrior tensed in a slight discomfort, and then he actually relaxed. The black web of veins seemed to quiver below the translucent surface of his skin...and then, astonishingly, impossibly, the blackness began to recede.

The flush of Quen's skin returned to a more natural reddish-brown hue.

Yeli choked out a sob. Tears streamed down her face. She put her ear to Quen's mouth so she could feel his warm breath. He remained unconscious, but it was obvious to see how much easier he was breathing already.

Ixchel's eyes went wide and then she fell to her knees, touched her forehead to the cold floor, and began to mumble a prayer under her breath as she clutched her turquoise and shell necklace in her hands. Gehro went to his knees beside her and also thanked the gods, but in his own quieter way. Gehro rubbed Ixchel's back, which seemed to soothe her somewhat.

Rakulo had seen more shocking things than this. He put his hands together in supplication and thanked each of the medicine people, and Reuben, in his own language. They seemed to get the gist of what he was saying.

When he turned around, Eliana and Amon were standing there with the tall, scar-faced Earth warrior they called "Major."

"Rakulo," Eliana said. "We have some news. Can you talk?"

He nodded and they walked a few paces away. Rakulo stood so he could keep an eye on Quen and the others while they talked.

"We think we figured out where Lucas and Remethiakara are hiding," Eliana said. "We're taking the fight to them."

His hand instinctively went to the scar in his abdomen. "Then I'm coming with you."

Eliana nodded. "I thought you might say that."

Major Bautista said something to Eliana, then grinned at Rakulo.

"He says you're a true warrior." She hesitated for a moment. "And you're very brave, but he wants to get you some real weapons—a gun."

"What is a gun?"

She pointed to the handheld weapon strapped to the major's belt. "Like this."

Rakulo had seen Earth-warriors with the major carrying that weapon and others like it, all projectile weapons that made a spear look docile by comparison.

He gladly returned the major's wicked smile. "I'd like to learn."

The major laughed and clapped Rakulo on the shoulder.

"I'm worried, Rakulo," Eliana confessed to him. "We underestimated the god-pretender before. I'm worried that we're missing something. How do we defeat him?"

Rakulo remembered lying on the cold floor at the top of Xucha's tower. After he lost the fight and the god-pretender stabbed Rakulo in the gut with his own knife, Xucha had left him to die while he turned his focus to saving his eggs. Rakulo had seen Xucha carry the eggs through a dark portal into a secret lair.

The god-pretender had escaped then, but only after he got most of the eggs—the ones Rakulo didn't destroy—to safety.

"Wherever he's hiding on Earth now, I know he won't be far from his eggs."

"Do you think they're with him?"

"Either there, or somewhere nearby for safe keeping. He risked everything to save those eggs on Kakul. He must be doing the same thing here."

"The one thing I don't understand is why he's cooperating with Lucas."

"Maybe Lucas has something Xucha wants? You said he has a Translocator of his own, right?"

Eliana chewed at her lips. "Yeah. That must be it." But she didn't seem convinced.

"Either way, I'm with you." He looked past Eliana at Quen and the others surrounding him, at the rest of his people napping on the floor or pacing around the warehouse restlessly.

Someone had found a ball, and the children were playing with it at the far end of the great cave in an empty corner.

"My people will never be safe as long as the god-pretender is still out there. We have to end this, for both our worlds. Only then will we be able to return home."

Rakulo followed Major Bautista up a few levels to a side room that was heavily guarded by his men. Even more of the large, thickly muscled warriors loitered in and around the room, polishing their weapons on long tables, fitting and refitting helmets and bulky vests, or sharpening long blades that made Rakulo's knife look like his mother's favorite new sewing needle by comparison.

Rakulo struggled with his thoughts, overwhelmed at the sight of all that deadly power together in one room. Throughout his life, obsidian knives and flint spear tips had been scarce, hoarded by the warriors for their hunting weapons, and by families for various household purposes. When the major reached the far end of the room and began unbuckling cases and laying weapons out in a row, Rakulo's curiosity overcame him.

"All the guns. Yours?" he asked, parroting a phrasing Eliana used when she first began to use his language. Direct yes or no questions were easiest to decipher.

The major smiled and nodded, then rattled over a rapid explanation that Rakulo could barely follow. He didn't need to know the meaning of the words, however, to understand that the major was describing the weapons he was laying out on the table, as he pointed to each and let Rakulo heft their metallic weight in his hands.

"This is a p90," he said, dropping a small black weapon, vaguely rectangular in shape, into Rakulo's hands.

It was heavier than it looked. Instinctively, Rakulo pointed the business end at the wall and away from people. The major nodded approvingly. He hefted the rifle to his shoulder, sighting down its barrel as the other men in the room were doing.

The small gun felt awkward. Rakulo set it carefully back down on the table and shook his head.

"No? How about this one?"

He handed Rakulo a smaller gun like the one the major had strapped to his hip, small enough to be held and fired with one hand. The major called it a pistol. It was much lighter than the other, but felt almost puny in his hand. He feared strapping it to his own leg in case he accidentally shot himself. Hard to imagine that such a small thing really do any damage. At least with a knife, he felt comfortable.

The major frowned when Rakulo shrugged and set the pistol down as well.

They went through each of the items arrayed on the table one by one, Rakulo picking up and testing each as he inquired in his halting English about the weapon's purpose. He carefully shied away from anything that the major said went *boom*—accompanied with an expansive gesture.

It wasn't until they reached the melee weapons that Rakulo really began to feel comfortable. The blades they had, even the large ones, were incredibly light and well-balanced. Rakulo eagerly added a larger knife to his retinue to accompany the smaller blade Amon had given him. The new one had a wickedly curved blade and a larger grip, and it suited his personality just fine.

Then they came to several instruments whose purpose he couldn't quite make out. They were all made of smooth, black metals, like the majority of the guns and blade handles. His eyes skipped over most of them and came to rest on the last in the row, a blunt stick about half the length of a well-cut spear, with two prongs at the business end.

The major picked up the weapon, the pale scar along his jawline curving as his lips turned up into a vicious smirk. He extended the black cylinder between them and pressed a button near the base with his thumb. A blue-white crackle of lightning arced between the weapon's prongs.

Rakulo took the lightning stick from the major, swung it experimentally through the air. The major nodded, apparently satisfied that they had found what they had come looking for. Rakulo continued to heft the weapon, testing it as a club, stabbing it out and pressing the button from different fighting positions—crouched, overhead, on one knee, even lying down. He'd found himself in exposed positions fighting Remethiakara before. It was never a bad idea to be comfortable with your weapon in any position.

When he stood back up, the major handed him a belt to secure the lightning stick to his body.

Rakulo inclined his head to Major Bautista. "Thank you."

"Believe me, the pleasure is mine." The major grinned.

Rakulo strapped it over his shoulder. He practiced drawing the weapon from under his left arm several times. Thrusting forward as he drew, Rakulo pressed the button and watched the lightning jump between the prongs.

If they encountered Xucha again, as Eliana believed, this time Rakulo would be able to face his fallen overlord with a weapon equal to the task.

32

NEW EXPERIMENT

"Are you sure it will work?" Lucas asked.

"I am." Remethiakara cast a disdainful glance across the purple and black organism that had grown over the array of computers, rendering the monitors and holograms useless.

He wouldn't say it to Lucas, but this cradle was a hack job by any measure. It was a hack job compared to the elegant lines of his fallen mothership's bridge, and a hack job compared to the balanced system of the tower he'd so painstakingly grown from a seed on Kakul.

That masterpiece had taken a century's cultivated patience to grow, with roots that wound deep into planet's crust, both sustaining and sustained by it.

This was a deformed monster, a combination of human computers and his own people's living biotechnology.

But it would do the trick.

The cradle had finished growing over the computers, and now stretched to consume the platform around which the stabilization sphere was positioned to spin. Tendrils had even grown up to twist around the rings of the sphere itself. A moist sucking sound drifted across the echoey lab as one of the organism's tendrils wrapped around an alloy ring and grafted onto itself. These roots would help channel the energy of the star shard from the cradle to the stabilization sphere. Just like the roots of his tower carried nutrients in to feed the jungle, and carried nutrients back to feed his eggs—a symbiotic relationship—so, too, this cradle would control and feed the monstrosity he'd been forced to create.

It was ugly, but functional. Remethiakara didn't have the luxury of time to worry about beauty, as would be his natural inclination. Not while his offspring were in danger. This all-consuming cradle was the best he could do under the circumstances. Remethiakara turned to Lucas and bared his teeth in imitation of the human smile.

The man glanced fearfully at the platform. Then in a smooth voice, he said, "Let's have a demonstration first, shall we?"

Remethiakara nodded. It was not an unreasonable request. "Do you have a volunteer?"

Lucas swallowed and strode briskly across the lab to the group of spectators gathered there. The men had dispersed for several hours while Remethi-akara worked, but were now gathered again to witness the demonstration of the machine's new abilities.

Lucas argued with the group for a minute. A wiry man with short-cropped blond hair and big ears that stuck out from the side of his head actually laughed in Lucas's face. Lucas scowled and swore back, sending spittle flying to slap across the taller man's cheek. In retaliation, the wiry guy shoved Lucas. A scuffle broke out.

Remethiakara's nostrils fanned open into a genuine smile as he took a deep, satisfied breath. He hid the expression by turning away slightly.

Someone finally broke up the fight. Lucas emerged from the group with blood smeared across his scarred mouth. He crossed the room toward the ramp, fuming and sweating noticeably.

"This better fucking work," he hissed at Remethi-akara. And then, yanking off his perfectly knotted tie, and dropping his crisply ironed overcoat to the ground, Lucas strode up the ramp and took his place on the platform in the middle of the sphere of rings.

Without hesitation, Remethiakara sent a truethought directive to the cradle. The entangled rings began to spin, activating the Translocator. Near his feet next to the cradle, the star shard emitted waves of heat that he felt through his armorsuit. The chitin covering the platform on which Lucas stood twitched and grasped upward, coating Lucas's legs up to his knees.

"You may not enjoy the process, my friend," Remethiakara said, "but it will certainly *work*."

He sent his truethought at the hack job monstrosity and gave the man exactly what he wanted.

A glimpse of terror passed over Lucas's face. Surprisingly, he gained control of his expression after that tiny betrayal, and stared defiantly at the Hawkwood executives across the room.

"Gentleman," Lucas said, his voice steady despite his obvious distress. "My job is not to give you what you want, but what you *need*. You may not agree with my methods, but when I brought you the Translocator plans, you saw my vision and agreed to fund the machine's construction so that you could gain a strategic advantage over the enemy. Now, you will have not only that advantage, but also, if you have the guts to claim it, the ability to create the unstoppable army you've always wanted. Your enemies—"

Lucas's words cut off with a strangling sound as Remethiakara pushed energy from the star shard through the cradle and into Lucas's body, feeding into his molecules until they were vibrating at a high enough frequency to perform mitosis.

The tentacles entwining each spinning ring of

the stabilization sphere flashed with a bright white energy, interlacing like a web around Lucas.

The image of a clean-cut bearded man in a sweat-soaked white shirt wavered as Lucas's body seemed to pull apart, warping and twisting in unnatural directions, like a heat mirage in a desert.

Crackling snaps emanated from the arch. The metal poles vibrated as they channeled the energy of the star shard, emitting a deep hum that ran like a deafening current through the room.

If Lucas was screaming, no one could hear it. Remethiakara watched, fascinated, as Lucas arched his back, contorted his face in pain, cramped his fingers against his abdomen. Then there was a flash of light. Remethiakara lifted his arm up to protect his eyes.

When he lowered his arm and the red spots cleared from his vision, he saw that there were two Lucas's standing in the sphere—nearly exact replicas of each other. Using his truethoughts, Remethiakara reached out and released the cradle's hold on Lucas's feet.

The chitin retracted into the base of the platform.

The two Lucases strode to opposite sides of the platform and inspected their lips in the reflective surface of the rings.

One nodded sadly. His mouth drooped down at one side.

The other took a deep breath and raised his lips in an even, balanced smile.

They walked down the ramp together, one of them limping slightly. Balanced-smile Lucas pulled a pistol from his suit jacket on the floor, and without a moment's hesitation, shot his clone in the head. Blood sprayed into the air, and the dead Lucas crumpled to the floor.

Remethiakara's nostrils widened. He quickly suppressed them, forcing them back to slits with an effort, just in case anyone had caught onto his facial expressions and their true meanings.

Lucas was playing right into his hands. Now if he could just get access to his offspring…

"What did you do that for?" the wiry man demanded.

Lucas shrugged. "I couldn't stand the competition."

No, Remethiakara thought. *You did it because he was a cripple and you wanted nothing more than the satisfaction of murdering your own self-inflicted weakness.*

"Now," Lucas said to the group of executives who, like him, were now smiling broadly even as blood pooled around the body of Lucas on the floor. "You see that I have the guts to claim it. What about you? Will you be remembered for creating the greatest army this world has ever seen? Or will you bow to your cowardice?"

The wiry man clapped Lucas on the back. After an excited discussion, one of the most muscular men in the group volunteered to be the next test subject. When he got into the sphere, they all looked expectantly at Remethiakara.

"I want access to my offspring," he said.

Lucas rolled his eye. "Fine. Yes."

Remethiakara lobbed a truethought experimentally at the cradle. Lucas's hand reached up and scratched an itch in the sharp-edged beard that framed his now even, balanced smile.

"Show me to them."

His eyes went distant for a second before he nodded. "I will. But we have no time to waste." He glanced at the Translocator. "How do I use it?"

Remethiakara considered this, then nodded. There was no harm in letting Lucas believe he still had the upper hand. Remethiakara placed a gauntleted hand on the organism near the star shard and drew energy into himself. The chitin morphed into a flat, perfectly smooth indigo surface at waist level. Lucas set both of his hands delicately onto it, shaking with excitement.

Remethiakara closed his eyes to focus on the image in his mind. In the center of the smooth surface, two large buttons appeared, each inscribed with cutout black letters. He'd taken the letters from what had been printed on the human tech keyboard the organism had consumed. The instructions needed to be familiar and were thus written in their own language, making operation by the humans possible.

Familiar was easier to trust.

One button read "Shift." The other, "Escape."

In each of them, he froze the truethought command corresponding to their functionality, so that anyone could operate it with those buttons.

Remethiakara pointed at the first. "This one will initiate the procedure. The other command will cancel it. Do not use the second command unless it is absolutely necessary. If the procedure is cancelled in the middle, the results will be...unpleasant."

Without hesitation, Lucas reached out and slapped the button labeled "Shift," activating the quantum cloning machine for a second time. The organism coated the legs of the muscular man, who drew a sharp intake of breath, then arched his back as the energy flowed into his body.

All eyes remained fixed on the muscular man as Remethiakara followed Lucas out of the room.

It was strange that he hadn't been able to sense the location of his offspring since he returned from Antarctica. He longed for the faint pulse of their presence. Wherever Lucas kept them, contact with their presence was cut off for him.

The mountainside facility was large, but easy to navigate. There were only four major hallways, two running north to south in parallel, and two east to west, like a giant cross. The living facilities—dorms and bathrooms—were located in the square space in the center where these four halls intersected. As Lucas approached the dorms, he turned sharply right and took Remethiakara down a darkened, unoccupied hall on the east wing, and then down a smaller offshoot in an unused part of the facility.

Or so he'd been led to think. This place was huge, with locking double doors at each segment of the intersections. The guards had discouraged him from exploring the dark, unlit hallways. Without his helmet—which he also sorely missed—Remethiakara's night vision was as poor as his human companions, so he hadn't bothered. Most of Remethiakara's time had been spent in the housing units or in the south wing at the cradle room. He was aware of the northern exit, but had never seen it. It made a sort of sense that the unoccupied eastern wing was where Lucas was taking him now.

Fluorescent bulbs inset lengthwise into the ceiling flickered to life as they passed and then died behind them. The silence between them became brittle. The rap of Lucas's shoes on the tile sounded in the still air.

Remethiakara's tongue kept flicking out to lick his teeth—a sign of irritated anticipation—and his hands had been overtaken by a slight tremor by the time they finally reached a large metal door at the far end of the east wing. Wordlessly, Lucas entered a code, followed by a scan of his eye.

"How have you blocked my senses?" Remethiakara demanded. The anger in his voice didn't come through the translation with the vehemence he would have given it in his own language, but that was probably a good thing. He was shaking with anger. Now that he knew they had been right here the whole time, and he'd never once been given access to them to check on their well-being…it was the height of offense. Who did this little worm think he was?

"We've done no such thing. Just put them in this room and left them."

"At the same temperature as you keep the rest of your rooms?" Remethiakara demanded.

"Well, yes."

The lock clicked and the door fell open an inch. Remethiakara slammed it open, accidentally punching a hole in the drywall as the door struck the wall. He strode into the room, his eyes roving for any sign of his eggs.

The room was some kind of storage closet. Disintegrating brooms were stacked in one corner. Dust-covered shelves lined the room. There, in a small plastic container with the lid on the floor next to it, were his four eggs.

His poor, dried out, dessicated, half-starved unhatched younglings.

"No…"

Remethiakara fell to his knees. His gauntlets hovered over each egg once, twice, searching for the faint pulse that would signal life.

There. A beat, and then two. So faint as to be almost imperceptible. But there.

He sent reassurance in their direction.

"Get out," Remethiakara said, standing and turning to face Lucas.

"What…" Lucas's eyes darted to the eggs, and his eyes widened in realization. "I didn't know. Look, you can clone them now. You built the cradle, I really don't mind if you use it, I—"

Remethiakara unhinged his flexible mandible, thrust out his sharpened back row of teeth, and howled his anger.

"GET OUT!"

33

NERVES

Amon rubbed his sweaty palms on the front of the bulletproof vest. The stiff Kevlar dug into his armpits and chafed as jet engines roared in the background. They had been flying over Europe for a couple hours now, and the closer they got to the Hawkwood hideout, the more nervous Amon became. It was only Eliana's sure, long-fingered hands reaching over to squeeze his forearm that kept him from puking his guts out. He was extremely nauseous, as if the space bends had never let up. He'd felt perfectly fine until he got onto the plane, but maybe Reuben had been right to worry.

There was something even deeper, too. In his heart, he knew that mounting pressure was a familiar foe. Old enemies are sometimes more recognizable than the best of friends.

"This is worse than I ever felt before public

speaking," he confessed to Eliana. "But there's no crowd of reporters waiting for me this time."

"It's just nerves. I'm getting butterflies in my stomach, too. What we're about to do is hardly advisable. But we need you because no one else knows the Translocator blueprints like you do."

She reached down and intertwined her long fingers with his own.

"I'm under no delusions. I would make a terrible soldier," Amon said. "The major is leading the assault and he made it very clear that our job is to stay back until his team has taken the facility."

"So what is it, then?"

Amon reflected. The last time he'd felt this nervous was just before unveiling The Auriga Project, at the gala where Eliana disappeared. The news crews and the large audience present that night made him so nervous he sweated through his suit before he even got on stage.

Deep down, he realized now, he wasn't really frightened of the press so much as scared to death of failure. He would gladly have given his own life rather than fail. Furthermore, he'd taken on a great responsibility when he was granted the funding to build the Translocator for the Lunar Terraform Alliance. If the project failed—if he failed—billions of dollars would have been wasted. No one would hire Fisk Industries for anything again if Amon let them down when it mattered the most. His reputation had been on the line that night, and with it the livelihood of all his employees at the company. Failure with The Auriga Project would have caused his whole legacy—his company, his fortune, his campus—to fall into ruin and collapse in on itself like that fallen pyramid they left behind on Kakul.

What made him so nervous now was that Lucas held that legacy firmly in his hands. If the traitor pulled off whatever evil stunt he was planning, no one would remember what a milestone The Auriga Project had been, even despite the accident. The scientific achievement of quantum teleportation directly to the lunar base would be forgotten, and all the public would remember would be the heinous crime committed by Lucas and Hawkwood—a legacy of fugitive terror and senseless murder. And Amon would be the man who failed to stop him.

"We have to put an end to this," Amon said. "I'm scared sick thinking about what Remethiakara and Lucas are planning to do. I already feel like I have the blood of the people he's murdered on my hands. Whatever perversion they're scheming now will be worse than that, I just know it."

"Don't talk like that. It's never too late to do the right thing."

"I know." Amon glanced down the aisle of the passenger plane, where Agent Moreno was fidgeting restlessly. "But I can't bring Agent Moreno's partner back from the dead. Or anyone else who—"

"Look at me," Eliana said. "The detective chose his job, just like I chose mine and you chose yours. You are *not* responsible for Lucas's actions. Only for your own."

Amon nodded even though, deep down, he remained unconvinced. "What will people think?"

"Who cares what other people think, Amon? You know you're doing what's right. I know you're doing what's right. That's why everyone—from the Marines to the FBI agents to Reuben and Audrey back in the lab—is working with us, planning to put their lives in danger for the same cause."

"Speaking of risking our lives, we must be close now."

Major Bautista had risen from his seat in the front row. He stepped into the cockpit for a moment, then returned to address the cabin.

"We touch down in less than an hour. As far as we can tell, Hawkwood still doesn't know we're coming. Intelligence passed on by General Wade reports that less than a dozen men have been seen coming or going from their location. They use helicopters to shuttle supplies into the mountains, but based on what's arriving we estimate that no more than thirty people are inside. Jet fighters from Ramstein Air Force Base are already en route—they'll patrol a thirty-mile airspace around our location while we make the assault, radio in any news of incoming reinforcements from

Hawkwood, and work to head them off. Any questions?"

Apart from a few throats clearing in the cabin, silence.

"Good. Last chance to take care of your personals, by the way," Major Bautista said, glancing up the row to where the few civilians were sitting—Amon and Eliana, and in front of them Rakulo.

A cold sweat broke out on Amon's neck. His hands began to shake, and he quickly disengaged his fingers from Eliana. "I have to pee," he said, getting up and hurrying to the galley at the back of the plane.

Amon squeezed into the tiny space and flicked the lock shut. Fluorescent lights flickered to life inside the bathroom. He reached down and tried to pick the toilet seat up, fumbled twice. He paused, took three deep breaths through his nose, and then finally managed to lift the toilet seat.

Amon tried to keep the sound of himself retching into the toilet to a minimum as the plane descended.

The bitter aftertaste of bile still coated Amon's palette as they hiked up the icy, windswept back of the mountain. Each of them wore headlamps with the Marines in the front and back of the group carrying large spotlights. The footing was treacherous, but they didn't have far to go.

Despite the terrain, they were hardly in the most dangerous position. Amon would wager that they were barely even in the fight at all. A concussion in the distance sounded hollowly. He felt it in his chest more than heard it, like bass from a concert speaker.

"That must be the major," Eliana said.

Amon nodded. The major had led the first strike team, six squads of twelve men apiece, to storm the front door. Another unit of a similar size provided backup for him. That put them at four to one odds to outnumber how many people they estimated were inside. Meanwhile, the team Amon and Eliana moved with had been directed to find a sneaky route inside through what they suspected were the vent shafts.

Some of Amon's tension had been worked out by the physical exertion of the short hike. Instead, a taut knot of worry now throbbed base of his skull. It was a probably just a tension headache. He did his best to ignore it. "Do you see anything?"

"Intelligence said the entrance would be somewhere in this area. We must be close."

Someone tapped Amon on the shoulder. He glanced behind him where Rakulo walked, his face wrapped in a balaclava and wearing more clothes than Amon had ever seen on the native warrior. Like Amon and Eliana, Rakulo wore a black Kevlar vest beneath his coat, but also carried a shock stick—a kind of modified cattle prod and bludgeoning weapon—that looked like it could do a lot of personal damage. Rakulo also carried a bowie knife large enough to embarrass the crocodile hunter himself.

Rakulo pulled a flashlight from his pocket and jerked his chin up ahead. He aimed the spotlight uphill to the right, and in the beam of the spotlight, wispy white plumes rose out of a metal grate for a few feet before being cut away by the cold night winds.

There was no loose snow on the grate, but the crossbars seemed coated in a permanent layer of ice.

"Huh," Amon said. "Less steam than I expected a MegaPower core to require."

Eliana looked at him, her face suddenly pale. They both knew that a lack of steam meant that the nuclear capability was only running as a backup. The *other* source of power must already be in use.

Another concussion drummed through his intestines, followed by the distant *rat-tat-tat rat-tat-tat* of machine gun fire—a lot of it, directed in controlled bursts.

"Piece of plan?" Rakulo asked in his broken English.

Amon shrugged. Eliana shook her head. "I don't know."

Ahead of them, a few men at the top of their unit

took turns slamming the butts of their rifles into the ice-coated vent grate. The ice cracked and began to chip away.

Rakulo hurried up to the front to help. By the time Amon and Eliana had reached the vent, men were working at the exposed bars with laser cutters in their gloved hands. Finally, one of them lifted the grate away and dropped it in the snow.

Rakulo peered over the edge into the black pit of the vent shaft. It slanted down at a 45 degree angle parallel to the downward slope of the mountain up which they'd hiked.

Holding the shock stick close to his body, Rakulo hopped in and slid feet first down the shaft.

Amon directed his thoughts at his stomach while a dozen of the Marines cursed and jumped in after the brazen Mayan warrior. Convinced that he had nothing left in his stomach to puke up, Amon helped Eliana into the shaft and then clambered in himself.

34

BY DARKNESS

Remethiakara decided that he'd been patient for long enough. The time for waiting was over.

He'd spent the last twelve Earth hours rehydrating the two remaining eggs that clung desperately to life. Getting nutrients to the embryos without a proper feeding system was difficult, but not impossible. They needed to be fed if they were going to make it through the night, so it wasn't like he had much choice. He'd known that from the moment Lucas stepped out of the room. Still, he fretted over the smaller of the two eggs. It wasn't perfectly symmetrical anymore—the shift out of zero G probably did that—and it had taken on the greenish-white veins that often led to premature hatching of a stillborn. Only a small percentage of the hardiest younglings survived such an ordeal.

One thing at a time, he chided himself.

It was the middle of the night now. With any luck, his companions were fast asleep, and he would encounter no resistance. He'd often used this tactic on Kakul, sneaking through the Wall to check on the feeding systems he'd built into the soil of that biospace. It was easier at night; the humans saw less and asked fewer questions.

Remethiakara lifted the plastic bin in front of him like a basket. Liquid sloshed softly in the bottom of the container. The water was a handspan deep and made for an awkward burden, but it was nothing his armorsuit couldn't handle. Enough cloth padding had been stuffed around the young egg so that it wouldn't knock against the side of the container as he walked. Thankfully, now that they were properly hydrated, the younglings' shells had become somewhat more flexible as well. The second egg, he left behind. It was well concealed and safe enough, for now. This smaller one with the green veins was a higher risk, and couldn't wait.

He stepped out of the storage closet and into the dark hallway. Once again, the overhead lights flickered to life in his immediate area. As he moved, the lights ahead blazed to life and those behind guttered out, so it felt like he was in a bubble of exposed light, blinded to what was in the dark mere feet ahead of him through the glare. When he'd gone out at night on Kakul, Remethiakara still had his helmet, which provided a function that improved his poor night vision. When he got clear of this mess, the first thing he planned to do was form himself a new helmet.

Remethiakara encountered no one until he reached the dormitory area at the center of the floor plan, and the lighting returned to normal. He stopped.

Cheering, shouts, and the clink of glass knocking together drifted from the direction of the mess hall.

That was odd. There was no way that so much noise could be made by so few people. Had more arrived while he was tending to his offspring?

Then it hit him—the cradle's new cloning ability. In the last half a day, Lucas and his friends must have been very busy playing with their new toy.

But what did it matter to him? He didn't care how many of them there were, they couldn't stand against him with a star shard. Besides, a party drowning in liquor, as this one undoubtedly was, would provide even more of a distraction than a sound sleep, especially in this large of a building. By the time they figured out what was going on, he would be long gone.

He strode on, increasing his pace as he took the long way around the central housing unit to avoid the mess hall. At the far end of the southern wing, flanking the door to the cradle room, two guards were slumped in chairs and snoring. A dozen brown bottles were lined up like dead soldiers on the floor beside them. They were still asleep when he pushed the door open with the plastic bin. One of the guys snorted awake as the door swung shut behind him.

The cradle was farther along than even he expected. He listed to a stop as he stared at the now enclosed platform.

They certainly *had* got a fair amount of play out of their new toy, hadn't they? The tentacles now wound completely around sphere of concentric alloy rings. The purple organism had grown between them so that it made a completely enclosed sphere, save for an arch-shaped gap in its center.

"The time for waiting is certainly over."

"What's that, sir?"

Remethiakara turned, not realizing he'd projected the words aloud through his suit. The bleary-eyed guard was standing in the doorway.

"Nothing."

"Sorry, sir, uh…Mr. Lamotte said no one was supposed to be in here without him."

"Yes!" Remethiakara said. The guard blinked. He was young—barely more than a kid, with tattoos along his neck and a three-day growth of black stubble. Remethiakara could tell he was getting uncomfortable because his words were being projected from the armorsuit, but his "mouth" wasn't moving. He opened and closed his mandibles with the next words to give the child a sense of confidence. "Of course, you're absolutely right. I'll get him. Watch this."

Remethiakara set the plastic bin with his youngling down inside the enclosed sphere of the cradle, feeling a sizzle flicker through his body as he did so. His heart leapt with joy knowing that proximity to the cradle would comfort the youngling. Its heartbeat increased in pace. It could sense it, too.

The cradle was another feeling entirely. The sensation that organism transmitted was sharp, hollow, and insatiably hungry. Unchecked, it would grow like a cancer to devour this mountain. Fortunately, he didn't plan to be gone that long.

"But I don't—" the guard said, biting off his words.

Remethiakara strode past him and hurried down the hallway, not pausing to listen to what the kid had to say. As he turned the corner, approaching the cacophony drifting from the mess hall, he saw that kid had resumed his seat, ramrod stiff and pale.

After peering into the mess hall and determining that Lucas was not to be found in that knot of sweating bodies, he found Lucas's room and knocked lightly.

A woman's voice drifted through the door. "No, come back..."

"Just a minute," Lucas's voice said. "Damn. Where'd I put my shirt? Ah, whatever."

The door swung open. A rancid waft of sex and sweat washed over Remethiakara, but he didn't let his natural revulsion show. "Maintenance."

"Maintenance? What are you on about?"

"The cradle needs maintenance. Come with me."

"Can't it wait?"

"No."

Lucas sighed. "Fine. All right. One second."

The door shut in his face. Remethiakara waited patiently.

When the door opened up again, Remethiakara saw the back of a broad-shouldered, voluptuous woman wrestling another man down into the tangle of sheets. For a moment, he thought it was Lucas, but then Lucas stepped into the hall, wearing sneakers and a white tank top, and snapped the door shut.

He leered at Remethiakara, who took off at a fast walk, forcing Lucas to jog to keep up.

An annoyed tone replaced the man's lustful expression. "You planning to tell me what this is about?"

"Maintenance. You need to learn how the cradle works in order to keep it from getting out of control. It requires significant upkeep."

Lucas's brain skipped right over the upkeep aspect. "Out of control? The hell do you mean, 'out of control'?"

Remethiakara shrugged. "You sought to distort the quantum disentanglement properties of your machine so that it became capable not just of transporting matter, but of replicating it. This is the side effect; the organism itself replicates. While I was working, I looked into your knowledge databases—there is an extraordinary tool called the internet your machines all had access to, quite remarkable in its way although very much a manual research process—anyway, there I found reference to what your doctors call 'cancer.' Have you heard of this cancer?"

Lucas was just staring at him now, the whites of his eyes rapidly widening. He flared his nostrils, but unlike Remethiakara's people's reactions, that was not one of pleasure. Heedless, Remethiakara barreled on.

"The organism is like a cancer. It will replicate itself and consume everything in its path to feed it as it grows, unless you do the work required to contain it. First, if you want to continue to use the cloning abilities, you must make sure the cradle has enough energy to sustain it. The star shard has a way of protecting itself, and won't let itself be consumed beyond a certain point. Soon, you'll have to switch the cradle back over to the nuclear reactor. That will work for a time, if you create a feedback loop that siphons some of the power, in the form of electricity, directly into the cradle. But even radioisotopes deplete eventually. If I had time, I could build a truly symbiotic system—much like I designed on Kakul, you see. The people there helped me maintain it. But even that would take a decade or two to construct.

We have to make do with what we have in the mean-time. There is much to learn, and very little time. Now, the first thing to understand is that the cradle does not react well to fire. Next…"

The tall man's reactions were slow, but drastic. First, he shook with anger. He opened his mouth several times to interject, but Remethiakara ignored him, prattling on over top of him each time he tried to speak. Then Lucas became very pale and quiet, obviously considering how best to react to this over-bearing situation. Remethiakara made sure not to give him an opportunity to speak until they were nearing the guards at the door of the cradle room, who were more attentive now and had pushed the beer bottles back behind their chairs—but not completely out of sight.

"Sir," the young guard said. "I told him no one was allowed in there without—"

"You're both relieved of duty," Lucas snapped. "Get the hell out of here. We have work to do and I don't want anyone else snooping around."

Taking a deep breath, Remethiakara strode into the cradle room, headed for the plastic bin. Lucas came into the room behind him, mumbling, "Work to do? What the hell did I say that for?"

"Shut the doors, please," Remethiakara said, using an academic tone, which he learned on the internet would put modern humans like Lucas off their guard and make others complacent. Lucas obeyed, his expression still vague from his bender. "Now, here's the crux of the situation."

Still introspective, Lucas came as Remethiakara requested, glancing at the sphere of rings. "My god, it's nearly woven itself together hasn't it?" He tilted his head to one side. "Did you intend this?" Lucas let a hand drift out and rub against the inside of the sphere just a few feet over his head. His fingers came away sticky with the residue the cradle gave off as it replicated. He wiped his fingers on his pants.

With Lucas distracted, Remethiakara gingerly pushed the cloth covering to the side of the bin. The cloth came away from the wet shell of the egg with no issue. However, as he lifted it, the egg broke and splintered in his gauntleted hands.

Remethiakara pulled energy from the cradle and poured it into the youngling within the fracturing eggshell. The air crackled with electricity. *Not yet, not yet*, he begged silently.

The shell of the egg held. The shape of the creature could be seen through an oily film. It stilled as Remethiakara's wishes flooded into its nervous system.

"What's the matter?" Lucas said, obviously concerned.

"You must see this. It is imperative for what you must learn. Please. Come quickly."

Lucas looked as if he wanted to shake his head

and back away, but he overcame that urge and knelt down next to the egg.

The door to the cradle room smacked into the wall as it opened. The young guard stepped into the doorway—in spite of his nerves, fulfilling his blasted duty as a guard. "Mr. Lamotte? Some people are poking around the facility at surface level. I was told to notify you."

The eggshell cracked fully. A pale, thin arm reached out and reached haphazardly around in the cold air. When it found the surface of the chitin that coated the platform, it dug in deep, and the tremors subsided. The arm was withdrawn a moment later.

Though Lucas made as if to stand again and respond to the guard's prompting, Remethiakara thrust out one arm and seized him by the throat. Lucas's eyes popped as he turned to look at Remethiakara—shocked. Realization dawned in his eyes, but by then it was too late.

Remethiakara heaved his arm forward and slammed Lucas's head into the hard chitin coating the floor of the platform, breaking his nose against the rigid material with a sickening crunch, and knocking him unconscious in a single swipe.

The egg cracked at the same time, and out rolled a pale creature in a segmented ball. It unfurled into a long body with pincer claws on its front arms, four eye stalks, a long tail that deepened to red at the tip.

The creature parted its mandibles and let out a joyous trill.

"Beautiful," Remethiakara breathed. It was farther along in its development than he expected—farther along even than he dared to hope. Perhaps the brief but intense proximity with the mothership's stalwart nature had strengthened it; perhaps it was the star shard's power he'd infused it with as a last-second reflex to keep the egg safe. Whatever the reason, he was glad, and a deep joy suffused him.

Remethiakara reached out and drew a blade across the big artery in Lucas's broken neck. Blood spilled down into the organism-coated floor of the platform.

"Drink, youngling," Remethiakara said. The chitin beneath Lucas's unconscious, half-clothed form picked up some of Lucas's blood and held it in a small bowl at the level of the creature's mandibles.

His youngling slurped at the bowl greedily.

When it finished, it fell on Lucas's exposed neck and ripped into his skin, its fresh-hewn claws sharp as they would ever be.

At that moment, a thunderous explosion shook the mountain. Dust rained down from the high stone ceilings. A gurgle escaped Lucas's throat the youngling tore into his flesh.

A heavy thud came from near the door. The guard hunched in a low squat, clutching the open door in one hand, the door frame in the other.

A second explosion rocked the room. The guard stumbled and splayed to the dusty floor. He glanced between Remethiakara and the long hall, where red and white lights had begun to twirl.

Remethiakara descended on the guard before the boy had time to push himself to his feet. His neck snapped like a dry twig.

Remethiakara swept past his body. The other guard who had been stationed outside the door was long gone. Remethiakara sprinted into the red and white flashing hallway, headed back to the east wing to retrieve the remaining egg.

The explosions couldn't have been good news, but he didn't plan on waiting around to find out what they were.

35

MOONLESS NIGHT

The vent shaft was as dark as the sea on a moonless night. Rakulo and the soldiers were the first to dive into the inky black deep, their agile bodies making barely a splash.

Eliana came next, less agile and more clumsy, clambering and banging on the tin walls of the shaft. Amon's warm presence and rapid breathing followed her like a lifeline as they struggled to keep themselves from plunging too quickly down the sharp angle of descent.

Eventually the shaft made a hard right and narrowed as it continued to delve into the mountain. Goosebumps broke out on the skin of her neck and arms as the bulky polyester of the heavy winter coat rubbed up against the narrowing walls. Then the metal vent enclosure gave way to a carved stone chimney—even less forgiving than the flimsy sheet tin had been.

They caught up with the soldiers then, the last man only ten or fifteen feet ahead of her in the shaft. No one spoke. In silence, they continued to crawl forward until the sound of gunshots interrupted their dusty shuffling. Their sense of urgency took on new meaning as shouted orders and the sharp, deafening *rat-tat-tat-tat* of automatic rifles resounded through the stone. As they moved forward, the sounds grew louder, echoed more, as presumably the stone walls thinned.

"Now I wish we'd stayed home," Eliana whispered.

"Too late to turn back now," Amon replied breathlessly.

Whispers trickled from the front of the line.

"Found an exit," the soldier in front of her passed on the message. "It leads into what looks like a small office. Bulldog squad is sticking with you, ma'am, while the rest move ahead."

Eliana nodded her silent thanks to the soldier. She was glad to be in the back, coming in the sneaky way, instead of storming the front door like the major and Agent Moreno.

But her hands still shook in the darkness, and small rivulets of sweat tracked down her cold neck. Only Amon's presence behind her kept her from curling into the fetal position and staying there until the sounds of gunfire abated.

She wasn't allowed the luxury. One by one, the men dropped through a rusty grate that had been fixed into the floor a century ago. The stone was only an few inches thick there—someone had obviously spent a lot of time or money to carve out this tunnel as a fresh air intake.

The four soldiers from Bulldog squad lowered Eliana and Amon into the office. The room was a patchwork of shadows, hung with dust, and piled with old wooden furniture and heavy metal stools. A chalkboard spanned one wall, running the length of the room. A path through the dusty old furniture had been cleared from where she stood to the door, which opened into a hall that refracted with flashing red and white lights. Sounds of fighting cracked down the hall, breaking up the steady ululation of an ancient klaxon alarm she was only now picking out from the rest of the racket. The soldiers dashed out into the gunfight two at a time, shooting as they moved and then taking cover behind stacked boxes or in depressed door frames as bullets ricocheted down the corridor.

After a minute, it was only Bulldog squad—four soldiers—Rakulo, and Amon in the room with her.

"Two at the front, two at the back," said the soldier who seemed to be in charge—the man that had helped her into the room. "You three stay between us. Got it?"

Numbly, Eliana nodded.

Two of them dashed into the hall at a forty-five degree angle, zigzagging around trash, debris, spent smoke grenades, and more old furniture. Twenty yards up, they hit the ground, taking cover behind a mahogany desk, the scroll top of the antique already chewed up by bullets.

"Your turn," the remaining soldier said—he had a sharp chin, and brown green eyes in a tan face. "Try to keep your head down. Ready? Go!"

Eliana took a deep breath, and ran, crouching low, trying to make as small a target of herself as possible. Something sharp pinged off the ceiling over her head. She screamed and froze. Amon put one hand at the small of her back and shoved her forward.

Eliana darted to the wall behind the flimsy cover of the mahogany desk and made herself as small as possible. Amon piled in next to her and then Rakulo. Contrary to how she felt, Rakulo seemed alert and calm, not even sweating. He shrugged out of the winter jacket and drew the bowie knife from inside of it, rising up slowly to peer over the desk.

Rat-tat-tat-tat.

Rakulo ducked back down and flashed her a feral grin as bullets thunked into mahogany. Splinters went flying, several of them drifting down into her hair.

Eliana's whole body shook uncontrollably. Glancing at Amon, she saw that he was in even worse shape. His face was pale and drawn, his skin drenched in sweat. He wiped his hair out of his eyes and panted heavily.

The two pairs of soldiers from Bulldog squad made incomprehensible hand signals to each other. Then the pair next to them shoved off the wall and sprinted toward a recessed doorway another twenty yards up. Risking a glance over the desk for herself, Eliana saw that a four-way intersection lay about the same distance beyond that doorway. The Marines were in the process of securing that intersection. Bulldog squad had fallen behind to help Eliana and Amon, and they were trying to catch up.

As the front pair reached the recessed doorway, a sharp *crack* split the air. Shards of glass and the brains of the first soldier splashed against the left wall. A lanky mercenary with a red crew cut kicked the door open and stepped through, simultaneously pumping another round into the shotgun. A white horse head logo on his chest was splattered with red. His combat boots crunched over glass.

The remaining Marine kicked at the knee of the Hawkwood mercenary. It popped as the lanky man's knee gave out. The Marine fell on the redhead, screaming. They got tangled up and tripped over the body of the other soldier.

A strong hand yanked Eliana to the ground. Rakulo sprang up and heaved the small knife overhead. The blade thunked into the base of the Hawkwood man's neck. Then there was gunfire as the Marine, who had pulled out his handgun, managed to squeeze off a round. The mercenary went still.

Rakulo hurried over and helped the lucky Marine up. They dragged their fallen comrade into the room, leaving a trail of glistening blood on the floor.

Rakulo beckoned for Eliana and Amon to join them. They ran, staying close together, leaning on each other for support. He directed her when she flinched. She held him when he stumbled, careful to step over the blood slick.

The two soldiers in the rear advanced to the mahogany desk. Then Rakulo and the living soldier moved to the corner. Eliana and Amon followed. They moved like this, leap frogging from desk to doorway, from crate to corner, from one questionable cover to the next through the deafening noise and dizzying twirl of red lights until they reached the intersection.

While the Marines provided cover fire, they passed through the intersection and paused for a breath when they were safe on the other side.

Eliana saw that the Marines had managed to

construct a hasty barricade of doors and overturned tables, and were slowly advancing with it down a broad, low ceilinged hallway where the majority of the fighting seemed to be concentrated. Presumably —her sense of direction had completely abandoned her by this point—that was also the direction in which Major Bautista's force was making their assault, effectively pinning the enemy between them. It was slow going for the Marines. They fought for every inch. The hallways where the battleground centered were poorly lit, half of the fluorescent bulbs set into the ceilings already shot out, with loose wires and bulbs and brackets hanging down.

"I thought Major Bautista said there were only a few people bunkered down in here," Amon said. "This looks like a goddamn army!"

The air grew thick with bullets again as the enemy returned fire. One of the soldiers in Bulldog squad shoved Eliana and Amon and Rakulo down the hall when a flash bang was lobbed in their direction.

When they were clear, Rakulo stepped close to her and asked, "Where is Xucha hiding?"

Eliana had a brief moment to be surprised to hear him speak in English. "I'm not sure," she said. "But he must be here somewhere."

Rakulo and the three guards still accompanying them peered warily around him into the darkened rooms as they passed.

"We need to find the Translocator," Amon said. "And Lucas." He had recovered his breath somewhat, but was still twitchy.

"Wherever it is, I'll bet that's where Remethiakara is, too."

"What if we went around?"

They moved onward into the large underground facility, away from the fighting. In this direction, the offices gave way to what looked more like dormitories, with kitchen facilities and bathrooms interspersed. It was an efficient design that centralized the utilities and built everything else around that core.

Eliana lost track of time for a minute as she puzzled over the construction of the place. As an archaeologist, she was used to evaluating floor plans of strange buildings. She'd already built a mental map in her mind of this one. If this one was symmetrical, it would have the arm they came down, the arm where the Marines engaged Hawkwood, and another arm right about...

They turned the corner and she saw it—another wing identical to the first. Only this one was completely blackened. About fifty yards up, she saw a flash of light moving with a figure in it. The figure disappeared around the corner.

Rakulo must have seen it, too, for his breath drew in sharply and he flatted himself against the wall. He caught her eyes.

"Don't do anything stupid," she said. "You know he's dangerous."

"How can I ever forget that?" Rakulo thumbed the scar on his abdomen, visible since he'd dropped his winter coat back by the vent exit. He unhooked the shock stick on his belt and thumbed the button. A jagged streak of blue lightning jumped between the nodes at the striking end. "This time, Xucha is not the only one holding lightning in his hands."

Eliana was blinking at the sudden switch to his own language for those two sentences when someone shouted, "Eliana, look out!"

Amon, who had never gone more than two paces outside of Eliana's reach since they arrived, stepped forward, wrapped his arms around his wife, and twisted, putting himself between her and the danger.

There was a small pop, and something whistled by her head. Another two soft pops sounded.

She hunched up and looked down at her navel. Amon's hands, clasping hers, phased out and became semi-transparent, wavering in her vision like a heat mirage. Her own arms and clothes did the same. She could see her own footprints in the dusty floor through her shoes. Then she felt a cold burn, sharp and sudden, pass *through* her body where her left shoulder met her neck.

Microscopic needles spread like fire across her skin.

The Marine, who stood in front of her now,

staring in the direction of the shooter and bending his knees slightly, was not so lucky.

The bullet that had passed through Amon, and due to contact with him, through her, struck the Marine in the eye.

His head snapped back.

He stumbled against the wall and sank to the floor, lifeless.

Her arms and clothes and Amon's hands snapped back into solidity.

Rakulo yanked Eliana and Amon sideways into a cutout in the hallway lined with wooden benches bolted to the wall. The alcove provided a slim berth against which to shelter themselves from sight of their attackers.

"Amon! Amon, are you okay?"

"I'm fine," he insisted, pushing her hands away. "At least, I think so."

She reached out and put her hand against his cheek. His skin was clammy and pale. "We've gotta get you out of here. Reuben was right, you never should have left home."

A firm shake of his head was interrupted by a sudden tremor that crawled along his whole body. Amon groaned, his neck muscles tensing as he twisted in two directions at once.

Literally, two directions at once—half his molecules twisting left, the other half twisting right, in a confusing blur of motion.

He clenched Eliana's hand so hard she thought he would break her wrist. She squeezed back, gritting through the pain. "Breathe," she said. "I'm here with you. Breathe."

He forced air through his nose. After a second, the tendons in his neck relaxed slightly. The visual heat mirage stopped.

The taller of the two Marines, enraged upon seeing their comrade killed, lifted his rifle to his shoulder and sprayed bullets down the hall in the direction of the shooter. He roared as he held down the trigger.

A second later, his clip snapped on empty.

Before he could draw his sidearm, a dark-haired man with a perfectly trimmed beard leaned out of a room—one of the dormitories—with a small pistol in his hand, the silver barrel of the gun extended by the long black tube of a silencer affixed to the front.

"Watch out!" Eliana called. But it was too late.

Lucas pulled the pistol's trigger twice. His aim was perfect, landing two shots in the soldier's neck, in the gap between his body armor and helmet.

The soldier groaned, lifted his own sidearm from the holster on his leg, and fired back. His shots went wild, pinging off the floor and walls. Lucas disappeared back into the room, unharmed.

As if that wasn't enough of a shock to her system, a half dozen men came around the corner at that moment—redheads with crew cuts, she saw.

"Impossible," Eliana whispered before pressing her body against Amon and Rakulo in the corner.

Three short, controlled bursts of rifle fire sounded, and the injured soldier fell to the ground.

The last soldier with them checked the magazine on his carbine and set his jaw. "I'll cover you," he said. "Go."

All Eliana could do was stare. But Rakulo grabbed her wrist in one hand, Amon's in another, and yanked them both in the opposite direction, toward the darkened hallway.

As they turned around, Eliana risked one glance back. The last soldier fired from the alcove they'd been using as cover.

Six identical redheads with crew cuts, wearing the same face as the man she'd seen killed not ten minutes before.

"Am I hallucinating?" Amon asked. "Or did those men all look the same?"

"You're not seeing things," Eliana said. "I think we just figured out what Lucas is doing with the Translocator."

"Quantum cloning?" Amon muttered. But he was already so pale that his skin tone didn't change, though she felt that hers might have. "Jesus."

As the gunfire ceased, they cut into the darkened hallway and increased their pace.

36

FIGHTING SHADOWS

Rakulo stalked down the darkened hallway, with Eliana and Amon following close behind.

He walked in a pattern, taking several careful steps, then crouching low to the ground and cautiously using the lightning stick to illuminate the area around him. Amon and Eliana gripped each other's arms and staggered forward into the glow of the light, then paused for breath. Rakulo moved forward again, avoiding sharp corners and other random objects crowded into the shadows.

Like the hallway into which they'd first arrived, the floor was slick with dust and smelled of mold. There were crates and chairs and furniture stacked haphazardly against both walls. It almost seemed like the people who once inhabited this strange cave had gotten it into their heads to start packing up to leave, only to be forced to abandon the place in a hurry—like his people had been forced to abandon their home in a hurry. Rakulo wondered what terror had chased these people away, and what they'd done to deserve it—if anything.

He'd often imagined his people packing up and leaving the village of Kakul behind. In his mind, it was a balmy morning, flooded with sunshine as the people he loved gathered around him. The mood was joyous and infused with hope, for they would be embarking on a journey to a better place.

But that dream had been stolen from him.

Rage boiled into his body and sharpened Rakulo's focus. He'd come here for a purpose. Now was not the time to get distracted by a child's idle daydreams.

After they had gone about twenty feet into the darkness, the overhead lights began to flicker on in their vicinity. Since Rakulo had seen someone moving through the darkness and bringing the lights on earlier, he expected this would happen eventually and was prepared for it.

Rakulo reached up with his lightning stick. A blue spark jumped, the bulb burst and the light went out.

"Good thinking," Eliana said.

Something rustled nearby...a vaguely familiar skittering, no louder than a whisper.

"Shhh." Rakulo put one finger over his lips and

held an open hand out toward Eliana, pleading for silence and stillness.

She obeyed. Even Amon, whose every inhalation seemed painful now, gripped his breath between his teeth for a moment.

As they held still, something crawled forward on the opposite side of the darkened hall, gliding under a table that had chairs stacked atop it, then navigating around a wooden crate that propped open the door to an empty room. It was just a tiny shadow, low to the ground and only visible in outline.

But even in the darkness, it was a shape Rakulo recognized—smaller than the ones that had attacked the village, but many-legged, with two pincer claws held up above the ground in front, and a tail that arched over its body in the rear. The creature was only as long as the distance from the tip of his fingers to his elbow.

At the sight of the vile creature, memories of the injustice done to his people filled his mouth with the taste of ash. He tightened his grip on the lightning stick.

But something made him pause.

A missing link that had been bothering him since that last-ditch effort to fend off the scorpions finally fell into place: Xucha and the scorpions were *connected.*

The scorpions came in through the holes he'd made in the Wall. Presumably, they had always been there, but it was only once Xucha had been chased away that they came forth.

Without their God, they had no one to care for them … no one to feed them. They were hungry.

He grudgingly admitted that they didn't initially attack the village in cold blood. At first, they came looking for food. Their first victims were the maize stalks in the fields, not his people. It was the scorpions who were responsible for the death of the maize plants. They were churning up the roots, looking for something to eat. Of course they were. There was only desert beyond the Wall.

And when they couldn't find what they were looking for out there...they went after Rakulo's people.

No.

They had gone after the turkey leg, and accidentally hurt someone. Then *his* people had retaliated.

Maybe these scorpions didn't come to their village with a harmful intent after all. Maybe they weren't evil.

What were they, then? Most likely, they were just animals. But he knew one thing for certain—they were Xucha's animals.

And that meant that Rakulo could give no quarter.

Rage burst through the dam of his careful control.

Rakulo stalked into position, then silently heaved

back with the lightning stick. The jagged line of blue energy crackled by his ear.

He thrust the weapon down as the pale, segmented body of the creature turned. It came up on its hind legs and hissed at him, vicious and unafraid despite its obvious size disadvantage.

A black leg stepped in front of the lightning stick before the arc of energy could touch the creature. For a moment, Rakulo thought it was Eliana, and a momentary pang of betrayal stopped his heartbeat.

Then he looked up, and realized he was staring not into Eliana's eyes—but into the face of the god-pretender.

Rakulo gritted his teeth in both surprise and battle lust. Xucha wore no helmet! The skin of his face was an iridescent shade of rough purplish green, with slits for nostrils and surprisingly human-like eyes. The god-pretender's lipless mouth twisted in anger.

Instead of frying the scorpion creature, Rakulo's weapon seemed to fuse to the black material coating Xucha's leg—what he'd honestly always thought, until this moment, was his skin. From the point of impact, a wave of energy peeled up the god-pretender's body, blue-white lightning crawling over the black cloth that clung to Xucha's humanoid limbs, starting where the lightning stick made impact and moving in a flash to his neck and fingertips.

Smoke rose from Xucha's body in a small cloud, refracting the flash of light. Xucha hissed with pain and fell back as the scorpion beneath him darted for cover.

In the flash of light, Rakulo saw that the god-pretender was protecting something in his gloved hand—one of his eggs!

Rakulo danced forward, battering Xucha about the body and arms with the staff of the lightning stick in an effort to force him to drop the egg, and perhaps even immobilize him. He didn't know what the lightning stick had just done, exactly, but the pain in Xucha's face was obvious, and Rakulo pressed his advantage with all his might.

Rakulo had never been a match for Xucha in hand to hand combat. A sharp pain shot through his abdomen as his strikes began to pull the wound Xucha had given him open again. Rakulo ignored the pain. He swung the lightning stick up at Xucha's chin and was thrown off balance as the god-pretender dodged him.

Xucha took three staggering steps backward, and seemed to regain his breath, to settle into a lower gravity.

Rakulo glanced over and saw that Amon and Eliana were retreating back the way they had come. That was good.

He turned back in time to see Xucha make a blade with his hand and slice down through the air, a motion that Rakulo had seen decapitate men in the past.

Instinctively, he tensed.

Nothing happened, and Xucha's face twisted in rage.

Then he came barreling at Rakulo.

They exchanged blows in the near darkness. Unable to see his attacker, Xucha landed a vicious kick to the back of Rakulo's knee that sent him to the ground, and won him a foot to the nose.

He rolled away and came up facing Xucha, blood dripping down his face.

Shifting the egg to one arm, the god-pretender blocked and parried his attacks with one arm better than any of his warriors.

As they exchanged blows, Rakulo came to a second split-second realization—although the lightning stick seemed to have disabled some of Xucha's powers, the god-pretender was stronger than Quen, and faster than Yeli, even with only one hand to fight. But the lightning stick had done something—his unnatural speed and strength was certainly diminished from their last fight, as was his seemingly magical control of invisible deadly forces.

Encouraged by this realization, Rakulo roared and pressed forward, swinging the lightning stick with abandon at the darkest shadow in the dim hall.

He landed three blows around Xucha's head. A

sideways strike at shoulder-level forced him off balance.

The god-pretender stumbled back, tripping over a small crate.

Rakulo dropped the lightning stick and drew his knife. He went in for a killing blow, slicing down with the blade at Xucha's neck with an overhand motion.

On his descent, the baby scorpion launched itself up at his face, legs extended.

Rakulo flinched back and redirected his attack.

The blow that was intended for Xucha speared the overgrown arachnid straight through its soft, young abdomen.

Xucha, unbalanced and unable to prevent Rakulo's attack, let out a primal scream of rage. Not the irritated hiss of before, but a mental howl of infinite grief bound in a vice of white-hot fury that stabbed straight into Rakulo's mind, bypassing his eardrums completely.

The scorpion's body twitched and writhed on the end of the blade. Sensing his advantage, Rakulo gripped the pincer claws and head of the bug in one hand, and ripped the knife through its body and poisonous tail, eviscerating it.

Xucha's scream bent into a choked snarl. He launched himself up, like the scorpion had, and reached for Rakulo's throat.

Rakulo danced back and struck his head—hard—

on a doorframe behind him that he hadn't seen in the darkness.

Xucha took the advantage, and with his free hand, drove his fist into Rakulo's face. The mottled, shadowy greys of the unlit hallway tumbled end over end. Rakulo slashed blindly into the darkness with the knife, and made contact with something before he fell.

Rakulo braced for continued blows to rain down, but something must have changed the god-pretender's mind.

By the time Rakulo staggered to his feet, Xucha was stumbling away down the darkened, crowded hallway with his egg in his arms. Rakulo took aim to throw the knife at him, but it was too dark to be sure of his target. He could just as easily hit Eliana, or a wooden crate. Wood scraps scattered across the floor as Xucha hurried. Boxes tumbled when he stumbled into them in his escape. The alien finally emerged into the light at the intersection. A deep gash on his face seeped blackened blood and the egg was carefully cradled like a ball in his arm.

Had he fought me with one arm? Rakulo thought, incredulous. *And he still managed to outmatch me and escape with his precious egg.*

Realizing he was still gripping it in his hand, Rakulo dropped the bloody, still-twitching body of the scorpion to the shadowed floor. He bent down and cast about for the lightning stick until he found it. Thumbing the spark of energy on, Rakulo pushed the button into the "hold" position and used it to look around. Amon and Eliana were nowhere to be found.

If he didn't finish this fight, his people would never truly be safe. Rakulo was determined to kill the god-pretender or die trying. He used the lightning stick to light his pursuit.

37

CORNERED

Remethiakara worked his way carefully around the block of dorms, choking back his grief and occasionally wiping away the stream of blood that seeped from the deep cut on his cheek, shaking the warm liquid carelessly to the floor.

His other hand was wrapped tightly around the egg—his last hope.

If Remethiakara was to have the slightest chance to rebuild a life for himself and his progeny, he needed to keep this youngling alive and get him somewhere safe.

The cradle would be able to transport them. Unfortunately, this would leave him without a star shard. He couldn't separate the shard from the cradle quickly; nor could he both take it with him and use it to power the machine that would send him forth simultaneously.

So no star shard—but he was out of other good options.

At the thought, his body grew weary. The fight with the young warrior had been vicious. Without the assisted leverage of his armorsuit, his arms, already tired from the fighting and the past several days' exertion, grew heavy and leaden as he moved through the hall.

Sensing his weakness, Remethiakara dug down into what little energy he had left, and moved boldly through the halls. He knew that his armorsuit would still stop most edged and projectile weapons, but since that electric shock disabled its other abilities, his usually reliable attack and defense functions were inaccessible.

Remethiakara managed to evade the two small armies that engaged each other in the western wing rather easily—it was impossible, however, to avoid the bodies. From the darkened east wing out of which he'd emerged, Remethiakara worked his way to the cradle room at the far end of the southern wing with no incident. He stepped over a great many dead clones with identical faces. It looked like only four or five of the soldiers had been cloned, but that dozens of copies of them had been created. It was not a pleasant experience; once they had the clones, they probably realized they could avoid the unpleasantness themselves if they just kept recloning the clones. He hoped they left the shard with enough power to get him clear of this blasted planet.

No guards flanked the entrance to the cradle room this time. As he approached the closed double doors, a tiny cautious force gave him pause. He heard a voice coming from inside. His psychosomatic senses were dulled without the armorsuit's amplification abilities, but he thought he sensed three beings in there, two of whom were responsive to his truethoughts. Peering through the crack in the door, he saw Eliana and Amon there, together. Eliana glanced at the door, sensing him, her brows drawing down.

Across the room, Remethiakara recognized the other person, and cursed.

The third man was Lucas—standing with a gun in hand, pointed at Eliana and Amon.

Remethiakara gently eased the door shut before they could see him fully.

Fool! Remethiakara should have grabbed a human weapon from one of the dead clone soldiers, but he'd been so caught up in his own thoughts that he'd not thought to.

He hurried away, intending to take a gun from a dead clone's hands. At least one of them would probably still have a weapon.

But before he made it halfway down the hall, the Kakuli warrior stepped into view at the end of the hall.

Remethiakara stopped.

"Ancient suns," he muttered in frustration.

Rakulo began to run toward him, letting out a shrieking battle cry.

38

BLOODY MIRACLE

Trembling under Amon's half-conscious weight, Eliana fled from the fight, crept out of the shadows, and hobbled away.

The theory of what Lucas was doing with the Translocator hardened into verifiable fact in her mind as they retreated back into the hallway they'd just tried to escape from a moment ago. Although the shooting in the immediate vicinity had ceased and the area seemed to be vacated, the bodies of the three Marines Lucas had killed remained sprawled lifelessly on the floor nearby. Theirs weren't the only bodies, either. The Marines had managed to take out a half dozen of the red-headed clone soldiers in the showdown. In the end, bulldog squad had been badly outnumbered. But where had Lucas gone?

Amon stumbled to the side. She braced her free

hand against the wall on her right. "Hang in there, Amon. Stay with me."

Amon responded with a nod and a few labored breaths. She didn't know how much farther he could realistically make it in this condition. She needed to get them both somewhere safe as soon as possible. He was too heavy for her. She wouldn't be able to carry him by herself if he passed out. Eliana eyed the closed doors near them as they passed, wondering if that would be a good place to hunker down, or if there was an unpleasant surprise hiding inside.

They continued down the hall, moving painfully slowly. Amon wheezed in her ear. Her knees trembled. She adjusted her hand on his waist, but he kept sliding down.

They passed a dozen dorm rooms, an entrance to an empty mess hall, and then a set of bathrooms. Finally, they stepped around the corner, and came face to face with her worst nightmare.

Lucas was standing in front of her, rubbing the barrel of the pistol's silencer against the edge of his beard.

"Well, isn't this sweet," Lucas said. Then he frowned. "You don't look so good, Amon. I could help you with that…if I wanted to."

Amon glared at Lucas from eyes with dark circles under them. Somehow, he found the breath for words.

"Go…fuck yourself." He coughed weakly. "Asshole."

Lucas smiled sadly. As he walked forward, Eliana realized something.

"Your face," she said. "It's healed."

Could he really help Amon? An impossible hope welled in Eliana's heart.

When she caught a malicious twinkle in Lucas's eyes, her hope shriveled and died. Lucas would never help Amon. He only helped people when it benefited himself. She'd known of his selfishness from the first time she met the smug bastard.

"That's right, darling. It's a bloody miracle."

"It's something."

Lucas took a few more steps closer so that he was right up in Amon's face. Eliana wanted to move back, but with Amon's weight leaning on her, she was afraid she would drop him. She stood her ground, and hoped it made her look braver than she felt.

Amon brought his chin up, staring up into Lucas's face, defiant. "No, thanks." He coughed with his mouth open, making sure to spray Lucas with spittle at the same time.

Lucas gritted his teeth and shoved the barrel of the pistol under Amon's chin while he wiped his hand with his other face. His perfectly symmetrical face. Not a scar or a freckle in sight. "Come with me. I want you to see something."

Walking around behind them, Lucas nudged Eliana between the shoulder blades with the gun. "Move."

Eliana found the strength to put one foot in front of the other. Lucas prodded them down the long empty hallway—this one, unlike the darkened wing, was clear of debris and furniture, and had been swept clean of dirt and dust.

Lucas pushed open the double doors at the end of the hall. "After you."

"Such a gentleman," Eliana said. She hobbled just inside the room, then paused to let Amon catch his breath.

Lucas shoved past them and hurried over to…something.

Eliana recoiled when her brain recognized the machine—it was a cradle, like Remethiakara had put her in on Kakul. She shuddered and took a few more painstaking steps forward.

Like the cradle in Xucha's home, this one was a dark purplish in color. Unlike that one, this cradle was not compact and arranged precisely—it was not smooth, but rough on the surface, gnarled, and lumpy. It had grown over several objects on the right —was that the sheet of tempered glass of a holodeck? The chitin extended to the left, and formed into a massive sphere the size of …

"Holy shit," Amon huffed. "That's the…Translocator."

"It was," Eliana said.

Lucas hurried up the ramp, unfazed by the sight of the Frankenstein machine, and crouched down next to what Eliana thought was a familiar body. She almost looked away—she'd seen enough dead bodies in the last thirty minutes to last her a lifetime—but some spark of recognition took hold of her gaze and forced her to look closer.

The head was twisted at an odd angle. The face was obscured and blackened with blood...no, she realized, the face was actually *gone*. It was just a scar of black and red flesh. The brains had been torn into by something sharp, and bits of grey matter were scattered across the floor.

Still, she recognized the body to which the face belonged.

And, apparently, so had Lucas. "That son of a bitch," he muttered.

Lucas put one hand over his mouth. Gripping the pistol hard in the other hand, he stood and slowly backed down the ramp, turning away, sliding his mouth into the crook of his elbow in an attempt to mask the smell, which Eliana was just noticing as it wafted across the room.

The smell of death.

Amon began to chuckle, then choked as his laughter twisted into deep wracking coughs. She ducked out from under his arm and turned to face him, mouthing, *What the hell is so funny?* with her back to Lucas.

Lucas lifted the pistol, leveling it at them across the room. "What are you laughing at?" he demanded.

Amon continued to cough several more times. The fit finally passed, and he drew in a deep breath, and then another. She caught his eyes.

There was a moment of confusion, and then understanding passed between them.

Eliana rounded on Lucas, taking four steps away from Amon at the same time. "You're not the *real* Lucas Lamotte!" she said. "You're just a photocopy. That's how you healed yourself, isn't it? You made a clone. The scar and your paralysis weren't embedded in your genetic code, so you thought you'd make a duplicate, and voila! Brand new Lucas doll, good as new."

"Shut up," he snarled, shifting the pistol to point directly at her. She barreled on, looking straight into Lucas's face and hoping she didn't lose her nerve.

"I hardly need to *say* anything." Eliana gestured to the corpse bleeding out inside the spherical shelter overgrown with that cradle organism. "The proof is in the brain pudding." She snorted in mock laughter.

"He's not the original, either!" Lucas sneered, obviously not realizing that he was handing her even more firepower without forcing her to pay for it.

Eliana laughed harder—this time, real laughter dredged up from some dark and twisted part of her soul. "Oh, that's good. You're the copy of the copy! Third rate leftovers! How can you possibly measure up as a man? You won't ever be as good as the original."

Her chest shook as she giggled.

"You want a man?" Lucas said, yelling now. "Look at this pathetic excuse for a man you call your husband. Look at him!"

Lucas shifted the pistol, now shaking in his rage, to point at Amon again.

"Do it," Amon huffed between breaths. "You… coward." Though his voice was low, the words hit Lucas like a punch to the gut.

"Fuck you!" Lucas took several menacing steps forward. "You never gave me the respect I deserved."

"You never earned it."

"I was there from the beginning!" Lucas insisted. "I built that damned company for you."

"You built it *with* me. And then…you…betrayed me."

"I don't need to prove anything to you," Lucas snapped.

"Only a fraud has something to prove, Lucas," Eliana said, drawing his attention back to her. "You know in your heart that's what you are now. Not just second in command. Secondhand. Lucas Lamotte, a photocopy of a fallen man. A fugitive. A fake."

Lucas let out a scream of frustration and shifted

his aim between Eliana and Amon, wavering and uncertain where to direct his anger.

She knew then that he would kill them both. She could see him battle with the decision—did he want to kill Eliana first to watch Amon suffer? Or did he want to kill Amon first and get his revenge right away?

Before he could make the decision, a battle cry echoed from the hallway beyond, drawing every-one's attention to the double doors.

The doors burst open. Remethiakara ran in, clutching an egg close to his chest.

Rakulo shouldered the swinging door open behind him, his bloody-bladed bowie knife gripped blade down in one hand, the activated shock stick crackling with blue-white lightning the other.

Lucas's aim with the pistol swung back to Amon as he seemed to come to a decision.

Amon's body began to shiver, faster than humanly possible, and his form began to blur.

"No!" Eliana shouted.

Lucas squeezed off two rounds.

39

PARALLEL EXPERIENCES

Sweat soaked every inch of Amon's skin, and his heart hammered in his chest. It felt like he was trying to catch a waterfall in his arms. The energy coursing through every molecule of his body was too much to handle. Overheated. Overpowering.

For the last few days, Amon had been a bundle of nerves, anxieties, and fears wondering what Lucas and Remethiakara were planning to do with the other Translocator. The thought that plagued his mind constantly was, *What if I can't stop them?*

Now that he was here, it was obvious what he had to do. Amon couldn't change the past, but he could affect the course of the future.

Like his experiences with public speaking, Amon tortured himself in the days and hours and minutes leading up to the event. But once he got on stage, there was only the doing, only the action, to focus on. Nothing else mattered. Recite the words. Perform the movements. Make eye contact with people in the crowd. That was always how he got over his stage fright in the end—he leaned into it.

So Amon leaned into the cascade of energy. He let go of his nerves and his fears and opened himself to allow the tsunami of energy to wash over him.

The world moved in slow motion. The look of shock on the alien's face was kind of funny. He never imagined Remethiakara to be surprised by anything. The ancient alien had been one or several steps ahead of them this whole time. Yet there it was, undeniable on his scaly, vaguely humanoid, noseless and lipless features—a look of shock.

In contrast, the pure determination plastered on Rakulo's face, an expression that ignored everything around him and was not capable of shock, was positively frightening.

Amon glanced back toward Lucas, and found himself looking straight down the narrow barrel of the pistol's silencer. Lucas had shifted his aim from Eliana back to him, and brought his other hand up to support the gun. His perfectly kempt beard was twisted in an hateful expression.

Amon let go completely; the energy coursing through him split his molecules apart like a sunburst.

Eliana screamed.

Two gunshots fractured the air of the cavernous room.

The bullets passed through where Amon had been standing a moment before and buried themselves harmlessly into the rock wall fifty feet back.

He focused on controlling that cascade of energy pouring through him.

Directing the flow of the current toward Lucas, his molecules suddenly *flowed* through space.

When he materialized beside Lucas, Amon was already bringing his hand down. Lucas flinched back in surprise, but not before his pistol clattered to the floor.

Amon kicked it away.

Lucas fell on Amon, both hands at his throat.

———

Amon dissolved before her eyes, and then materialized next to Lucas, completely unharmed. The two fell to the floor, grasping at each other's necks.

Realizing she'd been frozen still in the crosshairs of Lucas's gun, Eliana broke free, taking three steps toward the discarded pistol.

A chill swept from her fingertips all the way to her scalp at the thought of what she meant to do. Her stomach churned as she picked up the gun, lifting it in both hands.

It was heavier than it looked. She had killed a

man, once, in self-defense. Did she have it in her to do it again?

That seemed like a lifetime ago. She adjusted her grip, tensing the lean muscles of her arms. Raising the gun to the level of her eyes, she sighted down the elongated barrel.

Lucas had his fingers wrapped around Amon's throat, and he was squeezing hard.

"Stop!" she yelled. "Let him go, or I'll shoot!" The two men ignored her, utterly focused on each other. Amon got his hands up under his chin and managed to pry a few of Lucas's fingers back. The bearded man snarled and tried to drive his forehead into Amon's nose.

Amon's body dissolved again and materialized a few feet away, twisted awkwardly. Lucas collapsed in a heap at the sudden absence of a body beneath him. Her husband scrambled up and managed to drive a booted foot into his former second-in-command's neck with a relentless brutality, before Lucas could recover from smashing his face into the floor.

When he tired of kicking, Amon grabbed Lucas and tried to haul him to his feet. That was a mistake. Lucas wrapped his arms around Amon's legs and yanked him back to the ground. This time, he straddled Amon, got his hands up, and began to press his thumbs into Amon's eye sockets. When Amon craned his neck away, Lucas used the leverage to knee her husband in the crotch. Amon cried out in pain, bucked Lucas off. They rolled over and over, fighting for leverage.

Eliana shuffled around, trying to get a clean line of sight with the gun. What if she missed? She'd only shot a gun once or twice in her life, and even then she didn't like the feeling. Watching people shoot guns on TV didn't do much to train one in the use of a firearm. Her arms began to quake.

"Shit," she hissed. Eliana let the gun drop to her side. She'd never be able to be sure of her target when the two were that close together, tangled up and wrestling. She needed to get them apart.

A grunting sound from behind reminded her that Remethiakara and Rakulo were also in the room, having it out in their own fight. Like Eliana, the initial gunshots had caused them both to pause and watch the strange thing that was happening with Amon. By the time she turned around, however, Rakulo was clubbing Remethiakara in the head with the shock stick. The alien, cradling an egg to his chest, was limping and stumbling toward the ramp up to the Translocator's stabilization sphere.

Rakulo tripped him and drove a foot into his side, driving the breath from his lungs. Remethiakara used his body to protect the egg from Rakulo's attacks, but didn't make any move to stop him or really fight back.

The alien half-turned back to look at Eliana, eyes wild, teeth bared. For a brief moment, their gazes locked. Eliana experienced a slight dizziness, and then she gasped as a wave of sympathy washed through her mind, wresting control of her emotions a thousand times stronger than before.

"Stop," she said. "Rakulo, don't hurt him—"

She cut herself off as she tried to fight against her feelings. She knew he was manipulating her emotions somehow, but she couldn't just stand by and watch him hurt Remethiakara.

Damnit, but I have to do something!

An idea came into her head—not a half-baked plan, or a fuzzy mirage, but a fully realized, perfectly crisp, singular image, coupled with an awesome feeling of power and the inevitability of complete control.

Sprinting between the two pairs struggling against each other, Eliana stepped onto the cradle organism coating the floor. Firm yet forgiving, it thrummed with electricity, like walking in her socks on a carpet charged with static—even through the rubber soles of her hiking boots, she could feel the pins and needles.

Someone shouted behind her. Maybe it was a warning, maybe it wasn't even directed at her. The words didn't register. Eliana was incapable of stopping now.

The organism seemed to recognize her. As she approached, the mass that had overgrown what must have been the holoprojector, computer towers, and screens, suddenly rose up and smoothed out into a hollow that matched the shape of her body.

She turned around and pressed herself into the space, letting the cradle enfold her and support her weight.

She took a deep breath, steeling herself to face the innate animalistic fear of what she knew would happen next. When she had dreamed of this moment —of returning to the cradle—she had been filled with apprehension. She certainly experienced that now, but there was no time to dwell on it. There was no room for doubt. Only movement.

Tendrils unspooled from the material near her head, sliding slowly into the cavity of her ears.

Synapses fired, making a million connections at once.

She gasped as the rest of Remethiakara's vision began to piece itself together in her mind.

Rakulo snapped his head to the side when he heard a vicious pop.

The Kakuli warrior watched, fascinated, as Lucas, who had his teeth sunk deep enough into Amon's forearm to draw blood, loosened his grip and screamed. Amon bent Lucas's pinky finger back it broke at the third joint.

Rakulo smiled, glad to see his ally gaining the

upper hand. Amon now had the fingernail of the man's pointer finger touching the back of his wrist, and was forcing him back toward the god-pretender's abomination at the back of the room. The blood streaking down Amon's arm and onto Lucas's hand was enough to prove that whatever powers Amon had just developed, he didn't have full control over them.

However, the moment Rakulo took to pause and look over at the other duel granted Remethiakara enough time to scramble to his feet and stagger a few steps toward the ramp.

The ramp, Rakulo realized, which led up into the spherical cocoon of the abomination built by the god-pretender. Who else could have built such a thing? The rough but strangely forgiving material looked just like the inside of Xucha's tower had. Even now, the memory of the firm, scaly, and strangely forgiving feel of the stuff was vivid in his mind. The barely-healed scar on his abdomen pulsed with sympathy pains—a reminder.

Remethiakara was following Eliana, who used the vast empty space in the large cave to skirt around the dueling men and alien and run toward the abomination. As she approached, the scaly material morphed and seemed to encase her. Little tentacles wrapped themselves around her neck and wriggled into her ears. Rakulo gave an involuntary shiver.

But he hadn't come this far to let Remethiakara have his way. Rakulo heaved back the lightning stick and hurled it like a spear. It struck the god-pretender in the head before clattering to the ground. Rakulo lunged forward and seized a fistful of Remethiakara's suit—a soft, flexible material like leather—in one hand, yanking him to his chest and holding his large knife to the god-pretender's throat.

"What's so funny?" Rakulo demanded in his native language. The alien's nostrils were flared, and there was something like lust in his eyes. "What did you do?"

Remethiakara stared at him, but seemed unable to respond. His nostrils flared.

There was a great keening sound, a flash of light, and a feeling like a skin drum being struck with a hammer deep in his chest.

The cocoon-like sphere began to spin, lumberingly at first, and then rapidly gaining speed.

"What have you done? Make it stop!"

Rakulo's ears popped. His skin prickled with goosebumps as the temperature in the room dropped ten degrees in the span of a heartbeat. There was a flash—not of light, but of shadow—a sort of inverse flare. Inside the sphere, a rift had opened—a smaller rift than Rakulo had seen Remethiakara open on Kakul. But a rift big enough to walk through standing up.

Remethiakara, who had been limp and staggering

just a moment before, suddenly twisted with surprising agility and elbowed Rakulo in the solar plexus, driving the air from his lungs.

The god-pretender lunged forward, holding out the egg in one hand.

There was a moment when Remethiakara knew with certainty that Eliana would resist him.

He was on his knees, letting the native warrior land blow after blow to his body while he protected the last precious youngling in his arms, when they locked eyes and it seemed, for a moment, as if she would refuse.

She could have, if she wanted to. He knew she was strong enough. He just had to hope that his truethought directions were more compelling to a prepared mind.

He thought she would resist...but then she didn't. Eliana turned and ran to the cradle, opened herself up to its power, and it was all he could do not to let out a yelp of triumph and joy.

For a moment, he actually dropped the act he'd been putting on for Rakulo, and walked toward Eliana.

He didn't get far. Rakulo yanked him back, held that big alloy blade to his throat. The young warrior chief shouted in his ear, demanding answers. Remethiakara had become adept at their language over the millennia, and didn't need to rely on the translator in his armorsuit to understand the young man's words—it was his voice box that the evolution of his species' truethought biotech had rendered irrelevant, not their hearing. Rakulo was demanding to know what Eliana was doing, and to stop her. But with the vocalizer broken, he couldn't formulate a reply that the young man would be able to understand. So he said nothing.

Eliana interfaced with the cradle as if she was born to it. He'd never seen a human take to his race's biotech with such ease. The time he'd spent indoctrinating her on Kakul, gaining access to her emotions and making her sensitive to his truethoughts, had finally paid off.

He hoped she picked a viable location. He had come up with the plan at the last moment, projected the vision through the cradle with his truethoughts. It didn't matter where she chose, so long as it was far from here.

Eliana's curvy human form was backlit by the white-hot energy coursing through the cradle interface. The stabilization sphere began to spin, causing even Lucas and Amon to halt their struggle against each other and stare at the spectacle from their encumbered position on the ground.

It didn't take long. Just a few seconds for the stabilization sphere to get up to speed, and then there was that familiar flash of shadow that would be his salvation.

From the floor, Amon and Lucas craned their necks back and stared even while they continued to struggle. This was not the first time they were seeing a cradle create a space-time rift—but the first time they'd seen it from the origination point, which was more of a spectacle.

Twisting his body suddenly, Remethiakara jerked out of Rakulo's grasp easily and dashed ahead. Up the ramp he ran, holding out the egg in his hands.

Without the power of his armorsuit to augment his abilities, however, Rakulo was as quick, if not faster, than he was.

Within arm's reach of the event horizon—which, if crossed, would transport him through to safety—something snagged on the back of his armorsuit.

Remethiakara stretched his arms and held the egg out in front of him even as he himself was jerked to a stop.

The egg parted from his fingertips. Inertia sent it tumbling through the air, to be swallowed by the rift. As the egg crossed the event horizon and somatic contact with the youngling was lost, Remethiakara felt a surge of relief.

Turning, he found himself face to face with Rakulo and the blade of a very large knife.

Bloodlust filled the warrior's eyes, his face a mask of determination.

Remethiakara looked into Rakulo's brown eyes. Knowing that his last youngling egg made it clear of this violent, forsaken planet—that his offspring had a chance to survive—was all that mattered.

Remethiakara had lived a long life. He'd done his duty. Now, like the mothership, he could be at peace.

He flared his nostrils and let his mouth fall open. *Do it*, he urged, sending an encouraging truethought in Rakulo's direction. Without proper indoctrination, he would only feel the truethought's power subconsciously. But given his obvious desire, it was motivation enough.

"Your reign of terror is over, Xucha," Rakulo said. "The god-pretender is dead."

The sharpened blade of the young warrior's knife sank into Remethiakara's chest, where the human heart was located.

His heart was located lower in his abdomen, but it didn't matter. The blade pierced his upper set of lungs. He held Rakulo's gaze until the edges of his vision turned black and he suffocated.

As Rakulo sank his large knife into the body of the alien who had terrorized him his whole life, Lucas finally gained the upper hand on Amon. Exhausted and sick as he was, the strength finally left his hands, and Lucas managed to twist out of his weakening grasp.

Lucas stumbled toward the dark rift that had suddenly appeared within the modified Translocator's stabilization sphere.

Amon staggered to a standing position, his breathing shallow and heavy. He had very little conscious control of the power that enabled him to flow his molecules through space. Each time he rematerialized, he felt a more intense pressure on his body, as if a human-shaped bed of nails was pressing on every inch of his skin—from the *inside out*. If he gave a second to stop and think about the pain, he feared he might be overwhelmed by it.

One thing he had noticed, however, was that the more he thought about trying to disassemble his molecules, the more he willed it, the less likely he was to be able to do it. He'd tried several times to squirm out of Lucas's grasp this way while they wrestled on the ground, but was only successful one time out of ten. The deep teeth marks and blood streaming down his arm were a testament to his failures.

The strange ability seemed to be tied to his instincts and nerves. Like how your brain moves your leg without thinking about it when the doctor hits you in the right spot with a rubber hammer. Only his instinctive reactions—driven by fear—

seemed to enable him to reassemble his molecules at will. Like a muscle he hadn't learned how to use.

As Rakulo was dragging the alien's body back away from the rift, Lucas altered his course and began to run toward Eliana.

He's not going for the rift, Amon realized. *He's going for my wife.*

A deep fear shot through him. Amon didn't know whether Lucas was trying to hurt Eliana, or if he wanted to wrest control of the machine from her, and use it for himself. Either way, it didn't matter. His concern for her safety made it easier to shove the pain in his body down and away from his mind. Amon staggered forward, running at Luca's back with intent.

He blinked and suddenly he was between Eliana and Lucas, running at the man's front. He didn't stop.

Amon grabbed Lucas's shirt and tried to force him back. Lucas dug his feet in and resisted. Gripping his forearm and wrist, Amon pressed back.

He blinked again and they were *both* standing inches from the black rift.

Lucas turned and saw that his back was to the event horizon. Amon readjusted his grip, squeezing Lucas's broken pinky finger in his hand, as he simultaneously prayed that he wouldn't accidentally dematerialize again.

For whatever reason, he didn't. Amon pushed

back until Lucas's hand with the broken finger was touching the veil of shadow hanging in the air. And then he pushed through it.

"Eliana, turn it off!" he shouted, scraping the bottom of the well of his dwindling strength as the pain slammed into him once again.

The rift fell like a curtain, shrinking from bottom and top simultaneously. Lucas screamed, clutching half a hand to his chest. The broken pinky was gone, along with his ring finger, half his middle finger and most of his palm. They had been severed cleanly, as if with a laser or a maybe a guillotine. Blood began to gush out even as Amon watched. The sight made him light-headed.

Amon brought his own hand up, expecting to see the same. Instead, he stared numbly as the molecules of his hand slowly coalesced before his eyes, like a hologram solidifying into flesh and bone and blood.

Then the bed-of-nails pain hit him like a truck.

As he fought to keep the pain from overwhelming him, he saw flashes of the room around him, but without focus.

He blinked as Agent Moreno and a cadre of Marines walked around the room far above him. Handcuffs rattled and Lucas was hauled past him, a blood-soaked cloth pressed to his severed hand.

A strong man with a scar across his jaw lifted Amon, and laid him on a stretcher. Blackness, flashes of light. Glancing over, he saw Eliana—watching him with her green eyes. No, she wasn't smiling. He blinked and saw that her eyes were closed.

Amon opened and closed his mouth, swallowing as he tried to take a breath. There was so much pressure on his body. He reached his hand out and laid a hand on Eliana's stomach. She was still breathing, thank God. Amon finally managed a breath of his own.

Then unconsciousness took him.

40

DOWNLOAD

When Eliana woke next, her heart was pounding. The drone of jet engines finally allowed her to place herself—she was on a military cargo plane with a small cabin. Amon, breathing but unconscious, was strapped into a stretcher on her left. That and the sight of Rakulo, drowsing in a seat nearby, worked together to keep her from having a panic attack. Apart from the three of them, this cabin was empty.

Once she had caught her breath and her heartbeat had returned to a normal pace, she woke Rakulo and made him fill her in on what happened after she lost consciousness in the cradle. He told her how Major Bautista and his Marines had finally managed to overcome the contingent of clone mercenaries that Lucas had created using the modified Translocator. The rift that Eliana created pulled so much power from the arch that the lights in the whole facility went out. That gave the better-equipped Marines, with their night-vision goggles, an opportunity to out-maneuver and outgun the mercenaries' defenses, and finally overwhelm them.

A squad of Marines led by Major Bautista arrived in the southern wing of the facility moments after Eliana blacked out. A medic had treated Lucas's wounds, and he was now being escorted home in a separate plane, guarded by a dozen Marines and monitored by a medic. They intended to return him to the United States and make him stand trial for his crimes.

She knew Amon would be thrilled to hear that. The trial would take time, but seeing justice served would give him closure.

As for Remethiakara, Rakulo informed her that the alien's dead body was zipped up into a body bag and put in cold storage in the cargo hold of the plane.

"Do you want to see it?" he asked.

Eliana shook her head. "I think I've seen enough."

Rakulo pursed his lips and laid a hand on her shoulder for a moment before he let it drop back to his lap.

Eliana thought back to the moment she had entered the cradle. The vision in her mind of what Remethiakara wanted her to do was so crystal clear when it happened—the kind of mental clarity a woman only experienced once or twice in her lifetime. Knowing that nothing would ever be that clear again was akin to losing a limb.

After a long pause, Eliana said, "Remethiakara wanted me to send the egg to safety. He didn't care about his own life—as long as the egg was safe, he could die happy. I know that for a fact. I guess a lot of people feel that way when their children are in danger, right? Can you blame him?"

"No, I guess not. But he brought it upon himself. Anyway, the egg is gone. Unless you know where you sent it."

Eliana blew out a shaky breath. "I could probably tell you if I used the cradle again. But I'd really rather not."

"What was it like?"

"I felt like I could see the whole universe, Rakulo. A million different worlds, all interconnected."

"Could you reach them all?"

She shook her head firmly. "Not all of them. Only some were accessible to me. The others had been, once, I could tell that much. But they weren't open to me. In the end, Remethiakara didn't care where I sent the egg—as long as it was far from here."

"He thought he had won. Right before he died, I could see it in his eyes—he thought he would get away with it again."

"He almost did. I would have been fine with that as long as he left us in peace."

"He wouldn't have. My people would never be at

peace as long as he was out there. I couldn't let him live, Eliana. "

She could see the guilt in his face. He didn't feel any better about what he'd done than she did.

"I know that," she said, laying her hand on top of Rakulo's and smiling softly at him. "I don't blame you for anything. You did what was necessary—that's one of the reasons I believe your people look up to you so much. You always try to do right by them."

She glanced down at where Amon lay unconscious. She had it easy. Rakulo had a whole village to care for. She just had Amon, and she had nearly lost him.

He was safe, if unconscious, now. His chest rose and fell as he snored softly. She finally thought she understood how Amon felt about keeping her safe. How could she ever have been angry with him?

"Why does doing the right thing have to hurt so much?" Eliana said. "I just wanted it to be over."

Rakulo turned and gave her a tired smile. "I know exactly how you feel."

41

NOTHING FOR A LITTLE WHILE

"That's a job well done," General Wade said. "Especially you two. The Fisks have some guts, and I'll never forget your dedication to the mission. I was skeptical sending you both to Switzerland, but I'm glad you proved me wrong."

Amon had regained consciousness after Reuben put him back in the hyperbaric pressure chamber in Austin. Rather than the claustrophobic panic he had experienced before, it was with a tremendous sense of relief that Amon watched his breath fog the plastic lid in front of his face. A close brush with death does a lot to give a man a sense of perspective.

"Thank you," Amon said. "But I think Eliana deserves most of the credit. She saved us all. I just passed out."

"Not 'just'," Eliana said. "You did a lot more than that."

"Yes," General Wade said, looking at photographs the Marines took on a tablet in his hand. "I heard the story. How were you able to do what you did with that…what did you call it?

"Cradle is the word Remethiakara used," Eliana said, "and I suppose it's as good a thing as any to call it. But I honestly don't know, General. Remethiakara put the idea in my head, and maybe because I was introduced to the cradle before, I was able to do what he wanted."

"Impressive," he said. "I hope you don't mind, but my people are going to have a few questions about that."

"I'll help answer their questions and help however I can," Eliana said. "Honestly."

General Wade inclined his head slightly, signaling that he accepted her subtle apology in a classy way like the southern gentleman he was. Now that the general knew that what Eliana had been feeling was not entirely her fault, he understood better. They had had a short discussion about it early, and seemed to be on good terms again.

"What are we going to do about Lucas's Translocator?" Amon said. He needed to know the answer.

"I, too, would like some assurances there," Agent Moreno piped in.

"Don't worry, gentlemen. The military is already taking care of it. Our people are working on transporting it back to the United States for safekeeping. It's a big job, and they're being careful about it."

"So you'll just keep it in an underground warehouse somewhere? Like, what, Roswell?"

General Wade gave him an enigmatic smile. "It's more likely that we'll keep it here at the Lunar Austin Research Center, Mr. Fisk. But rest assured, folks, the days of Lucas terrorizing people with it are over."

Amon nodded. This wasn't his campus anymore, it was a part of something bigger now. He was starting to be okay with that.

This seemed to satisfy Agent Moreno as well. He had dark circles under his eyes and looked very tired, but relieved.

"I bet you're looking forward to getting your family back," Amon said to him.

Agent Moreno looked at Amon through the glass. "More than you know."

Amon glanced over at Eliana. "I think I know."

Agent Moreno smiled. "Of course. Sorry. I'm exhausted. Of course you know."

"Thank you for your perseverance, Agent," Amon said. "One day I'll be able to get out of this hyperbaric chamber and give you the handshake you deserve."

"For now," Reuben said, walking over from where he'd been working on the Translocator, "you'll stay right there and I'll shake his hand for you." Reuben and Agent Moreno clasped hands. Eliana and Audrey each gave him a hug.

"Thank you," Amon said again. "And thank you, also, for having the foresight to remove a piece of the star shard and bringing it back here for us to use."

Agent Moreno nodded. "I figured you could use it."

Reuben bobbed his head and gestured to his red-headed assistant. "Amon, you'll be pleased to know that Audrey and I have run some tests, and now that we have a new star shard, the power issues we were experiencing with the Translocator before have been mitigated. The shards are like fuel, and we were simply running out of it. Having a baseline for what another of the star shards looks like has also allowed us to define a power-measurement system. It's a very strange material, and reads differently depending how you charge it. You see—"

Amon raised a hand inside the hyperbaric chamber. "Let's spare our audience the technical explanation. I do have a question though. Can you use the star shard to reverse what happened to me?"

Amon tried to be careful to keep the desperate hope out of his voice. Eliana still heard it. She laid a hand on the upright hyperbaric chamber and gave him a reassuring smile.

"Maybe," Reuben said, obviously hedging. "Let's see how it goes. At the very least, I'm confident that we'll be able to reduce the time you need to spend in the chamber and get you moving around again. I can already see improvements since your return, and you can't stay in there forever. Audrey and I are working on creating a wearable device—like a smartwatch—to monitor your condition when you're walking around."

"Thank you, Reuben," Amon said. "I mean it. You're a good friend."

"I'm just glad to see you home, boss. And your lovely wife. You two deserve a chance to relax. Maybe now you'll get the opportunity to try. You can do that, right Amon? Relax?"

Amon's gaze locked onto the lovely emerald eyes and high cheekbones of his wife. She was even more beautiful now than she had been when they married. "I think I can manage that."

They all laughed.

"Can we just do nothing for a little while?" Eliana suggested. "I would like that."

"The most brilliant idea I've heard in years," Amon said.

42

HOME FOR GOOD

Rakulo's return to his people turned into a jubilant celebration in the steel cave that had become their home. Eliana produced delicious wine from somewhere that rivaled the flavor of even the berry wine that Gehro brewed in his cave on Kakul.

Quen, too, had recovered in the time Rakulo had been gone. Rakulo cried when he saw the big warrior smile and settle his hand on Yeli's shoulder, and embraced them both.

In the days and weeks that followed, Rakulo and his people grew restless, and were allowed to venture forth into the city that Eliana called "Austin" in small groups. It was a strange place, full of vehicles and buildings beyond anything Rakulo had ever imagined.

It also felt distant and cold, for it was not his home.

The more Rakulo saw, the more he decided that he wanted his people to be able to return to Kakul. He was crazy for ever wanting them to leave. Sure, they could probably make a new place for their people here—Eliana assured him it was possible. And Rakulo definitely still wanted to range farther out on his own, for he felt in his heart that he was an explorer.

But his mother and Gehro? The families who had lost their friends and relatives and everything they owned in the fight with the giant scorpions? They just wanted to go home. As their leader, it was Rakulo's responsibility to make sure that happened.

Since Amon was still in recovery in that glass container most of the time, once Rakulo confided in her what he wanted to do, Eliana threw herself into helping with the project. It was easier than Rakulo expected to enlist General Wade's help. Once Major Bautista was on board, though, things really started to happen.

With the help of the Major and his men and their powerful guns, Rakulo hunted down and killed every last scorpion they could find in the jungle of Kakul inside the Wall.

Then, thanks to the technical assistance of Reuben and Audrey—and Amon, too, giving ideas from inside the hyperbaric pressure chamber—they brought sheets of metal from Earth to Kakul and patched the holes in the Wall. In a few places, they left a hinged door—firmly secured from the inside, with a padlock to which Rakulo was given the keys.

This patching effort alone took a couple weeks, much longer than it took Rakulo to make the holes. But that was how life worked. It was always harder to repair the damage you made than to cause it in the first place.

Finally, though, it was time to lead his people home.

In the span of a single hour, they packed their scant belongings and gathered in the Translocator room.

Eliana gave Rakulo and his people the gift of more dried food and water, plus additional tools and supplies they could use to rebuild their village. Rakulo thanked them profusely.

Then, in small groups of seven to eight people, carrying their belongings on their backs, Reuben sent them through the Translocator back to Kakul.

When the last of the villagers had gone through, Rakulo turned to Eliana.

"Goodbye, Rakulo," she said. "If you ever wish to visit us, or if you ever need help again, use the bracelet to get in touch, and Reuben will bring you back to Earth or send one of us to meet you."

"Thank you," Rakulo said. "I will if it's an emergency. But I'm hoping that from here we can make our own way."

"You'll always be welcome here, my friend," Amon added.

"Thank you, Amon."

"Godspeed, Rakulo."

Rakulo waved at Amon through the sheet of glass. His grasp of their language had improved greatly in the past couple months, but he still didn't understand many of their expressions. This one was particularly odd.

"I don't need god's speed," Rakulo said. "I think we can do just fine on our own."

They laughed, and Rakulo, though he didn't fully understand the joke, joined them. Eliana gave him one last tight hug, then held him out at arm's length. He could see the tears gathering in her eyes. "Take care"

"You, too."

"Goodbye." Rakulo waved to the others. Then he strode into the Translocator sphere. There was a flash of light, a lurch, and a moment of dizziness.

And then, at long last, he was home for good.

***

Thank you for reading *The Ares Initiative*!

If you enjoyed this story, you'll love *Culture Shock*, the first novel in a new sci-fi mystery series! Turn the page for an excerpt...

CULTURE SHOCK (EXCERPT)

Chapter One

I heard the rumble of the engine long before I saw it. You couldn't mistake the sound of Alek's 1971 Chevelle SS. Tipping my chair legs to the floor, I crossed the cramped office and peered through the window.

The blinds were half drawn, as usual. You can never be too cautious in my line of work. I'd have ballistic glass installed if I could afford it, but the last time I was that flush with cash I spent it getting my truck paneling replaced after chasing a wanted felon into a tornado in Oklahoma. Glancing over my shoulder at the bills stacked on my desk, I shoved down the nearly suffocating wave of melancholy that washed over me.

Sliding my finger between the yellowing slats, my nail scraped the filthy glass. When was the last time my office had been cleaned? A year? Maybe two? I told myself the ingrained layer of grime gave the place a homely, "don't bother breaking in" sort of feel, which was good for security. Truth was that lately, cleaning the windows had been the furthest thing from my mind.

The growl of the engine grew louder until the cranberry red hot rod finally rolled into view. The car really was a beaut. Shining chrome trim, glossy black wheels, and one of those 409 big blocks under the hood. It was the kind of car I'd always admired and never been able to buy. Hipsters and hood rats making their way to their favorite watering holes for the evening craned their necks to admire the machine as Alek coasted to a stop behind my beat-up black Ford pickup.

No matter how often I dreamed of one day owning a vehicle like that, my current preferences inclined toward function over form. You can't haul much of anything in the trunk of a Chevelle, and I couldn't risk drawing an entire block's worth of eyes when conducting surveillance or tailing someone who might be in contact with my target.

Alek stepped onto the curb and pretended not to notice the people rubbernecking at his ride. With a casual glance, he looked both ways before crossing the street.

Alek Ludwig was a bondsman, one of the biggest in the city. He had a fancy downtown office within spitting distance of the Travis County Courthouse, and his business ran radio ads and late-night TV commercials. "Big wig Ludwig's got your back," they sang. Just like you'd imagine, with a catchy jingle and everything. I liked to give him a hard time about the ads. He was always a good sport about it, as long as I'd eventually admit that the jingle made one hell of an ear-worm, to which he'd reply that he didn't mind being needled about the song as long as it bought him toys like that Chevelle.

The man was portly, which I think is a term that's still considered politically correct. Skinny legs made him look like a beachball mounted on two twigs. Even in this heat, he wore cowboy boots, jeans, and a pale yellow button-up shirt with sweat stains blossoming beneath his arms. His head bore a graying fringe of hair, and his hairless pate reflected the hot Texas sun until he disappeared through my building's front door.

Turning, I reached across my small office to unlock the door, then resumed my seat at the desk. The door didn't exactly hit the desk when it opened, but the fact that I managed to fit a desk and two chairs in the space was a minor miracle. The carpet, a brown floral print, was as thin and worn as it was drab. The only other furniture in the room was a dented mini-fridge in the corner, and a metal filing cabinet whose main purpose was to prop up the coffee maker.

While I waited for Alek to climb the stairs, I turned my attention back to the stack of bills, and then to the dated laptop I was supposed to be using to pay them. Moving my fingers across the sticky trackpad, I clicked a link on the banking website.

What happened next made my skin crawl. The click seemed to set the office lights to flickering. That was ridiculous, of course. I was far from an electro-tech genius, but I knew enough to know that clicking a link on a website couldn't cause a power outage. But the single overhead bulb winked out and my laptop powered down of its own accord.

Muffled curses bled through the thin walls and told me that I wasn't the only who had been affected. Small comfort.

A second later, the power returned, and with it my laptop. On the screen now was not an internet browser, but a bright blue screen.

Gooseflesh prickled along my arms. *What on Earth?* The battery should have kept the laptop alive even without the power. I muttered a few choice curse words. Three firm strikes of my palm against the keyboard did nothing to bring the machine back to life. Imagine that.

Sighing, I closed the laptop and dropped it into a drawer so that I wouldn't be tempted to chuck it out the window like I wanted to. After all these years, I thought I might finally understand my father's Luddite attitude toward computers.

There was a quick rap on the door.

"C'mon in!"

The door cracked and Alek poked his head through, taking in the office with a single sweep of his gray eyes. He held a folded piece of paper in one hand, and a cold stogie jutted from his mouth.

"Those things are going to kill you."

Alek grinned around the cigar. His voice came out gravelly, like his lungs were coated with enough tar to fill a swimming pool. "We all die, Gunn. Might as well go out doing something I love." He held out the folded paper. "Think this is for you."

My blood went cold when I recognized the handwriting visible through the paper. I took the note from him and swallowed a groan as I unfolded the custom stationery.

***

Anderson,

Your rent is past due. Again.

You've always been a good tenant, and I really appreciate you helping me find Lottie when she ran away last week, but rescuing cats from rooftop bars doesn't pay the mortgage or my property taxes on this building.

This is your final reminder.

Sincerely,

Cathy Burns,

Property Manager, Sunshine Real Estate.

***

"You all right?" Alek asked.

"Must be a misunderstanding." The words felt hollow as they left my mouth. "I put a check in her mailbox on the first of each month."

At least, I thought I had. It must have slipped my mind this month. I shuffled through the pile of bills for a beat, then let them drop back down.

"You still write a check to pay your rent?" Alek asked. "Can't they just debit the money from your account automatically?"

I scowled at him. "Same dollars. What's the difference?"

Alek plucked the cigar from his lips and frowned at me. "I'm sorry I haven't had many gigs for you lately. I thought you were keeping busy with other work. If I'd known, I—"

"Don't worry about it, I'll get it taken care of. You didn't come here to talk about my finances." I shoved the note into my back pocket and sat on it.

The wrinkle between his eyebrows stayed, but Alek slowly began to nod. "Well, I've got a job for you. Pop out for a drink?"

"Thought you'd never ask."

A happy hour with Alek was one expense I never worried about covering. Still, I got to my feet slowly, trying not to reveal the eagerness I felt, and let Alek lead the way out. We'd become friends over the years, but pride is a funny thing; I didn't want him to think I was desperate. Work had been scarce of late, and while a single job wouldn't expunge my debts completely, the money would certainly help steer things in the right direction.

I closed and locked the door to my office. On this side, you could read *Gunn Bounties* in bold letters on the frosted glass. Beneath my business name, in a smaller print: *Anderson Gunn, Fugitive Recovery Agent.* The lock gave a satisfying click, and then the letters were only visible in afterimage as the hall went dark.

"That's starting to get on my nerves," Alek said.

"What gives?"

"Been brownouts all over the city today. Must be the heat. Or there are gremlins in the power lines."

"It's Austin," I said. "Weirder things have happened."

"Like the lizard man? Or the Cathedral of Junk?"

"Or that one time the mayor sent queso to the moon?"

Alek snorted and slapped his leg. "Oh man, I almost forgot about that!" He sighed. "I love this city."

We made it down the stairs in the darkness, using our hands to feel our way, and stepped out the front door. A wave of humid air washed over me and my skin broke out in a sheen of sweat. Even after seven thirty at night, it was triple-digit temperatures outside. The weather in Austin was pleasant for most of the year, but in the summer, it could become unbearable. I tried to ignore the way my jeans stuck to my skin as we walked.

My office wasn't in the high rise, big money buildings near the Capitol where Alek worked, but in a grungy part of Sixth Street on the east side of the interstate. I liked it here. The place had a certain open-minded atmosphere of good vibes that some people said could be traced back to Austin's roots as the musical heart of rock 'n roll. Divey bars, loud music, and good food were in abundance, especially on the fringes. The smell of charcoal and *al pastor* wafted past my nose. The trill of an electric guitar floated to my ears from a distance as someone warmed up their ax for the evening's first set.

At the corner, a windowless door led to our establishment of choice. An octagonal wooden sign jutting out over the doorway depicted a pig with one arm resting on the rim of a large cauldron. His other hoof, though lacking fingers, somehow clutched a large mug of beer. The pig's face held a tipsy yet mysterious expression, as if it knew the secret to one of life's many mysteries and was on the verge of being drunk enough to spill the beans. *The Poached Pig* was etched in an arch above the drawing.

The chime of a small bell sounded behind me. I turned and looked down the street in time to see an old man wearing nothing but a bright green thong cycle past us on a ten-speed bicycle, waving like a supermodel and grinning like a cartoon character. It took me a a moment to realize the grin didn't belong to him, but to the bright orange Garfield mask strapped to his face.

"Look," I said, nudging my friend with an elbow.

"Keep Austin Weird!" Alek shouted in solidarity.

I caught his arm before he turned as I spotted another flock of bikers headed our way. "Oh, I see. Must be World Naked Bike Ride day."

Odd little fact: Austin has no laws against public nudity. Which meant that the parade of beautiful women wearing their birthday suits and casually pedaling down the street in the same direction the old man with the Garfield mask had gone was perfectly okay in every sense of the word. Sure, they were a huge distraction to passing motorists, but this kind of thing wasn't considered all that unusual. It was a point of pride for the city: *Keep Austin Weird.* The saying was plastered on brick walls, printed on t-shirts, and impressed upon the minds of a local population dedicated to their eccentricity.

This particular parade drew more observers from the bars, but not fast enough. In less than a minute, the group of naked cyclists was gone, nothing but a blur of tan flesh cutting toward the horizon.

"It *is* warm out," Alek commented. "I hope they stay hydrated."

I chuckled, yanked open the door to *The Poached Pig*, and went inside.

Chapter Two

The place smelled like beer and barbecue with a hint of fry grease. Although the air conditioner hummed, it wasn't exactly cool inside, yet none of the regulars complained as long as the ceiling fans were spinning. A line of brass taps behind the bar poured just about every local brew you could imagine. Mirrors behind the shelves lined with liquor bottles made the bar look bigger than it was. There were no TVs—one of my favorite aspects of the place. Instead, an ancient jukebox leaned against the back wall.

As Alek and I slid onto the green vinyl bar stools, two fresh pints slid across the bar in our direction. The bartender and proprietor, Barry Morris, nodded a silent greeting, threw a towel over his shoulder, and took our order. Then he ducked through a half-door leading to the kitchen. The faint drone of a radio drifted out, mingling with Stevie Ray Vaughan's voice belting *Pride and Joy* through the tinny jukebox speakers.

I took a sip of the ale—crisp, slightly bitter, and refreshingly cold. Glorious. Alek let out a satisfied sigh as he folded his hands around his sweating pint glass. The silence stretched between us as we enjoyed the music, grateful for the moment of peace. It was the first time I'd felt anything close to calm all day.

Alek finally pulled out a manila envelope and

slapped it down on the bar. "Fresh skip here for ya, stud."

My heart slammed against my ribcage. I took another sip of my beer while I pretended to study a row of bourbon bottles on the top shelf.

With the most casual gesture I could manage, I lifted the envelope and pinched the metal prongs, then slid a finger and thumb into the opening and pulled a stack of papers free.

I scanned the bio and background information Alek had compiled, then let out a low whistle. "Cameron Kovak. What did he do to get his bail set at a hundred grand? It was only his second DWI."

"He somehow managed to plow his truck into a guy tending his neighbor's garden. One minute he was pulling weeds, the next, *bam.* Poor bastard nearly died of internal bleeding in the hospital, but he pulled through, thank God." Alek frowned. "The judge was pissed. She couldn't charge Kovak with Intoxication Manslaughter, so she set the bond high enough to sting. Kovak's wife called me to bail him out. I got the sense some kind of romantic spat precipitated the incident but, still, I thought I could count on her to get him to court on time. Guess I was wrong."

"Not necessarily her fault. Maybe something spooked him."

"Maybe. Either way, the wife can't find him, so I'm hoping you can."

Barry returned through swinging doors and slid a plate down in front of each of us. On mine, a Reuben on rye with chips. Alek got a club sandwich on sourdough with fries. Both toasted to perfection.

Alek dug in while I scanned through the rest of Kovak's paperwork—current address, emergency contact, cell phone number, employer. Didn't seem like he'd be too hard to find. With luck, the job would go quickly and I could pocket my usual ten percent fee in a few days. Ten large—my take on the hundred—would put me back ahead of the game and make sure I could pay Ms. Burns and keep the office. Dingy and dirty as that little place was, it was mine, dammit.

After what seemed like a well-considered amount of time had passed, I said, "I'll take it."

"Good." Alek bobbed his head. "Knew I could count on you."

I rubbed my hands on my jeans and stared at the untouched plate in front of me. Now that I had work to do, my appetite had all but disappeared. I licked my lips as I thought about my next words. Best to get straight to the point. "Got any other jobs lined up after this one?"

Alek took a bite of his sandwich and shook his head while he chewed. His appetite, it seemed, had not waned. "Not yet," he mumbled through a mouthful. "But if something comes up, as long as it doesn't interfere with you finding Kovak, you can have first dibs."

I had to inhale to make room for the fullness I felt in my chest at his reassurance. "Thanks."

"Gunn… are you sure you're okay?"

I waved him off. "I'll be fine."

I hid my face in my sandwich as I forced myself to take a bite. Although I wasn't hungry, old habits inspired me to put the food down. Couldn't afford to let it go to waste. Especially not one of Barry's sandwiches.

The lanky bartender stopped polishing the counter at the far end of the bar and came over to lean down next to us. "Did one of you fellas say something about a Kovak?"

One of Alek's eyebrow shot up. I took another bite of my sandwich and crunched down on a chip.

"Why?" Alek asked. "You know him?"

Barry thumbed back toward the kitchen. "Nah, just heard about him on the radio. Guy worked for the power company. They found his partner dead in a ditch this morning."

My galloping heart skipped a beat. I turned to Alek. "If that's true, we need to talk about hazard pay."

Alek wiped his hands on a napkin and pulled his phone out. "This is the last thing I need right now."

"Five percent," I said. Normally I wouldn't be jumping for joy at the thought of taking on extra risk to find a dangerous fugitive, but more danger meant more money. Fifteen grand would give me a three month runway. I'd finally be able to get ahead again.

"Hold on, hold on. I'll get to the bottom of this. If it *is* true, you know I have no problem including hazard pay. But first, you gotta be straight with me, Gunn. What's going on with you?"

Barry and Alek both turned to watch me intently. I could see the genuine concern on both of their faces. They were just trying to be helpful, but my situation dug at me enough that I wasn't enthused about sharing the details.

But you only get what you give, and Alek was the man with the money.

"It's just been hard to keep up. My old man was never any good with money either. Maybe I inherited his bad luck."

"Why do you say that?"

I thought back to the blue screen on my laptop. That wasn't the first computer I'd seen that on. Had a fella once tell me it was called the blue screen of death. I knew what it meant. "When did your family get their first computer?"

Alek shuckled, a wet hacking sound. "I'm a bit older than you are. I bought a Commodore 64 for the business the second year they had 'em. I was about your age then. Just getting my start."

"My parents bought their first one when I was a

kid. I was ten, it was the heyday of the PC revolution, and after arguing about the cost for several weeks, my parents finally caved and bought one. I think it was the realization they could do their finances with it, using spreadsheets, which my mom liked. You see, my dad was super scatterbrained—still is—and she invested a lot of time and money over the years in an attempt to upgrade the systems around him, thinking that would make her own life less chaotic. In reality, she just ended up doing the work herself."

Barry nodded. "Typical in that generation."

"Spreadsheets never made any sense to my father. He'd sit for an hour or two pretending to enter his receipts while he waited for her to come to his aid. When she finally did—often after cooking a meal for all three of us—he'd shrug and say, 'No reason to jinx a stroke of good luck!' as he picked up a paperback and stretched out on the couch." I sipped at the beer when I realized my mouth had gone dry. "He used to say quirky, carefree things like that more often, but he hasn't been interested in much except the bottom of a bottle since mom passed. I guess maybe she held together more than finances for him."

Alek and Barry had both leaned in while I was talking. I guess I was keeping my voice down unconsciously. They both straightened again when I finished.

"Hard thing," Barry said.

Alek pursed his lips. "Forgive my bluntness, stud, but what's that got to do with the price of eggs in China?"

I laughed without mirth. "Just had another computer go to the big clearance sale in the sky."

"Normally I'd cap it at two and a half, but today I'm feeling generous. I'll give you three percent. Deal?"

An extra three grand? Count me in. Alek stuck out his hand, and I shook it. "Deal."

Alek Ludwig returned his attention to his phone and searched the news aggregators while I took a half-hearted bite of my pickle and ate my sandwich. A loose plan began to formulate. I could start tonight by talking to Kovak's wife, the one Alek seemed to trust. If what Barry said about a dead body was true, I didn't want to waste any time.

Alek read a few more headlines and then cursed under his breath. "I'm going to have words with Kovak's damn lawyer. He should have called me the moment he found out about this. Look."

Alek shoved the phone into my hands. It was an article from *The Statesman*, dated today. The picture of Kovak from Alek's bond paperwork matched the mug shot I saw on the screen. This time I studied him more closely. Dirty blond hair. Big goofy ears. Smug smile. He had a splotchy birthmark at his left temple that would be hard to hide, even with a hat.

I skimmed through the text until I found the pertinent section. "'Police are investigating the murder of Dale Edwards, a lineman employed by CenTex Power & Light. His body was discovered south of Austin early on Friday morning. The cause of his death is as yet undetermined, but police are actively searching for his missing colleague, Cameron Kovak, who was reportedly dispatched with Edwards last night.'"

"Unbelievable." Alek chewed on his cigar, then spat a fragment of tobacco onto his empty plate. "Usually I'm a better judge of people."

I scrolled down the page with my thumb. "Wait a minute. Barry, I thought you said they found him in a ditch. Is that the ditch in the background?"

Alek squinted at the screen. "I can't tell. Don't have my glasses with me."

In the photo, yellow caution tape was just visible in the distance. It seemed to make a perimeter at the edge of the so-called ditch, the full circumference of which was hidden behind a copse of oak trees. I felt the sudden urge to go there and see for myself. Unless it was just the angle, the hole looked enormous.

"Some ditch," I said.

Barry's stoic face was unreadable. "Radio said ditch." He turned away, suddenly disinterested, and began removing liquor bottles and dusting the shelves beneath them.

Alek stepped outside to make a phone call, no doubt trying to get some more information from his contacts at the police department. I knew people there, too, but I didn't have the same kind of leverage.

He returned a moment later. "Sergeant on duty said the cop assigned to the case is Detective Sheila Gonzalez. She's still on scene."

"Well, I'll be damned," I said, as impressed by the name as with how quickly Alek acquired the information. The image of a tall, attractive Latina woman popped unbidden into my mind. Athletic build, proud green eyes, a thick mane of dark curly hair. She'd filled out in the years since we'd first met, but she was just as beautiful now as she had been then, and if possible, even more intimidating.

A soft laugh tipped me off that Alek must have seen something in my expression that amused him.

"You know her?" he asked. "The sergeant got weird on the phone when he found her name, made me think she might be new."

"Her father used to be the chief of police. Sheila transferred to Dallas so she didn't have to work for her old man, but now that he's retired, she's back in town."

"That's right, I remember now. But how do you know her?"

"We went to college together at Texas State."

"I see," he said. "You two seeing each other?"

"Nothing like that. We tried dating in college, but it never worked out. We were better as friends. Suppose we still are."

"Is it weird having her back in town?"

"I've known her forever. She's like one of the guys to me, you know? Maybe it's not a bad thing to have a friend on the force, though. It seems to have worked well for you. As much as I try to place nice with the cops, most of them keep me at arm's length."

"They're just doing their jobs."

"If you say so."

"You still got a thing for her, don't you?"

"What? No. C'mon."

Alek pushed his empty plate to the back of the bar and stood. "You do."

"I do not." I swallowed the rest of my beer and slammed the glass down, maybe a bit too hard.

"Have it your way," he said with another chuckle. "So what's your first move?"

"Isn't it obvious? I visit the scene of the crime and talk to my lovely detective friend."

"Oh, she's lovely now, is she?"

"Shut up."

He twirled his cigar expertly between his fingers, then bit it between his teeth again. "You know, now that Kovak's a suspect in this case, she's going to be looking for him, too."

"Even better. I like a challenge."

"I'm only paying you if you find him first."

My stomach roiled, but I laughed good-naturedly and gave him my most confident smile. "Come on, Alek. Have I ever let you down?"

Get *Culture Shock* now.

Though ample evidence suggests there existed a wide variety of languages and dialects among the ancient people of Central America, the author based the language of the *Kakuli* people on Yucatec Maya, the most commonly spoken—and well documented—Mayan language today.

Words, when borrowed, were taken from modern Yucatec Maya dictionaries and archaeological texts. Where English transliterations varied, spelling was chosen for consistency and simplicity. The sounds of the Mayan language are poorly expressed by English letters, so a rough pronunciation guide follows.

NAMES

Citlali

[kit-LA-li]

Dambu
[DAHM-boo]

Ixchel
[EESH-chel]

Kakul
[KAH-cool]

Maatiaak
[MAH-tee-ahk]

Rakulo
[Rah-KU-lo]

Tilak
[Tee-LAHK]

Uchben Na
[OOCH-ben Nah]

Watiya
[Wah-TEE-yuh]

Xucha
[SHOO-cha]

M.G. Herron writes science fiction and fantasy for adrenaline junkies.

His books explore new worlds, futuristic technologies, ancient mysteries, various apocalypses, and the vagaries of the human experience.

His characters have a sense of humor (except for the ones who don't). They stand up to strange alien monsters from other worlds... unless they slept through their alarm again.

Like ordinary people, Herron's heroes try to make the world a better place, and sometimes screw things up.

Find all his books and news about upcoming releases at mgherron.com.

Juliette Davis lives in an inner-city Melbourne suburb. She was born in New Zealand and finished her schooling and teaching qualifications in Wellington. On a visit to Melbourne the city put out its tentacles and seduced her. Having fallen in love she moved across the Tasman to enjoy this new love. She still loves the city and now calls it home.

A few years ago she changed her life and became a residential property manager.

Juliette has freelanced for a number of newspapers and style magazines where she has written about houses and the people who live in them.

When she's not writing she roams the Melbourne streets, watches people and the activity on the Yarra River, drinks coffee and eats food from around the world. Her favourites are Italian and Vietnamese.